On Shifting Sands

Other anthologies from Paradise Press:
Queer Haunts (2003; expanded edition 2013)
Oysters and Pearls (2010)
People Your Mother Warned You About (2011)
The Best of Gazebo (2012)
Eros at Large (2013)
Coming Clean (2014)
A Boxful of Ideas (2016)
We Want to Tell You How (2018)
Lost Places (2024)
Flash Dances (2024)

See our website for more information:
www.paradisepress.org.uk

On Shifting Sands

Moments of Change, Exploration, and Discovery

An LGBTQ+ Anthology

Edited by Hastie Salih and David Flybury

Paradise Press

First published in Great Britain in 2025 by Paradise Press,

www.paradisepress.org.uk

Selection copyright © Paradise Press 2025

The individual authors retain copyright of their respective contributions.

The authors have individually asserted their moral right to be identified as the authors of their work in accordance with the Copyrights, Designs and Patents Act, 1988

All rights reserved. No part of this publication may be reproduced, stored in a retrieval system, or transmitted, in any form or by any means, electronic, mechanical, photocopying, recording or otherwise, without the prior permission of the copyright holders. Nor may it be used to assist in generating AI content.

A CIP catalogue record for this book is available from the British Library.

ISBN 978-1-904585-93-0

10 9 8 7 6 5 4 3 2 1

Printed and bound by P2D Books Ltd, Westoning, Bedfordshire

Cover design by David Flybury

Typeset by Ross Burgess

Set in Cambria with headings in Tempus Sans.

It takes a village, it turns out, to make an anthology, and we have had the assistance of many in the production of this. So, first to our contributors who have generously offered their work for inclusion; then to other members of GAW whose advice and patience has been invaluable - particularly Ross Burgess, Jeffrey Doorn, and Peter Scott-Presland; and then to our families who have supported us throughout: thanks. It is to all of the above that we dedicate this book.

Contents

Introduction
   About Gay Authors Workshop   xi
   Paradise Press   xii
Talim Arab
   If   1
   When   2
Stephanie Dickinson
   People Watching   3
CJ Bowman
   A Love Poem   6
Roberto Lissa
   Arriving   8
Susan Miller
   Going Grey, no way   11
Craig Binch
   Finding Camino Craig   13
Jenny Bull
   Garden of connection   18
   Blackberries   19
Irene Lotta
   Gladys Born Again   20
John Fairlamb
   Epiphany   24
CJ Cass-Horne
   A Testament to Restore Faith   25
Gillian Jane Morris
   Changes and my Healing Journey   28
Ross Burgess
   The Hunting Party   33
Leigh V Twersky
   Red Cross   40
   A Duel   44
Patrick C. Notchtree

The Visit	50
Death in Custody	54
Loving Stephen	60
Elsa Wallace	
Out of the Frying Pan	61
Forsaken	65
Having Your Cake *AND* Eating It	70
Emily Hay	
Pessimists' Romance	74
Wonderbra	89
Catherine Meads	
When will they come for me?	96
Zekria Ibrahimi	
With Jules	97
On an empty Saturday in Soho	98
Soho in autumn	100
Not the fairest of fields	101
I glimpse	102
Carpe Noctem	103
Peter Scott-Presland	
The Belt	104
Age Concern	106
Truant	117
John Dixon	
Growing Up	126
Pit Stops	128
Only One Thing For It	130
Tarpaulin	132
Nairobi	137
Inscription	142
Kevin Crowe	
The Bench	147
The Platform	153
Hastie Salih	
A girl at last	158
Afterlife	160

The Journey	164
Twisted apple tree	166
Twilight	168
My Mother's journey	170
David Flybury	
A Clearer Idea of Everything	172
A Fresh Start	177
Jeffrey Doorn	
A Traveller's Tale	186
Ringing	195
Joshua Shepperton	198
Ian Everton	
Sam	204
People Just Don't Understand	207
The Fly in the Ointment	210
Bodicea Iceni	
Bereft	215
Blue	216
Second Daughter	217
Eleanor (Nor) Dow	
Ways of Belonging	219
Adrian Risdon	
Praed Street	227
Diana Dors	229
Patisserie: a Fairy Tale	231
Safeguarding	234
Rainer King	
What the Desert Keeps	235
The Island	239
The Grammar of Wanting	242
Les Brookes	
Three Chameleons and a Parrot	244
John Grendel	
The Boy Who Could Not See Himself	252
Allison Fradkin	
Soar Spot	263

Challah If You Queer Me	267
Hongwei Bao	
Long-Term Relationship	270
Blind Date	272
Blue	274
Elizabeth (Beth) Lister	
My Life on Shifting Sands	276
The Authors	
Author Biographies	283

Introduction

We are delighted to offer you this varied collection of LGBTQ+ poems and short stories, an unapologetic medley of novelists, writers and poets who will enthral, astonish or shock you with visions of life in the LGBTQ+ community – a mosaic of queer loves, heartbreaks, defiance, and humorous rebellions.

Echoes of Baldwin, Lorde, or Woolf may flicker through these pages, but our voices are authentic and unmistakably contemporary. *On Shifting Sands*, we are forward looking, keeping our footing, making progress, searching for solid ground – it's there!

Let's celebrate the magic, enjoy the symphony of soft and tempestuous sounds as our authors turn silence into stories, find the extraordinary in the every-day, or the spectacular once-in-a-lifetime. Sift through this collection to find your diamond or your flake of gold.

Hastie and David

About Gay Authors Workshop
Supporting LGBTQ+ writers since 1978.

GAW is an association of LGBTQ+ creative writers – poets, dramatists, fiction and non-fiction writers. Our aim is to support writers by providing opportunities to meet, read, discuss and develop their work with a view to possible publication. We hold monthly Zoom meetings and frequent gatherings. We have a quarterly newsletter to keep in touch, report meetings and publish members' poems and short pieces. We welcome members from all over the country – indeed the world!

Website: gayauthorsworkshop.uk
#join_GAW_to_join_in

Paradise Press
The imprint of the Gay Authors Workshop

Established in 1999 to overcome the indifference to LGBTQ+ writing in the mainstream publishing industry, we have published over forty books in print and e-book formats: prose, verse, and anthologies of poetry/stories/essays.

From fantasy and chilling tales of the supernatural to the memoirs of gay men who lived through the repressive years of the 1950s and 1960s, from acerbic humour to thoughtful poetry, from romance to mystery, there's a book for you! Our books may be purchased via the website.

Website: www.paradisepress.org.uk

Find us at linktr.ee/ParadisePress

Talim Arab

If

If the night parts us in sleep,
you are a waking dream,
a silver light tracing my skin.

If pillows are galaxies,
turning and twisting,
your body's a ballet of stars.

If the bed is the sea,
moon-pulled waves rising,
your breath a tidal lullaby.

If we wake in sheets
thinner than water,
your skin the sun's quiet kiss.

If morning brings desire,
and the bed is wider than the world,
still your shifting hand will reach,

reach for me.

When

When morning withholds light,
the bedroom dark as failure,
I hear a bird's hopeful melody.

When the night sky's a blackboard,
chalky stars; the moon studies me,
I chant your name, a whispered spell.

When the bed is winter,
sheets thin as snowflakes,
I remember the furnace of your chest.

When the pillow is flat,
dream-starved, feathers fallen from flight,
I trace a gold hair left on the empty bed.

When the bed frame is a book,
bodies changing stories,
I read of love lost and found

for you.

Stephanie Dickinson

People Watching

I wasn't expecting to be sitting in Gail's café right now, drinking a rather expensive coffee.

My car's being washed and I've treated it to the deluxe package. Half an hour, the man said so here I am. Half an hour's not long, but boring when you are on your own and have nothing with you to entertain you. People watching it has to be then. There's a young woman sitting at the table next to me. She has her laptop open and is intently studying something and at the table next to her a man is doing the same thing. Working from the café, rather than home, I suppose.

More interestingly, at the far end of the room there's a couple sitting who are actually talking to each other. I can't see the woman with her back to me but her companion is facing me so I can see that she is quite pale with freckles scattered across her nose. She has dark, shoulder-length hair and a half-fringe that she sweeps to one side every so often. She listens earnestly to her companion and responds with a smile, or a frown and several times running her fingers through her hair.

Her companion puzzles me. There is something familiar about her but I can't think what. She has short, cropped hair in that vibrant rich red colour that I have always secretly wished I could try. Not that Gina would have approved but now that Gina and I are not together any more I suppose there's nothing to stop me now. Except that I still have the light brown bob that I have had for the past ten years.

The dark-haired woman has got up and is heading for the counter. She points to two of the exotic cakes on offer and taps the loyalty card on her phone to the sensor. She must be a regular then to have their app on her phone. She is slim and athletic looking and I wonder if she usually eats the rich cakes on offer here or if it's a special occasion for her and her friend. She cuts the cakes in half, so they are going to share. Does that mean they know each well? Gina and I used to do that and we'd known each other for five years. I mentally shake myself. I must stop thinking about Gina and move on from her.

The woman carries the cakes through the café. She pauses at the laptop girl. 'Working hard, Jenny, I see', she teases. 'Working for Facebook now are you?' The girl looks up. 'It's my coffee break,' she grins. Dark-haired woman moves away and laptop girl calls after her. 'Hey Beth, are you going to the party on Saturday? You can bring your friend'.

Beth gives a non-committal shrug. 'Maybe', she says.

I feel almost triumphant now that I know that the dark-haired woman has a name. I also know that she has a sense of humour and might go to a party on Saturday.

Her companion is still a mystery though. I can see her vivid red hair and she is wearing a brightly coloured baggy shirt. I can see her feet under her chair. She has jeans on and red boots. Doc Martens, maybe? Gina had boots like that. I haven't seen Gina for three years. Could it be her? Maybe she always wanted cropped, red hair and now that she isn't with me decided to try it. I want to see her face. It's highly unlikely it is Gina ... but maybe ... I wonder how I can get a look at her when she is sitting at the far end of the room, facing away from me. I look around. There's a poster on the wall next to her by the back door. I could go up to it and look like I'm interested in what it is saying. Then I could casually turn so that I can see her profile. She might notice me and I can say something. Something about the poster, of course. I'd know then that, of course, she isn't Gina and I'd know what someone with such dramatic hair would look like. Probably she has dramatic make-up to match.

My phone buzzes and I look at the message. My car is ready to be picked up. There's a couple of other messages, too, and I answer them. I gather my bag and get ready to casually saunter to the back of the café to look at that poster. I just have to know for sure. I don't want it to be her but what if it is? I look towards the poster, and the empty table next to it.

CJ Bowman

A Love Poem
for dumb gay boys who think Disney is real

When Aladdin
Offers to show you the world
You know he's kinda lying,
But you'll go with him anyway
Because he has 2 big dark eyes
And you've had 2 big dark negronis,
And when you lie on his carpet
You're surprised how much it burns,
And how there are little dark crumbs
Sticking to your skin.
Later you look to the side
And see an ashtray and a half-empty glass
Of beer that just catches the sunrise
Shining, shimmering, splendid.

Instead, you'll go with the Beast
Because he reads lots of books
And he promises to eat you
The way he eats porridge.
But he's not out yet
So, everything you do together
is tinged with something
And he's always looking
Around and his great hall
Way, where you hide from his
Flatmates Is cold, so you tell him
One day he'll be a prince
But by then you'll be
Far far away.

Instead, you go with Hercules
Because you feel like
Zero and need a hero
And believe his pecs
Make him a good person.
But he says something strange
Over wine one night and
When you ask him about it
He tells you he also needs
A hero and you feel strange
Because you're not sure
You've seen this scene,
And you ask him what kind
Of hero? But he's not sure.

Instead, you open up your phone
And suck that guy who looks like
Jafar and then go for negronis.
A guy with bored eyes
tries to talk to you
In the bar but you ask him
To be quiet for a moment
Because you hear a cartoony song
In the background and it reminds
you of a feeling from before.

Roberto Lissa

Arriving

She's resting her head on Andrea's lap. June's eyes are closed; Andrea's hand strokes her hair, the blades of grass, soon to be yellowed by the heat, tickle her thighs.

Neither of them is saying anything. Andrea is going through her Insta stories, and June is just content with the lull of the wind.

They came to see the Lambeth County Show, in the air quote ironic way her university students would, and then found themselves enthralled by the charm of it all. To the extent that they had a low-key argument about whether shearing sheep was the humane thing to do as they watched a very chirpy Australian do a demonstration that looked a bit rough and tumble.

The day was hot and dusty, the portaloos not nearly as nasty as June expected and now, as the sky turns pink beyond the Shard, they are sitting in silence, full of apple cider and love.

Maybe this is the elusive thing she has been chasing all her life. This feeling right here, a mix of contentment and the ability to stay in the moment for once. To enjoy the feeling of Andrea's fingertips through her hair, the balmy breeze coming from the city, a woman ensconced in the cocoon of the here and now.

Why had it escaped her for so long? She had dated women before, so that was clearly not the issue. She had dated poets and feminists, Londoners from all walks of life and New Yorkers from various sides of the anxiety spectrum disorders. There had been femme and butch in equal measure, bisexuals that intellectualised everything and women who were, frankly, a bit of a hot mess.

Andrea radiated homecoming for June. They had grown in similar, generic commuter-belt places, attended similar schools and had parents with similar expectations. Respect for the monarchy, the hope that their daughters will reach the 1.3 kids and detached house nirvana, arguments about whether it's clotted cream first and then jam or vice versa, still pending a resolution after decades. They were not the same person, and obviously, their families were not the same, but there was comfort in not having to explain the subtext of things, in finding another human with as wide a range of conversation as hers, spanning from the *Guardian* Blind Dates to whether young people these days are really doing lesbianism right. Dinner could be beans on toast after a long day or some experimental vegan sushi and neither of them would bat an eyelid.

Not only did she do all the things June liked, Andrea never did things that June didn't like. June had kept a mental tally of those as well:

Andrea didn't refer to New York as the Big Apple.

She didn't tell her off whenever June was a total dick to her mum.

She did remind her she had been a dick to her mum once June was compos mentis to engage with the conversation.

She didn't ask about her exes, but if they came up, she would remember some minor detail. Oh the Linguistics PostDoc. The one who gave you chlamydia in Santorini.

She didn't have the wandering eye, but she could have a conversation about hot people's bodies in a matter-of-fact way that felt not threatening, like a doctor taking someone's vitals.

She didn't mind that June would say she didn't want a side of chips, but then let June eat more than half of her portion.

She did not judge her for her crazy rules about what not to eat and how not to eat it and, most importantly, had never asked her about her live-in arrangement with eating disorders.

Is it possible she had never felt this connected to another human before? She goes through the catalogue of women again, the ones that were all id and no ego, and all the men, a lot of them too much id and too much ego. The intellectuals with no originality, the people uninterested in debating *The Discourse*, and it was Andrea who maximised all of June's criteria, including the ones she didn't know she cared about until meeting her.

The evening light strikes a sense of possibility in her. She could propose right here and now, capture this elusive moment and freeze it in time, a specimen to be brought out at dinner parties for years to come.

'Do you remember when you proposed to me, babe? I dropped ice cream on myself and my dungarees were sticky for ten hours and you had so much cider and then we both lost our phones and couldn't get an Uber home. Still, it was the best day of our lives.'

A life ahead and an urge so immense, like a dam about to burst, that June is happy to do a whole U-turn on her aversion to The Institution of Marriage situation and buy a ring from the crystal healer's stall so that she can get on her knee right here and now.

It must be the cider talking, June thinks, as a mini burp travels through her oesophagus to die a little understated death in her throat.

'We've had too much to drink. Let's get kebabs, shall we?' Andrea says, as if reading the thoughts at the bottom of June's eyes.

Susan Miller

Going Grey, no way

When I was very, very young ...
And life was only about having fun
I thought that twenty seemed archaic
And it was a miracle that anyone older
Could walk let alone run
Turning grey, not today!

As a teen I saw my elders as sad and boring
Trying to impose rules that left me yawning
I was a terrible youngster and no mistake
We drank and smoked and thought we were cool
Looking back my asthmatic lungs now think: 'You fool'
Going grey, no way I say!

Getting to my twenties I was smoking and drinking
At Uni we spent hours in lectures
I guess we were thinking
We marched and talked and talked and marched
And that of course, left us parched
Going grey, that's the road to decay!

Then onto a job
Or even a career
Working and thinking,
Definitely still drinking
Writing the news
Even uncovering the odd ruse
Going grey, no way!

***

Travels took place, as life started to churn
Leaving one's family

Meeting new loves
Having adventures and taking one's turn
Always being told to keep trying to learn
Going grey, no way I say!

Death came crashing in
My granny was first and my world was shaken
I wondered about everything then
Certainties and equanimity taken
Life could never again be like it was when I was ten
Going grey, I don't want to be fey

So now I'm really getting on
Ticking a new age box on a form
And feeling the odd ache and pain
They say age is only a number
But I feel like I'm suddenly on a speeding train
Going grey, no way!

But then I look at others
Who are older but great
And still living with a with sense of fun
And I see it's possible to continue
I can even learn how to use a pun
Going grey, with a sway!

So go away aches and pains
Bother me no more
I'll stop saying my side aches when it rains
And go out and dance in the showers
Even ignore my hay fever and smell the damn flowers
Going grey, it's actually OK!

Craig Binch

Finding Camino Craig

It all began with a magical movie *The Way*, a great story which planted a seed of a desire to do something crazy like the Camino Santiago. Maybe it was a midlife crisis, a curiosity to find my lost self or a chance to turn off my busy brain and jump out of the rat race.

I bought and studied an idiot's guide and chatted enthusiastically with my friends and family about my latest whim, who nodded, politely expecting the inevitable. My two good friends were sold on the idea and wanted to join me. My husband on the other hand did not. His worst nightmare: walking all day when you could be lazing by a pool sipping a piña colada. Stubborn as I am the trip was planned for spring 2020.

Then Covid came along and ripped up our plans showing no mercy, along with a thousand other special moments – on a positive note: my friends got pregnant. The plan was on hold and the guidebook was tidied away until the madness subsided. 3 years slipped by, I was at a crossroads in my career and in my personal life, the itch was still there and it grew again with the desire to walk or maybe escape.

Spontaneously, I booked the flights – choosing the Portuguese Camino, a tribute to my Portuguese husband, now walking alone. I studied the guide again, watched YouTube videos on what to pack. I was loaned a backpack bigger than me, and I bought a pair of Skechers to take me on the path to enlightenment, naive and brazen enough not to care.

The Camino by origin is a pilgrimage. I'm not particularly religious but the notion was attractive nonetheless the less. I was just going on an adventure; the husband was not so pleased and tit for tat, booked a week in Cyprus whilst I was away, to lounge by the pool and soak up the sun.

I had not travelled alone for a long time, always reliant on my husband to book all our trips and multilingual of course he did all the talking. This time I was on my own, thrilled and nervous it was too late now.

I am a bit of a coward, so I arranged to meet up with some old friends who I had worked with in London now living in Porto. We had a lovely meal, catching up over a sweet Porto wine. The evening passed by too quickly, and I was suddenly on my own again in a strange city.

The albergue was clean but noisy and I was in a bunk room with six other strangers, of course I didn't sleep.

I rose early dressed, slung on my backpack over my already aching shoulder and walked to the cathedral, the starting line of the Camino Santiago, to collect my Camino passport.

Of course, the cathedral was closed, I checked online, and I had an hour to kill; a pastel de nata and a coffee later and I was back to the starting point.

I queued up and eyed up the other pilgrims, I detected French, Spanish and German accents. Professional gear and serious socks – me with my oversized backpack and Skechers, what was I thinking?

Camino passport tucked in my backpack with its first stamp still damp, I went in search of my first arrow, I found it nestled in the cobbled stones pointing me to who knows where?

One foot in-front of the other I marched into my adventure, excited for my grown-up treasure hunt looking for the little yellow Arrows adorned with a seashell the emblem of the pilgrim, the beacon to light my way.

Through winding city roads I began in earnest, worried that I wouldn't find my way, doubted myself, lost my arrow, backtracked and almost started again, now hot bothered and sweaty, trying not to panic.

Finally, I broke through the beautiful city, meandering through the suburbs and then a fork in the road: two arrows pointing in different directions? this wasn't fair!

I spotted a group of professional pilgrims, walking sticks clicking in unison heading to the right. They must know what they're doing, in blind faith I followed behind. A mile later the arrows ended and I found myself on a motorway. My guides dispersed. Grumpy, tired, I marched on blindly, traffic whizzing by on the dusty road. This was not the tranquillity I'd hoped for. Not for the first time I doubted my sanity, but stubbornly knew failure was not an option.

Tired and thirsty, only 4 hours in, I hadn't even the energy to take off my backpack, when, out of nowhere an elderly man on a bicycle was approaching, smiled a warm moustached smile said 'this is for you' in broken English and handed me a cold bottle of water. Before I could say thank you, he was on his way with a cheery wave. I must admit a tear rolled down my cheek. I felt like I'd been touched by an angel. A simple act of kindness was all it took! I drank thirstily and within a minute I found my sacred arrow and seashell. My mood lifted as I started off into the country lane with a renewed spring in my step.

I was enveloped in fields and small-holdings, winding lanes and blue skies – now that was more like it! After another hour I found my albergue, a converted monastery, a vision for my aching feet and rumbling stomach. I'd survived day one. That night we had a BBQ in the grounds, mixed with my fellow pilgrims from around the world – all with a different reason to be on is magical road.

My first walking companion and Camino friend was a jolly chap from Ireland, a retired publican in his 60s who'd already completed the French Camino. Putting me to shame, he marched the Camino as if it was a breeze and entertained me the whole day with his hilarious story telling.

The day passed quickly and we were soon checked into the next albergue, followed by a wave of other weary travellers. Bunk beds again in a room of familiar strangers, an open invite to dinner and suddenly I'm at a table surrounded by lovely people laughing and joking as if we were lifelong friends, sharing stories and tales of our homes and lives we'd left behind.

With full stomachs and the last of the wine emptied from the glass, the weary gaggle of newly found Camino friends ambled off to bed, sides aching from the laughter nearly as much as my feet.

My third day of walking, now well into the rhythm of the pilgrim lifestyle, boots strapped on, backpacks slung on shoulders and hats on heads the next chapter to my mystery tour unfolded.

This day I met Patricia, a young Portuguese girl on her first Camino, charming and lovely – with blisters the size of tennis balls on both feet. Unperturbed we walked together, quite a bit slower but from that point on I never walked alone again. I felt a duty to support my Camino friend, encourage her to carry on through the discomfort. I am forever grateful: for someone who usually rushes everywhere I had no option but to slow down, because of this I really got to smell the flowers. I soaked up the beautiful countryside, lush fields, quaint small holdings and country lanes. I was present in the moment truly and I loved every minute. Nothing mattered, no deadlines, no meetings, no stress, no drama, just a forward road of unknown adventure; I had no idea where I was, but I didn't care. My busy mind settled, my heart a little lighter. All my troubles were left behind and I felt free and like I never wanted to stop the adventure: I had discovered Camino Craig!

The days flew. By the end of my two-week hike on the penultimate night I sat at a table with 18 other fellow pilgrims and friends from all around the world to celebrate Patrícia's 30th birthday. The night was perfect, with wonderful Spanish food, good company, birthday cake and a table filled with happy smiles, laughter and music. None of us wanted the night to end.

The final day had mixed feelings: wanting to reach the finish line and the incredible Santiago cathedral, but also never wanting it to be over.

An early start and the final kilometres. We entered the historic city with gathering crowds of tourists and fellow pilgrims. The plaza and cathedral came into view as we entered the majestic end to our journey. Laughter, tears, hugs, exchanging numbers after we had dumped our rucksacks and posed for a hundred photographs: we'd done it!! Two weeks has been a lifetime and another world.

It was elation, pride and a slight shock of 'almost' back to reality. There wasn't so much a physical change after my experience, but a nod to remember what is important. Life is short and sometimes you need an adventure. With time to think I re-evaluated my life, and now two years on I'm divorced, in a new job, and I'm published as an author in an anthology. Before Camino Craig this wouldn't have been possible.

I have never been so grateful for an experience in my life. The wonderful people I met, without exception; the places I may never have seen; and the space to free my mind.

Reflecting back with my rose-tinted glasses, reminiscing on this magical almost Fairy-tale adventure, I smile to myself and remind myself I'm still Camino Craig, in between the drudgery of everyday life.

On my return I hung my Camino shell by the front door and went back to my meetings and managerial duties, and the life I had briefly left behind. But now you see, I have a secret weapon: I can close my eyes and take myself right back to those precious moments ... any time I wish.

Jenny Bull

Garden of connection

Olive tree breaking free
Rambling rose hips of generosity
Birch trees

   Dance

Moved – By the wind

Weeping silhouette – mysterious tree in midwinter leaf

We stand still in a garden
Intermittently drenched in flood light – that reminds us to let

Love

in
  tap
      tap
          tap
              of rain
on the shelter

I hold

Catching my attention
Like
a child saying forget-me-not

Stay still in this moment

and connect

Blackberries

Blackberries taste sweeter in the drowned desert on a path
    that runs out
between two bridges

I found a tree split in 3
    it took my weight
while I drank tea
Tried to work out if it was oak
or ash

Its identity cloaked
in moss
A beautiful tangle of neighbouring leaves

keep on spinning your way into the future

Stay on a path that feels right in this moment

Homes that look out and feel free

Homes that do knot

Irene Lotta

Gladys Born Again

He who sits in the heavens laughs (Psalm 2 verse 4)

God help me say the right thing, repeated Gladys with each flight of clattery steps up to the fourth floor. She was scared of the lift and the exercise was surely good for her heart, but seldom had she so grimly hated the shadowy stairwell as now, as she steeled herself not to bolt into her own little flat but to call on her new next-door neighbours. Before she had time to get in, take her coat off and decide to postpone it another day. So *God help me* continued more breathless and urgent each step.

Between prayers the soup kitchen haunted her. That, said the Pastor, was all that the local Churches Council had asked from their church, for a volunteer or two to do the soup-run on Friday and Saturday nights. Gladys had said she'd do anything to help the poor souls of this desperate town, and she certainly was no coward, as her resolve to talk to the new neighbours proved. She had no fear of violence, poverty or filth, clear in her own mind that suffering was part of the spiritual path in her service for her God. And she firmly believed that her God would protect her from any too terrible harm.

But her real fear, the fear that had driven her from the charity-shop and the magazine-selling on doorsteps, was deadlier to her spirit. It was ridicule, scratching away at the deep buried doubts she could only deny all the stronger when the ultimate cruelty came. The person who laughed at what Gladys believed in. From that, she knew only too well, God did not seem to see fit to protect her. The soup kitchen would be rough and ready, no place for polite manners, the volunteers possibly even readier to scorn her convictions than the down-and-outs queuing too hungry and broken to criticise – maybe.

As her thoughts made her ever more anxious, she returned to her prayer *God help me to know what to say God help me* repeating itself almost frantic in the unheard spaces of her head. To an outside observer, if Gladys' thoughts could be seen it would read like a mantra or rosary; Gladys of course would be horrified by the comparison with the religions of poor benighted souls which deviated from the pure truth which her stern but beloved Pastor had taught her. *God help me* she came up to the fourth floor landing, walked past her own doorway and rang on their doorbell. No turning back now, though she longed to; her duty was clear. She had overheard the rumours about them in the few weeks since they had moved into the flat. If the rumours were true, she could not fail as their very neighbour to offer them a chance to find a way out of their terrible sin. People said they were *homosexuals*. Oh, she was squirming with embarrassment. Poor Freddie, the Pastor's own son, who they all tried so hard not to laugh at, had confessed to these strange, perverted temptations, but with God's help had managed to resist them ... so of course it was possible ... *God help me God help me God help me ... Never mind soup kitchens never mind working don't be afraid if they don't understand* ... Tim, the younger man, answered the door – *Gladys isn't it – Andrew this is Gladys, our neighbour – thank you so much for coming – oh you've brought gooseberry jam, my favourite, how wonderful – Gladys this is Andrew my partner* ... She thought she would choke at their openness. No attempt, then, at hiding their terrible, unnatural sin. All her carefully planned, tactful introductions to moral and spiritual questions were blown away from her in her astonishment, but the younger man had gone away to make a pot of tea while the older man was taking her coat from her and asking her neighbourly questions about how long she'd lived there and what were the best local shops.

She was lost – but she had to – she had to invite them to come and hear the Pastor, who would tell them how to turn from their path to eternal damnation. Her eyes began to swell with tears at the difficulty of how to broach such a terrible topic with such pleasant people.

Gladys, is something the matter?

She couldn't possibly do it today – she would really have to get to know them a little better first – she would say nothing today.

No, I'm fine. But she wasn't, and found herself inventing a ridiculous story about a funeral and a bereaved woman who sounded uncannily like herself, until with a mixture of horror and relief, she found Tim with a clean hankie for her tears, putting his arm round her. For an excruciating few moments she found herself sobbing out loud, to her utter shame, in front of the two men.

Losing all hope of extricating herself from the alarmingly powerful lie she had crafted, she decided to sit as they advised, quietly sipping on the tea which Tim had made for her, against her wishes, with a deliciously comforting excess of sugar.

Soon, with elaborate apologies for her tears, she began to approach a passable performance of control and her usual self could field a few safer, respectable topics of conversation. She could even smile now at the two men who sat there so calm, unperturbed, strangely warm in their attitude.

So, she decided to ask them, have you moved here to work in the area?

Bombs and explosions were slight things compared to the shock.

We both work for the Church of England – we've been sent here to set up a refuge for the homeless. Andrew is running the drop-in, and I'm organising the soup kitchen.

As Gladys' tea-cup went flying through the air and her scream reached her own ears, two things happened.

He who sits in the heavens laughed at the springing of the trap at last, at the first chink in the armour. Seeing ahead through the slow, painful death of the old Gladys, while holding her soul tight through tears for her as the new Gladys travelled through blankets of fear towards life.

And as Gladys perceived in that terrifying moment that her laws and her scruples could be shackles and lies, for herself just as much as for them, Andrew and Tim were there with her to hold her and feel for her pain, in the warmth of their love for a journey they'd already travelled themselves.

John Fairlamb

Epiphany

Appearing:
Genuine appearing rather than a misleading apparition.

Understanding:
A genuine understanding and appreciation of the facts instead of illusions and alarmist conspiratorial theories.
Like an oasis in the desert as that inspires relief and hope in the weary traveller rather than mirage that plays mind games with desperate travellers who have already lost their bearings.

Religion:
Are the fruits of your faith, joy and peace and love
Or will your beliefs end in disappointments and frustration and anger?
Is your religion a crutch?
Is it full of fairy tales and simplistic moralism?
Or does it help you get in touch
with the person that you really are, and were meant to be –
the truth that lies beneath?

CJ Cass-Horne

A Testament to Restore Faith

This story was first published in Flash Dances *(Paradise Press, 2024) and is reprinted by permission.*

In the small town of Catfish-Paradise, Arizona, a kind-hearted middle-aged man named Timo Bumblethorpe lived a quiet life. He had always been driven by a desire to make a difference in the lives of those less fortunate, particularly the elderly who he believed deserved all the love and care in the world.

One sunny day, as Timo strolled through the town, he stumbled upon a flyer advertising a Care Home. Curiosity took hold of him, and he decided to pay it a visit. Upon entering, Timo couldn't help but notice the weary expressions adorning the faces of the residents. Loneliness hung heavily in the air, and Timo's compassionate heart ached for them. He knew at that moment that he had to do something to improve their lives.

Driven by empathy and an unwavering determination to right the wrongs he had witnessed, Timo concocted a plan. He would go undercover and move into the care home himself, experiencing first-hand the neglect endured by the elderly residents. And so, Timo transformed himself into a new resident, taking on the name 'Niko'.

As Niko settled into the care home, he quickly struck up a friendship with Clive, a charming gentleman residing in Room 23. Clive had called the Care Home his dwelling for the past twenty years since the loss of his partner. He shared heart-breaking tales of inadequate staff, negligence, and overall indifference from the current owners, an organization called Homeways Connect.

Motivated by his newfound ally's plight, Timo's determination grew stronger. He simply could not stand by and allow the residents to suffer any longer. After careful consideration and deep discussions with his wealthy lesbian aunt, Aunt Layana, Timo made up his mind. He would buy the Care Home, using their combined resources to make a change.

With Aunt Layana's financial backing and unyielding belief in Timo's noble endeavours, they confronted the owners of Homeways Connect. They demanded that the Care Home be sold to Timo and Aunt Layana, threatening to expose years of neglect and mistreatment to the press. Astonished by the unexpected turn of events, the owners agreed, realizing they could not stand in the way of Timo's determination to make a difference.

With the purchase finalized, Timo and Aunt Layana embarked on a mission to transform the Care Home. They hired compassionate staff, improved the living conditions, and organized activities that brought joy and laughter back into the lives of the residents.

As time passed, Timo's friendship with Clive blossomed into something deeper. They became long-life partners, standing side by side, ensuring that the elderly residents were given the love and care they deserved. The Care Home, once shrouded in neglect, became a beacon of hope and happiness.

Word quickly spread about the remarkable transformation at Catfish-Paradise Care Home. Families from all over America started choosing the Care Home for their elderly loved ones, knowing that it was a place where they would thrive. The Care Home became an embodiment of love, laughter, and gay pride, a testament to the power of one man's empathy and a community's unwavering support.

In the end, Timo's pivotal moment led to a change that brought light and happiness into the lives of so many. The town of Catfish-Paradise, once divided and indifferent, came together to embrace and cherish the elderly residents. And it all began with the selfless and compassionate heart of Timo Bumblethorpe, who never wavered in his belief that everyone deserves love and care.

Gillian Jane Morris

Changes and my Healing Journey

I have learnt that change, like it or not, is an integral part of life. Everything changes all the time even if we cannot see it. I am a Libran and Librans are all about balancing scales. I spent years trying to balance my work/life scales which were always tipped down on the side of work. Once I had balanced them, I soon discovered other 'scales' in my life that needed attention. One of the biggest was my change/stability scales.

I moved around and changed jobs a lot in my 20s and 30s. This was initially for my career but later it was mainly for my health. I found these changes difficult because I liked familiarity; seeing the same neighbours, staff, close friends and family on a regular basis, knowing my way around the town I lived in, feeling settled in a job and having a routine. Letting go, as part of these changes, was challenging for me and often very emotional. I struggled to let go of friendships, relationships and situations, or even belongings that I no longer needed. The latter may have come from my mother who was a bit of a hoarder and ended up with a house full of stuff she never used. In her case it was a consequence of experiencing lack during wartime in her childhood. 'Don't throw it out,' she would say to me, 'You might need it one day.' Despite telling myself I do not want to end up like her, I now find that I have far more belongings than I need.

I hate de-cluttering because it involves throwing out or giving away possessions which hold sentimental value for me. Old children's books with precious handwriting in them saying, 'From Nana with lots of love at Christmas xxx'. Ornaments and jewellery that are 'out of fashion' but which hold dear memories for me. A string of big blue plastic beads given to me in a paper bag from a patient of mine ... a very sick young boy who died shortly afterwards. Ornaments that immediately arouse memories of my parents and grandparents. A penguin, because my father loved them. Glass swans made by my paternal grandfather, who had been a professional glass blower. Squirrel Nutkin that always sat on my maternal Grandmother's mantelpiece and a brass bell from my Nana's Welsh dresser. How could I throw these out? I just have to find ways to incorporate them into my new home and current life. Sometimes I can balance the 'old and new' in creative ways that work.

I do find some change fun, exciting, and ultimately rewarding. I like to change my wardrobe and the interior décor and furniture in my home. I read, study and learn new facts and skills that often bring about changes in my life. I like art and craft and creating new and restoring old things. I love to go on trips, travelling, meeting new people and learning about their lives and sharing ideas.

I found relocating, moving home and exploring new places exciting, as well as challenging, and these changes in my life resulted in a wealth of experience in both my professional and personal life. They also changed and shaped my attitudes especially after experiencing different cultures when working and living abroad. As a medical student I spent four months in Canada on my 'elective' in 1985. I remember how this vast country was a whole new world to me with its beautiful national parks, towns and cities, huge shopping centres, delicious food and drinks, gadgets and inventions, including robots that had not made their way to the UK yet, but most of all the super friendly people. The staff in the hospital, including the consultant who was my mentor, were all very kind and friendly. They welcomed me and treated me as an equal. This contrasted with my experience in the NHS. As a medical student, and later as a junior doctor in the 1980s, some nursing and medical staff were quite unfriendly and difficult to work with.

Again, years later when I worked in Australia from 1997 to 2000, I was impressed by how friendly colleagues were and how they had a more relaxed attitude to life in general. Working under these circumstances was so much more pleasant than in the NHS. Although I could see that staff in the UK were generally more stressed because of the high demands and heavy workload it did not justify their behaviour at times. I often reflected on my working experiences abroad and I always tried to be as polite and friendly as I could to all staff from the cleaners to the consultants, regardless of how busy or stressed I was. Ultimately it made work a lot more pleasant for me and hopefully for them too.

Having struggled with health problems since my late 20s I have been on a 'healing journey' for years that involved introducing big changes into my life. Although my problems were physical in nature, requiring major surgery, I was aware of the mind-body connection and one of the most significant lessons I learnt was in regard to loving myself. This started when I first read Louise Hay's book, *You Can Heal Your Life* in which she teaches the importance of loving ourselves. It is not a selfish, self-centred, narcissistic love she talks about but rather a self-compassionate love.

With more insight into my caring for others personally and professionally and my 'people pleasing' behaviours, a lot of my beliefs and attitudes gradually changed. Eventually I changed how I spoke to and treated myself. I showed myself more compassion and I stopped tolerating certain patterns of behaviour in others. I learned about the importance of boundaries and how they could protect me rather than keep me distant and 'closed off' from others.

I was not overtly rejected by my family and my 'old' friends because of my 'alternative lifestyle' but there were definite changes in the way they treated me. I was not included in all major events and meetings as I had been in the past. I realised that this may have been in part due to my changed lifestyle and attitudes but the feeling of being rejected or just not accepted and included any more was heart-breaking as I still loved all my friends and family. I could not reconcile it until I eventually accepted that this was not a reflection of me but rather of them and their limitations.

I hate losing 'old' friends whether due to distance, disagreements or death, as they are impossible to replace, but I do like making new friends. Having recently moved house, again, I have made some new friends. They show great interest in my life and career and I surprise myself sometimes when I tell them about all the different jobs and experiences I have had. Their respect for me and my current needs is in contrast to interactions I have had lately with some of my 'old' friends, who seem to 'take me for granted' and are in denial of all my health issues and expect me to have the same energy and vitality that I had in my 30s!

Following the death of the three family members I was closest to, several close friends and my two beloved Siamese cats, my life changed dramatically. I struggled for years with the 'grief process' ... remembering, trying to process memories and feelings, forgiving, reconciling, letting go and 'moving on', but despite seeing several counsellors I got nowhere with it. Eventually with the guidance of an extremely talented art therapist I started to 'recycle' my emotions and memories rather than bury them or try to 'build my life around them' as I had been advised to do previously. Every time I expressed deep emotions she said, 'Can you put that down on paper?' I didn't have a clue what to paint so we just talked, but the process went on in my subconscious mind week after week. Then, surprisingly one session I painted a large ball of thick black and red, swirling brush strokes which I saw and felt deep within my heart. The black represented my dark, heavy grief, anger and hurt, and the red my passionate, energetic and powerful love. It remained like that, on paper and in my heart for a few weeks until, in my mind I saw it more like fertile compost or soil, full of energy and life that was able to change, transmute into and sustain new life. Then I painted beautiful flowers growing from it. They represented the energy I am now using to build a new life for myself in my new home where I am growing trees and flowers in my garden, sketching and painting them with colourful acrylics and gold leaf, playing my new piano from the music sheets my mother played from when I was growing up, making new friends and learning to love myself and enjoy my life just as it is.

The therapist asked, 'Are you the phoenix rising out of the ashes?' and I said, 'No. It is the energy from my feelings, my memories and my love.'

Ross Burgess

The Hunting Party

The day had started off well. The light mist over the Great River slowly cleared as the sun rose; there was a chill in the air as we started to gather for our hunting expedition, but it looked like being a fine day. During the summer we had been able to go out wearing not much more than some feathers and strings of beads, but today I was glad of the new tunic Mother had made me out of reindeer skins, laboriously scraped and sewn together, with a mammoth-hide belt. 'You're getting to be a good-looking young man,' she said, as she straightened my hair and beard. 'It's time you were going off to find yourself a wife – you know how much I want grandchildren, and ...' at that point she stopped, and made the sign against bad luck. My brother Swiftfox and his wife Wildbird had been trying to have children for several years now: she'd been pregnant four times, but each time the baby had come out dead, or died within a few days. Now she was pregnant again, but she looked sick, and old before her time, and wasn't eating.

'Yes of course,' I replied, but couldn't raise much enthusiasm at the thought of a wife. It wasn't girls I fantasised about at night.

We were all ready to set out, with our flint knives and flint-tipped spears. Thinsnake led us in the chanting, keeping time with his rattle. The chant asked for support from our ancestors, and forgiveness from the animals we hoped to kill, with some other stuff that had been part of the chant for so long that no-one knew any longer what the words meant. Thinsnake no longer came hunting with us. He sat around all day, in conversation with people or things we couldn't see, throwing special herbs on the fire and breathing in the smoke. But people seemed to think he did a good job by keeping evil things away, and when things went wrong he was always ready to tell us how we might have offended the ancestors.

Our hunt leader explained the plan for the day. A group of horses had been seen a couple of hours walk away. Horsemeat would make a welcome change from the usual reindeer flesh. They would be far too fast for us to catch them, so the aim would be to scare them and drive them towards the River; if all went well some of them would fall off the edge of the cliff and break their legs so we could finish them off easily.

But when we got there, the horses had gone. Some piles of dung confirmed that there had been horses there, but not for a while. The enthusiasm we'd set out with seemed to evaporate as we stood around arguing about what to do next. The sky was starting to cloud over, and I suddenly realised that my lucky necklace, with its carved mammoth-tusk beads, was no longer round my neck – the string must have caught on something and broken without my noticing. It had kept me safe on previous hunts, and I started to get anxious without it. Swiftfox was all for turning back – he'd promised to take back some tasty horsemeat for Wildbird in the hope that it would bring back her appetite, but now he was more concerned just to get home to be with her. Then someone noticed vultures hovering above the next hill – maybe this meant a recently dead animal that we could carve into meal-size chunks while keeping the vultures and hyaenas away.

The rain began to fall as we started up the hill. Soon it was falling in torrents, with loud thunder and flashes of lightning: maybe the ancestors were angry with us, or Thinsnake had made a mistake in his chanting and upset them.

The hill seemed to go on and on, as we struggled upwards. Soon I realised that I couldn't see any of the others. I called out, but my voice was drowned out by the thunder and the noise of the rain. Just then an enormous wild boar appeared from nowhere, running straight at me. I tried to fend it off but it brushed my spear aside and hurtled straight into me, tearing my leg open with one of its tusks. I fell down, hit my head on a rock, and passed out.

After a while I came to for a little and found myself being lifted up by a pair of strong arms, then I lost consciousness again.

Some time later – I've no idea how long – I awoke and found myself in what seemed to be a cave, with dim shadows moving about in the firelight. Someone was speaking gently in a language I didn't understand, and doing something to my injured leg.

Eventually, maybe days later, I came to sufficiently to realise that I was indeed in a cave. This time there was enough daylight coming in from outside for me to make out that there were five or six people there – but not people as we knew them in the village. I'd heard stories of the Bigfolk, and one day someone had pointed out a group of them in the distance. Mothers used to frighten their children by telling them that the Bigfolk would come and eat them if they didn't stop being naughty. Close up, however, they seemed much less frightening, just strange. One of them came over when he saw I was awake – he seemed to be the one who'd found me and been looking after me. We introduced ourselves by pointing to ourselves and saying our names. His name, as far as I could reproduce it, was something like Wolgong: I could never quite get my mouth in the right shape to say it as he said it, and he had as much trouble with mine, but we each laughed at the other's attempt.

His appearance was striking. Contrary to what I'd been led to expect of the Bigfolk, he was hardly any taller than me, but massively built, with a vast chest, covered in thick hair, and enormous muscles. He had a big nose, and his eyebrows sprouted from a very prominent ridge above his eyes, but he had no chin to speak of and his forehead was very low. But as strange as his features were, his colour was even more striking. All our tribe had dark hair and darkish skin. Wolgong's face and arms were tanned by the sun, but elsewhere, especially the parts normally covered by his clothes, his skin was decidedly pale, and he had red hair and a red beard. Somehow, despite the strangeness, he seemed quite attractive to look at. I had no means of knowing how old he was, but I did notice one or two grey hairs amongst the red.

Over the following days he treated my wounded leg with some sort of leaves, brought me things to eat (fish, small pieces of meat cooked over the fire, nuts and berries) and held me when the pain in my leg was so bad that I cried out. He shared the cave with a woman whom I took to be his sister, her man, and a couple of children, all of them with the same red hair and facial features. Between them they kept the fire going the whole time, and when the wind blew back into the cave the smoke became a bit overpowering, but they all seemed to be used to it. Wolgong and I chatted away to each other, with gestures; I managed to pick up a bit of his language, but I don't think either of us understood much of what the other was saying. As my leg got better, he encouraged me to stand up and hobble about a bit, holding on to a stick. At night he would cover me up in a heap of skins and furs and lie down nearby.

One day I noticed that my prick, which had been very lifeless since the accident, had started to wake up, and I absent-mindedly started playing with it. Wolgong saw me, and came over and hesitantly joined in. When he saw that I didn't object, he lay down next to me, held my prick in his big hand, and started stroking my nipples with his other hand. He had become very aroused himself by this time, and soon turned me over and slid inside me. Years ago one of my uncles had tried it on with me: I'd been appalled at the thought, and pushed him away, trying to make a joke of it. But this time with Wolgong, it seemed very natural, at least after the initial shock of penetration.

Time in the cave passed easily. I had nothing to do but get my strength back, eat the food that Wolgong and his family provided, and occasionally get turned over. But I was concerned that I'd been away from home too long. Probably a month and a half had passed since the unlucky hunting expedition: Mother would be very worried about me, and I was anxious to find if Wildbird had had her baby. So one day I decided to go back, and Wolgong came with me. It took us a while to find the way – I'd been unconscious when he'd brought me to the cave, and he didn't know our village. But eventually I recognised a path I'd been down before.

As we arrived at the village, Thinsnake was the first to see us. He spat in our direction, uttered a curse, his face a mixture of fear and loathing, and disappeared into his hut. I went straight to our hut. Mother seemed pleased to see me, but very downcast, and gave a start when she noticed my companion. 'Where have you been all this time? Why have you brought that ... person ... with you? Don't you know what's been happening here?' She soon told me the worst: it had gone badly with Wildbird when the baby was due to come. She'd been screaming in pain for a good part of a day, and Mother and the other women could do nothing for her. Eventually the baby came out dead and Silverbird herself died soon afterwards. I told Mother about the accident and that Wolgong had been taking care of me, but he himself seemed embarrassed and soon set off back to his cave.

After he was safely out of the way, Thinsnake turned up. He shouted that I'd brought bad luck on my family and the whole village by associating with one of the Bigfolk. 'How could you let him get close to you? They are not like us – they are animals, not people – you're lucky they didn't kill you and eat you. And you've affronted your ancestors by associating with them – why do you think Wildbird and her baby died?' I let him carry on like this for a while, as there seemed no point in arguing. But I started to feel guilty at the thought that maybe he could have been right, and the ancestors had been angry at me spending time with the Bigfolk – and maybe even angrier if they knew what Wolgong and I had been doing together in the cave. Could it really have been my fault that Wildbird died and that Mother still had no grandchildren?

When Thinsnake had gone, Mother turned to me: 'Swiftfox just stays in his hut,' she said. 'He won't eat, he won't let anyone come near him. It's down to you now. It's time for you to go and get a wife. You should do it soon, before the snows come.'

So in a day or two Mother got me ready for my next expedition. She'd patched up my tunic, which had got a bit blood-stained and slightly tattered, and made me a new necklace of what she said were seashells, but I didn't really know what that meant. She painted my face with the traditional designs, and put some eagle feathers in my hair. I took two of the other young men from the village to keep me company, and we took a couple of baskets of gifts – fine stone knives and axe-heads, animal skins, spears with new flint tips, wands carved from mammoth tusks, and all the usual gear for such occasions, but Swiftfox couldn't be persuaded to come with us.

After walking for a day and a half we came to a village I'd been to once before. We found the man who seemed to be in charge and explained why we'd come. He was friendly and told us there were several young women who might be persuaded to go with such a handsome young man. He obviously meant me when he said this, but it had been so long since I'd seen my face reflected in a still pond that I had to take his word for it that I was good-looking. No doubt the facepaint helped. One girl in particular took my eye. Her name was Redcloud, and indeed there was a slight reddish tinge to her hair, and her skin was paler than most of the others. We seemed to like each other, and her mother seemed pleased when I said I'd take her – later I heard there was a story that one of her ancestors had had something to do with one of the Bigfolk; Redcloud's grandmother had also had a pale skin, and some possible suitors had been put off by this. But somehow I had come to find pale skin attractive. I and my companions stayed in the village for half a month, and there was a big feast on the final evening to celebrate our wedding; some of the older men played flutes made of animal bones and banged drums, we all danced, and there was plenty of roast pig, fish, and fruit.

When we arrived home, it was again Thinsnake who was the first to greet us. He was friendly this time, although he looked slightly disturbed to see Redcloud. 'So you have a new woman,' he said. 'We will have good luck now – the ancestors are pleased that we've got rid of those creatures.' Something had happened while I was away, and I felt sick when I thought what it might have been. So after a day or so, when Redcloud was settled in, with Mother fussing over her, and even Swiftfox starting to take an interest in life again, I set out by myself for the cave, making a few false turns, but eventually finding it. All was quiet inside. There was no sign of life, the fire which Wolgong and his family had kept alight all the time I was with them had gone out, the hearth was cold, there were what looked like bloodstains on the floor, and there was a bad smell that made me not want to go further into the cave When I got back I asked Mother if she knew what had happened, but she changed the subject. The next day the snow started falling.

Author's note: recent research suggests that the ancestors of modern Europeans had dark skin and hair in Palaeolithic times, while the Neanderthals had red hair and pale skin.

Leigh V Twersky
Red Cross

For a long time when I was a little boy in the 50s, I wished I was a girl. Girls always seemed to be so nice and had so much more fun than boys. It was such an effort to do boys' things, which were boring. I'd rather play with dolls or draw pictures. My parents told me I should be glad I was a boy, it was bad not to want to be. I looked at the men in my life and felt I never wanted to be like them. In fact I knew I couldn't be. Terrified of having to wear long trousers, for that was surely the point of no return, I clung onto my shorts as long as I could. There was nobody who felt like me.

Very early 60s. I was about 8 or 9. School trip to the Zoo. Our teacher, Miss Botfield, was my favourite in primary school – Craven Park Juniors, Stamford Hill. Everyone loved her, and we missed her terribly when she got married, became Mrs Pook and left.

It was a hot summer morning. I was sitting at one of the window desks, third row back. Miss Botfield said that as there were 33 children in the class and the coach could only take 30, three of us would have to stay behind. Since everyone wanted to go – all kids love zoos – she'd folded 33 squares of paper into a hat.

'Three of these have a red cross,' she said. 'If you pick a red cross, you won't be able to go. It's the fairest way.'

She started with the window seats. The first two children went up and got their paper squares. Both blank. I was next. I reckoned there'd be loads of blank ones for me to pick. I was wrong. When I unfolded my paper, I saw the red cross, in that wonderful deep crimson biro ink. I was stunned. I'd drawn the first red cross. I think I knew I would and spent the rest of that lesson trying not to cry.

The day came and I watched the coach leave. Miss Botfield gave the three of us very easy work, and we read stories, played games and helped her tidy the classroom cupboards, where I found a copy of the *Observer's Book of Wild Flowers*, and asked if it was for me, for not going, but she said no. She told us picking a red cross was unlucky, but it could also mean something special.

Later that year, the group of children I used to walk home with via Chat's the corner sweetshop (no one knew the real name of the shop) had noticed a strange person with short, dark hair wearing a black jacket and trousers, unlike anyone we'd ever seen before. One day, we stopped the person, and I think it was Lynn, who asked, 'Excuse me, are you man or lady?'

The person looked at us and said, 'I'm a Lesbian.'

'What's a Lesbian?'

'Ask your mother.'

So I went home and said, 'Mum, what's a Lesbian?'

My mum was quite shocked. 'Oh, they're bad women who don't want to be like women.' She didn't explain.

If that was supposed to horrify me, it had the opposite effect. I was overjoyed. Now I knew I was not alone – there were other people like me who weren't happy with what they were. Somehow. I just needed to find them ...

Some years later, I was quite happy being a boy. I was about 15. The best back-handed compliment I'd ever received was from a boy at school. 'If you were a girl, you'd be beautiful.' I was thrilled. I liked the thought of being attractive, of flirting. I played with the idea of grown men wanting me. Of course, we'd all been warned about strangers ...

We were living in Ilford then, but I still went to school in Islington. Going home was a simple change on the Underground from Angel to Gants Hill via Bank. Trains were frequent and reliable then. Mid 60s. Swinging London.

Many of the other kids at school lived in North London and sometimes, if we were chatting about something interesting, I'd go with them to Kings Cross and then double back via Holborn. I loved exploring the Tube. I remember one afternoon like that. I'd got the Piccadilly line from Kings Cross to Holborn. I noticed a young man, not much older than me, staring at me, hard enough to worry me. He kept looking over. I was glad I was only going two stops, and got off at Holborn.

So did he.

I looked back. He was still looking at me. I got onto the escalator to get the Central line. He was behind me. I began to feel threatened. My heart was beating faster and faster. Was he one of those child killers? I quickened my pace. And so did he.

The interchange at Holborn is simple. The Central line is the other side of the station. There's a tunnel, which leads to the two platforms, seen from the ceiling like a big letter F. The first branch of the F is the stairs down to the Westbound trains, to Ealing Broadway or West Ruislip. The end of the F leads to the Eastbound platform for Hainault or Epping. I needed to go East.

Was he following me – or just on his way home from work to somewhere on the Central line? How could I know? I entered the F. He was right behind me. I passed the Westbound steps, slowly. He also slowed down, never taking his eyes off me. Sweat poured off my brow. My mouth was dry. I didn't want to end up in a newspaper article, discovered in a ditch after going missing.

I doubled back and ran down the steps to the Westbound platform. He turned round and came after me, fast. I held my breath. Sensed danger.

There was a train in the platform. The doors were open. I leapt on. Stayed by the door. He jumped on too. Stood opposite me. Leering, with eyes that try not to look, but take you all in. He was breathing heavily, as I was.

The hiss. The signal. The guard (they still had guards on the Tube in those days) had pressed the button to close the doors. Now or never. I just managed to jump out. The doors closed. Forever. I breathed a sigh of relief. As the train departed, his eyes were still on me, reproachful, longing, despondent. I smiled. I'd outwitted him. Escaped. The train accelerated. I'd never see him again. I was so happy, so clever! Grinned all the way home.

Later that evening, I was supposed to be doing my homework, but all I could think about was my secret adventure. Couldn't get that final look of his out of my mind. But then I started to wonder what could've happened if I'd not managed to run away. And spoken to him, asked him what he wanted. And I started to get turned on at the thought of where it could've led. He wasn't bad looking. Maybe he wasn't a crazy murderer. Not seeing him ever again now seemed more of a loss. Wasn't feeling quite so clever. And so I realized something else too, which I didn't have all the words for then, but you know anyway, something I'd always known but kept to myself, something Miss Botfield had said could be unlucky or something special.

My own, personal, life-sized red cross.

A Duel

Guy de'Ath entered the ballroom and sighed with wonder. It was his first ball here, and as a new member of society, a milestone in his development as a young gentleman.

The host, Sir Peregrine Landsworthy-Brough, had not yet come down to the ball. Brough Hall had been decorated with red roses and white lilies from the landscaped garden. Servants stood attentively with trays laden with champagne. An orchestra was playing a stately sarabande, to which many of the guests were dancing.

A cursory glance round had Guy marvelling at the sumptuous dresses and spectacular wigs of the ladies as they curtseyed to their partners. There seemed to be something not quite right, but he couldn't put his finger on what it was.

A merry jig started up. Guy was not ready to join the dance yet. He felt a sudden rush of nerves. Had he forgotten anything? He checked: handkerchiefs, white carnation buttonhole, cane and sword – just a short court sword for decoration – and his calves were suitably curvaceous. His red velvet court suit was the most expensive he could afford.

He went over the dance steps in his head and tried them out, dancing on the spot, and felt his wig. His snuffbox was full.

The de'Aths were newcomers to the area, having recently moved from Norfolk, and Guy had not made any acquaintances yet, so unsurprisingly he felt shy, but he knew once he had a drink inside him, he would be more confident. He wanted to start anew and this was his big chance. In Norfolk, he'd always dreaded any society occasions, never certain that he really belonged.

He took a flute from one of the trays and downed the champagne in one. It was heady and not altogether agreeable. He helped himself to another, having replaced his empty glass.

His crimson outfit really suited his sallow complexion and dark hair, he thought, catching his reflection in a mirror.

The jig ended. The dancers clapped and returned to their seats.

A footman, who'd announced Guy at the entrance on his arrival, struck a gong. The noise achieved the required silence it demanded.

'My lords, ladies and gentlemen. Your host, Sir Peregrine Landsworthy-Brough!'

Cheers and applause filled the ballroom.

A young man, similarly dressed in red, but sporting a gigantic powdered wig, began to descend the grand sweeping staircase from the gallery, his hand resting on the gilded banister. He was a bit older than Guy and of a similar, average height.

Guy thought he looked so dashing in his scarlet attire and was sure he had all the young ladies falling at his feet.

'My dearest friends,' started Sir Peregrine, surveying the ballroom as he spoke, 'and my dearest lords, ladies and gentle ...'

Here, he stopped and fixed Guy with a stare and marched straight up to him.

Guy's eyes widened with fear and embarrassment. Had he done something wrong, broken some arcane rule of etiquette? He had no idea.

Sir Peregrine grabbed Guy's lapel. 'How ... how dare you!' he thundered.

There were gasps and murmuring from the guests.

Guy wanted to die right there and then, but decided to be brave and stand his ground. 'I'm terribly sorry, Sir,' he squeaked timidly, 'I don't understand. How dare I what?'

Sir Peregrine laughed. But it wasn't a friendly guffaw. 'You have the temerity and audacity to wear my colour?'

Guy was dumbstruck. 'B-but I had no idea red was your colour, Sir.'

Sir Peregrine stepped back and looked Guy once over. 'Normally,' he roared, 'I would order Vicky Dyler here' – he pointed at the footman – 'to kick your backside out of my house and expect you to apologize profusely. But today of all days, my twenty-second birthday, this is all too much. There's no other way. I demand satisfaction.'

'Satisfaction?' Guy gulped. 'You m-mean ... a duel?'

Sir Peregrine chuckled and nodded once. Then he slapped Guy's right cheek. 'My challenge.'

More gasps.

The blood drained from Guy's face. Eighteen. Insulted and assaulted on what was supposed to be a bright new beginning but would probably turn out to be the last day of his life. Thank God he'd brought his sword, even if it was just a small weapon. He dared not refuse this challenge, lest he be branded a coward and shunned from society as a laughing-stock. No lady would marry him, although up till that moment he hadn't really given much thought to marriage. 'Very good, Sir,' he said. 'When is this to take place?'

'Immediately.' Sir Peregrine called to Vicky Dyler. 'You will be my second.' He seized Guy's arm. 'And who have you brought?'

Guy trembled and his voice was shaky. 'I ... I have n-no one, sir. I c-came alone.'

'That was careless.' He took in the panorama of guests. 'Anyone willing to second this ... this er boy, who dared to outdress me on my special day and from whom I shall have satisfaction?'

A young man stepped forward.

Sir Peregrine shook his head. 'Not you, Cornwallis. You know why. Someone ... anyone else?'

Eventually, another youth volunteered.

'Excellent, Sopwith. I thank you.'

Guy was too nervous to say anything. Sir Peregrine led him to the entrance, turning back once to address his guests. 'Enjoy yourselves. I shan't be long. Music pronto!'

They set off in silence. Sir Peregrine marched Guy, never once letting go of his arm, into the extensive grounds of Brough Hall. The sun was just beginning to set. An owl hooted and a bat flapped past in the sky.

This is all so beautiful, thought Guy, and very soon I'll be dead. He was not skilled at fencing and was afraid that his opponent would be confident and accomplished enough to kill him, or at least maim him. Sir Peregrine obviously didn't expect the duel to last long. Perhaps, Guy hoped, it would only be to first blood. He didn't dare ask. He tried to remember all the good things in his life, but the memories just wouldn't come. He couldn't help quaking with fear. Sir Peregrine squeezed his arm.

Presently they came to a glade in a wooded part of the estate. Guy noticed with despair that Sir Peregrine had a rapier, rather longer than his own sword. Maybe as they were unevenly matched he would be a man of honour and call it off. He was everything Guy admired, handsome and chivalrous. He saw they were similarly complexioned. They could be brothers. ...

'Sir,' he began, mustering all his courage, 'I am profoundly sorry to have offended you. However, I fear our duel will not be fair, for my sword is no match for yours. And when you have slain me, will my thus spilt blood really afford you satisfaction?'

Sir Peregrine ignored him.

'Surely we can just discuss this like gentlemen?'

Sir Peregrine looked at Guy. Then he burst out laughing, for longer than Guy thought polite. 'My dear fellow,' he said, once he'd recovered from his fit of giggles, 'I am demanding a rather different sort of satisfaction.'

Guy was dumbfounded. The seconds sniggered.

Sir Peregrine hushed them and, grabbing Guy's arm again, pulled him ten paces further into the woods. 'Relax,' he whispered.

'How can I?'

Sir Peregrine continued. 'I must say, you are one fine fellow and cut a right handsome figure in those red breeches.' He brushed his hand over the front of Guy's breeches and then felt the back.

'Oh, what a relief,' sighed Guy. 'But why all that fuss before?'

'Spectacle, my dear boy. You caught my eye and I simply have to have you. It'll be your birthday gift.' He proceeded to unbutton Guy's court coat and loosened his breeches. 'And I believe I caught your eye too.'

He held Guy's growing cock. 'That's some homage you pay me.'

The conversation ended abruptly here. Sir Peregrine wasted no time fucking Guy's tight arse, all the while rubbing his penis. Both came simultaneously.

They lay back on the warm grass. 'Thank you,' said Sir Peregrine. 'You've indeed given me satisfaction.'

'Likewise,' said Guy, somewhat breathless.

'You can be my companion and friend. You'll be at home here in Brough Hall. Now get dressed. Time to re-join the merriment.'

They got back to the glade, where Sopwith was giving Vicky Dyler a blow-job.

Sir Peregrine said quietly, 'Just to warn you. If you engage with Vicky Dyler in that way, wear a bib. He can be messy.'

Guy didn't know if he could laugh. 'But why did you refuse Cornwallis, Sir?'

'Oh, he's got the clap and shouldn't do much willy-wise. But come now, we must return to the Ball. Sopwith, very sensible stripping to your waist.'

A Duel 49

When they arrived and were re-announced by Vicky Dyler, there was rapturous applause.

'You will dance with me,' said Sir Peregrine.

Guy looked uncertain. 'But won't people ...?'

'Don't worry. Look around.'

Guy did, properly this time. And noticed the ladies were rather taller than those he'd known back in Norfolk, had thicker necks and inordinately large hands and feet. He'd never known why he always felt awkward in society with all its rigid rules. Now he did.

A gavotte started. Sir Peregrine bowed to Guy and they joined the dance.

Sir Peregrine was right. Guy did feel at home.

Patrick C. Notchtree

The Visit

*A poem describing my visit
to see Stephen in prison.*

I drive alone, glee mixed with fear
Along the now familiar way
I foresee your smile, your joy at seeing me
I fear your gloom, your basic misery.
What crisis has hit you?
What illness attacked you,
left by an uncaring system?
As I drive, my mind is full;
The sight of your face,
The sound of your voice,
Perhaps all too briefly, the touch of you.
And I know I will miss
The scent of you,
The taste of you.

The buildings squat low among the fields
As though the huge site tries to conceal
The depravity of its existence.
As I get near, I sound the horn
Our special code, in case you can hear
To lift your mood, your love is now near
My gaze tries to penetrate
The wall that incarcerates.
In the car park I pause, I am still free,
Empty my pockets, just coins, ID and a key.
Soon I know I will have
The sight of your face,
The sound of your voice,
Perhaps all too briefly, the touch of you.

THE VISIT

And I know I will miss
The scent of you,
The taste of you.

The electric doors take me in too,
But they bring me closer to you.
Search, rub down and then I'm through.
Look down the room, are you there yet?
Then to the shop hatch, I know what to get;
Lots of chocolate and very sweet tea.
(That's for you, much less for me.)
Along the big room I carry the tray
To where you are sitting, it's now our day.
And now so briefly at last I have
The sight of your face,
The sound of your voice,
And all too briefly, the touch of you.
And yes I do miss
The scent of you,
The taste of you.

You smile your smile, I sense your love
But kept under wraps in this public space.
Other cons, and screws watch this place
Not to mention the lenses above.
We talk, catch up, where is the letter?
Written last week, still not arrived.
Despite complaints, that gets no better.
But now for a time, so long deprived,
At last I have
The sight of your face,
The sound of your voice,
And all too briefly, the touch of you.
I really do miss
The scent of you,
The taste of you.

My eyes take you in, the pallor of your skin
Fed on so little, under two pounds a day.
Not surprising you look so thin.
The chocolate bar is pushed away.
It's now too rich, too much to eat,
On the edge of malnutrition,
More and more less of a treat,
I'm scared for your condition.
But just for now I have
The sight of your face,
The sound of your voice,
And all too briefly, the touch of you.
I long to have too
The scent of you,
The taste of you.

My eyes take you in, your hair to your toes
You are still there, despite being clad
In the blue prison clothes.
This respite from your pad.
We ask how can I help you,
Trapped in the prison of your past,
So you never see another screw,
And make you truly free at last?
But just for now I have
The sight of your face,
The sound of your voice,
And all too briefly, the touch of you.
And I so want as well
The scent of you,
The taste of you.

You live in the moment, I know
Your defence for the torment inside,
On release, where can you go?

The Visit

But we manage a laugh, a joke beside.
Then comes the call, 'Finish off now.'
The pain of knowing that now we must part.
I'll keep on coming, I made that vow,
I'll hold these memories deep in my heart.
But now I must leave
The sight of your face,
The sound of your voice,
And all too briefly, the touch of you.
And I so want as well
The scent of you,
The taste of you.

I walk to the door, go through the check,
I turn and look back, to see if you wave.
You're at the far end, I'm craning my neck
You get that last glimpse; you're being so brave.
Then I am out, into the sunlight,
Empty my locker and walk back to our car,
I sit for a moment, my tears out of sight.
Then the drive back, so near and so far.
As I drive, my mind is full;
The sight of your face,
The sound of your voice,
And all too briefly, the touch of you.
And I know I will miss
The scent of you,
The taste of you.

Death in Custody

A poem describing my feelings and the events after the suicide of my dear Stephen in prison.

They called my name, approach with care
Why have they come, do they care?
Two sad faces with the news I dread
My love, my friend, at his own hand – dead!
They take their time, let the news sink in
A fight in my head, I struggle with reality
Will I never again have the joy of
The sight of your face,
The sound of your voice,
And all too briefly, the touch of you?
And I so want as well
The scent of you,
The taste of you.

Condolences come from far and wide
Friends, both real world, and online too,
Our solicitor, even, who knows us both well.
And flowers from those who the visits provide.
But all I can feel is knowing that I
Can't have again
The sight of your face,
The sound of your voice,
And all too briefly, the touch of you.
And I so want as well
The scent of you,
The taste of you.

Police on the phone, coroner too.
So much grief but so much to do.
In a way it helps, it keeps you still there
Somehow 'alive', your short life to share

Just thirty-five, not really got started.
I'm pleading, begging, that I might yet view
The sight of your face,
The sound of your voice,
And all too briefly, the touch of you.
And I so want as well
The scent of you,
The taste of you.

Why did you do it? I know only too well;
A lifetime of grief from that childhood abuse.
And may that man, still free, yet rot in hell.
Your own errors too, compounding the damage
I weep and I cry, but what's the use?
Despite all I could do, it wasn't enough
I know I will miss, however tough,
The sight of your face,
The sound of your voice,
And all too loving, the touch of you.
And I so crave as well
The scent of you,
The taste of you.

I set it all down, five pages long
The trials of your life that led to this end.
From shattered boyhood you tried to be strong,
But the nightmares remained, but even your friend
Was not enough and you did reoffend.
You never hurt anyone, I know that is true,
But that terrible legacy was the downfall of you.
My life goes on but from now on without
The sight of your face,
The sound of your voice,
And all too loving, the touch of you.
And I so crave as well

The scent of you,
The taste of you.

They sent me the letters, written that night,
That you left me, reliving your pain.
Long letters, page after page
Outpouring of grief, torment and rage.
So hard to read, but they show you were sane,
'Balance of mind' intact, it's quite plain.
But now I must live without, for an age,
The sight of your face,
The sound of your voice,
And all too loving, the touch of you.
And I so need as well
The scent of you,
The taste of you.

I went to the prison to visit your cell,
The place where you ended your private hell.
I had imagined it Spartan and white,
But the reality was far from bright.
Rough plaster, painted dark grey,
Small and drab. Like an underground cellar.
A pigeon hole for a human being.
I sat on your bed, where you used to lie
But which you then used, on end, for the noose.
Your only way out from the torment of abuse.
I picked up your glasses, so personal, so you
That's when I cried, despite the nearby screw.
Was this the last place that ever had known
The sight of your face,
The sound of your voice,
And all too much, the touch of you?
In there I could sense
The scent of you,
The taste of you.

They held a short service in memory of you.
You had said they would, with prisoners there too.
You'd asked me to go, so how could I not.
A Christian service, as no doubt you knew
Which would have amused you, as you believed not one jot.
But it was warm and loving with many kind words
The prisoners spoke well of you, their pain seemed real too
I spoke about you, with words well received
About childhood abuse and the legacy it leaves.
Then I went away, they back to their cells
Unlike me though, they won't miss
The sight of your face,
The sound of your voice,
And oh so much, the touch of you.
And I mourn for as well
The scent of you,
The taste of you.

I wanted to see you, they offered the chance
To see you again, a final chance.
Steeling myself I entered the room
Curtained, quiet solitude, I held my heart numb.
As I got closer I saw your dear face.
As always the sight of you made my pulse race.
But then I was by you, and you were so still.
I stroked your hair: 'Wake up!' I wanted to shout
I thought you just might and brush me aside
'Gettoff me hair', and give me a clout.
Your hands were so cold, and I saw your slim chest
Misshaped under clothing, where postmortem had messed.
I realised again that despite this last look
This was the last I ever would see
The sight of your face.
No sound of your voice,

And cold, too cold, the touch of you.
No trace now forever.
No scent of you,
No taste of you.

Ashes to ashes, dust to dust
I sorted your funeral, as I knew I must.
As next of kin, it's all mine to do
I did my best, to honour you.
More people came than I thought might
I hope you think I got it about right.
As the curtains closed round with you in the coffin
I tried not to think of the coming cremation
As the shell that was you met its conflagration,
Knowing that now, never again
Will I ever again have the joy of
The sight of your face,
The sound of your voice,
The warmth, the love, the touch of you.
And I try to imagine
The scent of you,
The taste of you.

It seems unreal but I must face
In my life there is an empty space
I have my family, in which I am blessed
Unlike yours, who left you bereft.
I have the ground ashes, all left of you
I will take time to think what to do.
Maybe the stadium where your loved football team play
Some for a ring perhaps, so I'll always have you
Perhaps on the Med, where we spent such happy days.
But whatever I do, I will always love you
And do my best to remember
The sight of your face,
The sound of your voice,

Loving and kind, the touch of you.
And I'll keep in my heart
The scent of you,
The taste of you.

Loving Stephen

Is it wrong to love you so?
Your death was such a hammer blow
On those last visits each week
You could barely even speak
But you often did cry
As you just wanted to die.
Remember, remember the 4th of November
Suicide, hanging, a knot
The thought of your pain
As you hung from that frame
Drives me insane.
Life's not the same.
But I have your image all around
So many pictures of happy times
Us together, you were happy then.
Bittersweet memories abound,
They can never be done again.
But life goes on, my love endures
A part of me is always yours.
There is so much to you I owe.
Is it wrong to love you so?

Elsa Wallace
Out of the Frying Pan

Edgar, who identified himself as involuntarily gay, had the luck or misfortune, while taking minutes at the Parish Council, to be introduced to a zealous young doctor who on learning of his plight was eager to assist him un-gaying himself. Edgar unburdened himself of the difficulties of his life as an unfulfilled gay man to this sympathetic religious ear. And so a trial of standard procedures was attempted but none achieved success.

'I can't understand it,' said Dr Ruler. 'By my way of thinking you're halfway there, it only needs a little push. You've no time for Judy Garland or Bette Midler, and you can't get your head round Tchaikovsky. I don't see where the hold-up can lie.'

'I suppose I'm just meant to be a failure,' said Edgar despondently. 'Look at the way I furnished my flat, it's a disaster. We can't have Christian Fellowship coffee evenings in it.'

'There you are; that's going in the right direction. No gay man could have ruined a railway cottage to that extent.'

Yet it seemed impasse was reached until one evening the indefatigable Dr Ruler excitedly called him, offering an emergency consultation. 'No waiting list for you, my friend, here is hope at last.'

Closeted with him in the cold surgery Edgar studied the label on the bottle of yellow pills.

'It's all in Chinese!'

'Yes, it's a Chinese remedy. The translation is simple. One pill at night once a week.'

'I've heard dodgy things about Chinese medicine – this could contain all sorts: arsenic, mercury, tiger bones.'

'There's nothing harmful in them. It's herbal, organic from the foothills of Tien Shan. Look, I'll take one myself, that should reassure you. Though, ha ha, I don't need to be more straight than I am.' He imagined that four children proved his credentials, and he swallowed a yellow pill with a swig of tea.

'This will see you right. I guarantee in two years you'll be married with a baby on the way.'

'I'm not sure a baby is what I want. What I want rid of is being different, the worry of people finding out, all that.'

'And so you shall. This will change everything for you.'

'How did you come by them?'

'A missionary friend – he smuggles Bibles into Beijing. He's very successful. These pills are an open secret there. They've been using them for decades. Of course they won't export them – they prefer us to go on in our decadent way, makes it easier for them to take over the world.'

Edgar wondered if he were about to add, 'Damn clever, these Chinese.' He shook the bottle. 'I don't know. What proof have you got?'

'Proof? My dear chap, don't you read the papers? What more proof do you need? Because of the one-child policy there are more than eighteen million single, some say surplus, males in China – AND THERE ARE NO HOMOSEXUALS! I rest my case.'

Edgar was sceptical.

'Their Government has stated it as a fact,' said Dr Ruler, rapping the table for emphasis.

'Oh get away. There are gay Chinese in London. I should know. I've had unrequited love with noodles often enough.'

'That's because they stopped taking the pills, or never had them. These are Government issue, the real McCoy. Look here, I'll monitor you – I'll give you a check-up every fortnight, bloods, the lot. Now what do you say?'

Though he was dubious Edgar said yes.

Weeks passed and no change came. The men on the building site next his office were as desirable as ever.

'This is a dead loss,' said Edgar as the doctor clumsily siphoned off more of his blood.

'Have faith,' counselled Dr Ruler. 'After all, you've been ogling men since you were eight and now you're thirty-seven. Rome wasn't built in a day.'

Disheartened, Edgar almost abandoned his efforts. 'One can be Christian and gay,' he observed. 'What about Cardinal Newman?'

'Newman wasn't gay,' snapped the doctor. 'Just good friends. Newman was a saint. The total disappearance of his body shows that. It was a miracle. Normally a body, teeth included, could not vanish like that. He went on to a higher realm.'

'I sometimes wish I could,' said Edgar, in whom the new postboy was inflaming lustful thoughts of some power. 'Have these pills been tested on homosexual animals?' he asked suddenly.

'Animals?' Ruler gaped.

'Yes, gay animals. You haven't heard of them? I can't credit this. For someone planning to cure me you don't seem to have encyclopaedic knowledge of the subject. But I suppose there are no gay animals in China,' he added sarcastically.

'Never mind that. Look, have two pills this week. Call me as soon as there's a flicker.'

There was one tablet left when Edgar was aware that something was different. He awoke to strange sensations. His brain felt alive, pressing against his skull, like a head of fern-frond attempting to uncurl. Well, the pills were derived from some sort of fern so perhaps the feeling was appropriate. The usual morning depression and forebodings were absent and he almost ran out into the day.

The first woman he spoke to made him flush and his heart pounded pleasurably. He wondered if he might be imagining it, to please Dr Ruler, or was it all in his mind, were the pills mere placebos?

But no, what had been rather desultory feelings of friendship grew into something quite other. He became almost ashamed of the way he had treated this woman in the past. He had often ignored her, or taken her for granted. He had even borrowed money from her in an unconscionable and casual way. It was no exaggeration to say he had at times exploited her, traded on her kindness.

But now he mooned over his desk at work thinking of her. He longed to see her every day. To hear her voice, even on the telephone, was delicious. He dreamed rich daring dreams. He would not act on them immediately – instead he would be subtle. He would take her out to lunch.

To be sure he waited a couple of weeks before he did so and before informing Dr Ruler. The latter crowed in triumph.

'What did I tell you, just as I said! You doubting Thomas! I bet you will be a dad before you're much older.'

'I doubt that,' said Edgar. 'She's past the menopause, for a start.'

'What?'

'Oh, yes, an older woman,' Edgar confirmed with relish. 'In fact, my mum.'

Forsaken

He was taken to the island at night, the inky surround of sea and sky making the faces of the three men in the boat appear ghostly pale. As they reached the limited space for landing the boatmen spoke curtly to each other. The fettered man said nothing. They unloaded him and the boxes and bundles in silence, then glanced up at the building on the height, even darker against dark sky.

'There'll still be some potatoes in the field,' said one.

'We'll be back in six weeks, or later if the weather says no.'

They struck off his fetters and left him to it.

It was the island of Forsaken to which he was condemned as a traitor, and which usually was used for murderers of good birth. Therefore it wasn't quite as grim as might be expected. Part of the old keep had a weatherproof roof. Some few stunted trees remained in the walled plot of stony ground. There were good cisterns of rainwater. In the past pirates had occasionally landed and killed anyone they found, but that hadn't happened for some time.

He was adequately provided with dry goods, tools, oilskins and a cock and hen. This was a rare island, being rat-free – it was said previous occupants had devoured them and had also trapped and eaten any seabirds so incautious as to rest on the walls of the keep.

He stowed his possessions in the dry room and waited among them for the dawn, which the cock was pleased to announce. The room held a table, bench and bed-frame, all of which needed attention and though unskilled he managed to effect rough repairs. The two fowl he put into a small enclosure and dug a patch of shallow earth to provide grubs for them, as well as giving them some meal and seeds. Then he gathered dead shrubs and grasses to cook his own food. On the shoreline he had seen much seaweed which he could dry on rocks for fuel and eat whatever small life was in them. He would do this automatically, not really anxious to preserve his life but because he had no books and nothing else to do. He worked over the larger walled area and planted it.

He stared at sky and sea and brought them into his brain so that in the dark of night he still saw them. His fire and candles he used frugally.

The boatmen came again, as they had said, bringing further provisions. One remained with the boat; the other strolled about looking at everything with interest.

They were not allowed to speak to him so this one addressed his comments to the hen.

'You have high connections but they cannot shorten your stay. You must use your voice or it will dwindle to nothing. You feel alone but it may be preferable. Once there were two here. The result was unhappy, one of them had to go.'

It was a warm dry day and the boatman laid his coat on a wall. When he departed, he seemed to have forgotten it. In the pockets were a little flute, a candle, some nuts and seeds, some slips of plants, twists of paper containing sugar. The coat was superior to his own and he wore it gratefully when the wind blew cold.

One day when preparing more ground to plant, thin as it was, he came upon bones just under the surface: long bones from which he deduced where the skull should be and found it, the cranium crushed but the teeth perfect. There was a little chapel-room attached to the keep – no altar within, but a large cross cut into the stone at one end. He thought he might lift a paving stone and re-inter the bones there, only that night the ghost came and as he couldn't divine its wishes he covered over the bones and let them rest there in the sound of the sea and under a wild sky.

He had just had his small supper after shutting the fowls in their shelter, and had taken out the flute to essay a tune upon it (which pastime really did pass time, he had found) when, looking up, he saw the ghost smile at him where it had appeared in the doorway. He knew who it was from the perfect shape and whiteness of the teeth.

It seemed to him like a poet, with long straight hair, thin narrow face and hands, wearing a loose shirt with full sleeves, tight trousers and elegant boots. It shimmered pale silver-grey and looked not above twenty years old.

What should he say to it? After some thought and as it remained he said 'My name is Millin. Will you be seated?'

He gave up the solitary chair and sat on his bed.

The ghost inclined his head but sat on the table, swinging one foot gently and studying him.

Millin told the ghost why he was there, for treachery (he omitted the additional charge of blasphemy), and that he would be there for some time.

'So you are forced to share your island with me.'

The ghost nodded and smiled, but didn't reply.

Millin could think of nothing else to do but continue his flute-playing. The ghost slid on to the chair, rested his elbows on the table and listened intently.

'I am a mere beginner, not even an amateur,' Millin broke off to explain.

The ghost smiled. He was whitely opaque and created his own light until he faded out abruptly.

He appeared irregularly, outside while Millin worked or when Millin retired indoors. Millin became conscious of his own appearance and, not being able to shave, cut back his beard as best he could.

He greeted and spoke to the ghost in a friendly manner but he made no reply, though he did appear to comprehend him. He had tried to question the ghost, that he might answer yes or no with a nod or shake of the head, but though he knew he could hear him all he elicited was a gentle smile as though rebuking an impertinence.

Once he apologised for the content of his speech: 'I talk much of potatoes and peat-cutting, but that is what occupies my mind at present.' The ghost smiled a sweet boyish smile and made a deprecatory gesture as if to say 'Think nothing of it.'

Sometimes Millin met him walking on the rocky shore; the ghost would nod to him and go on his way.

When he tired of flute-playing in the evening Millin recited what poetry he could recall, some of which appeared to please but sentimental verses drew a sarcastic grimace.

Millin enjoyed his company though he was disconcerted when on occasion, as he faded, the ghost's face became skull-like.

He dreamed, and in his dreams, rarely, the ghost spoke to him. Smiling he said, 'I am a murderer, you know,' and 'I trust we shall always be companions.' His dream-voice was light and pleasant.

The fowls, released to wander as they willed, did well and even produced chicks. A butterfly was blown to land, and some terns, perhaps also caught by the wind, settled for a while. He thought they were intrigued by his fowls.

While the ghost often sought out his company, liking to watch him at work by day and listen to him talk in the evenings, he had his own life, disappearing for hours at a time. Sometimes he came upon him sitting on a wall staring out not toward the mainland but over the far western ocean. When the sun shone he seemed to revel in it, raising his arms to the sky and in that bright light more translucent than ever. There could be no doubt he was glad to be free of the grave.

The boatmen continued to bring supplies including a small flask of brandy as the autumn closed. Being his only contact, they had developed a proprietorial interest in him:

they were gratified to see him thrive and girded against the fierce months ahead.

One day they came before their time, disembarking a seasick official who announced he had brought good news.

'The conviction for treason is rescinded, other information having come to light. What is yours shall be restored to you. You need only recant the blasphemy and liberty is yours.'

The ghost, leaning against the doorframe, gave a start, then doubled up in mirth.

Millin thought for a few minutes.

'I do not recant the blasphemy,' he said.

'Should you like more time to consider?'

'No, thank you.'

'I shan't make this journey again.'

The ghost executed a mocking bow as the official made his unsteady retching way down to the boat.

Too late Millin thought, 'I should have asked the name of the ghost man. He might have known it.'

That night he told the ghost, 'As I woke you from your grave, I can hardly abandon you. And besides, now I shouldn't care to lose you.'

It seemed to him that the ghost's lips formed the words, 'Nor I you.'

Which made him wonder, as he lay on his rough bed with the glimmering presence beside him, whether, had he recanted and returned to the mainland with the boatmen, the ghost might have, after all, accompanied him across the strait. But it wasn't a gamble he would take.

Having Your Cake *AND* Eating It

I like to think that I am lesbian simply because I am in love with Rosabel and we happen to be women. She is the only person I have ever loved. It is on account of her personality I love her, for I have had many girl friends before, but they have been friends only. I cannot, however, ignore the influence my family may have had on my character and disposition. My three older brothers had probably conditioned my parents in their child-rearing technique, so by the time I was born they were disinclined to alter their methods and I was brought up, more or less, as a fourth son. This attempt at equality was regarded by me with ambivalence; at times I liked the freedom and lack of discrimination, at others I was jealous of my friends who were treated 'like proper girls'. For instance I was pleased and annoyed that I was expected to take turns with my brothers in overhauling the car at weekends, and I was flattered and furious when my father, complimenting me on a new white silk blouse, said to me, as he might have done to one of the boys, 'Very handsome, you look like Lord Byron,'

My parents were eccentric to start with and I liked that, but was annoyed that an aunt had to prod my mother into buying me my first bra, irritated that an 'outsider' should have to remind her that I was female. The price of a teenage bra staggered my mother; she held up the wisp of broderie anglaise and embarrassed me and astonished the assistant by exclaiming, 'Good Lord, that's as much as for rugby shorts!'

Homosexuality was mentioned once in our house and then by a visitor, a casual acquaintance who chose to remark that he had heard that Tchaikovsky was 'queer'. Obviously determined not to let this non-musical person hold the floor, my father answered coolly, 'Aren't we all?' 'How true!' beamed my mother, for though she and my father enjoyed disagreeing on almost every topic, she believed in presenting a united front to visitors.

I really had no suspicion that I would ever fall in love with a girl; I think it was competition with my brothers that made me notice with a sense of triumph that my girl friends were not only prettier than theirs but more intelligent too. I went through a phase of hoping they would marry my friends so that I might have the sisters-in-law of my choice.

The only assertion of my femaleness I made was in taking up cake-baking and decoration.

'Rebecca, I can't think all this cake-baking is good for you psychologically,' said my mother one day.

'Why not?' I was concentrating on my speciality, a four-layer sponge.

I swear she was about to answer, 'Your brothers don't bake cakes,' but caught herself in time and instead said vaguely, 'I don't know, I'll look it up. Anyway you'll have to move your icing gear out of the spare room, I might need it for Clement.'

Our cousin Clement came to live with us. He was newly engaged and hoped to save money by lodging with relatives.

'Rosabel is such a charming girl,' my mother told me. 'Very talented.'

'Can't be all that talented,' said my father. 'Got herself engaged to Clement, didn't she.'

He was contemptuous of Clement on account of his meanness, legendary in our family.

Rosabel came to tea. Expecting an ordinary pretty little thing, I was totally unprepared for this tall beauty with a narrow unusual face and shining swathes of red hair arranged to resemble the bud of a strange flower.

'Delicious cake, wish I could bake like this,' Rosabel said to my mother. 'Do give me the recipe.'

'Do you bake too?' said my mother with evident disapproval. 'Good heavens.'

'Rosabel only does it for fun,' said Clement. 'Rebecca does it professionally.'

'Oh dear, do you think this recipe would be too advanced for me?' asked Rosabel widening her extraordinary grey eyes.

'Not at all.' I muttered on self-consciously about walnuts and buttercream.

A few weeks later I was ridiculously pleased when Clement said, 'For God's sake give Rosabel another recipe, it's nothing but walnut cake at her place.'

Inevitably I was asked to make their wedding cake. Clement's eyes gleamed at the thought of saving money this way, but I had mixed feelings, being by now aware of the extent of Rosabel's attraction for me as I could not avoid seeing her almost every day.

Deciding that a clean break would be best, I took a tiny flat the other side of town. My mother fussed slightly about my living alone and after two weeks telephoned to say she had found me a flatmate.

'But I don't want one,' I said angrily, for if I could not live with my 'rosa bella' I did not intend to live with anyone.

'It's Rosabel. She's been let down badly over this other flat, was definitely promised it and now they tell her not for another six months.'

So Rosabel came to stay. I thought, 'Well, we won't be together much, she'll be out with Clement.' But Clement's meanness meant no theatres or restaurants. I feared he would be around every evening for a meal, but to my surprise he only came to supper once. Rosabel said he had taken up a correspondence course.

I made a start on the cake and Rosabel helped with chopping the fruit. It was winter and we spent cosy evenings indoors, Rosabel watching me doing the lattice-icing or helping me plan a huge fabric collage for the sitting-room wall. She would keep buying things for the flat, a cane mat, a chunky blue glass vase, and brushed aside my protestations that I should pay her for them. I said, 'What will Clement say about your spending spree?' She pretended not to hear. I gave up trying to cut myself off from Rosabel and drifted in the warm current of her company. We were lunching together every day, in her favourite cafe. 'In summer we'll take sandwiches to the park,' she said. I wanted to say, 'But you won't be here in the summer,' but it was such a horrible thought that I could not voice it.

Just before Christmas my mother telephoned wanting me to come over and admire her book reviews.

'I'm in the middle of icing,' I said. 'No, not Christmas cake, wedding cake, Rosabel's.'

'Rosabel's? Didn't I warn you about your cake-madness?'

I turned to Rosabel. 'My mother says your engagement was broken off weeks ago – why didn't you tell me?'

She just went red and fidgeted.

'What am I to do with this cake?' I glared at it, hating it now in all its rose-festooned glory. 'A nice fool you've made of me – I'd never have done all that work on it for anyone else,' I said recklessly.

'Couldn't we keep it?' suggested Rosabel diffidently. 'Well, eat it, I mean?'

'Eat a whole wedding cake ourselves!'

'We could send pieces to my old school pals,' she said thoughtfully. 'And there's your family, and people at the office.'

It's a three-tier cake – I suppose it is just possible that we may have finished it by the time our first anniversary comes around?

Emily Hay
Pessimists' Romance

The 1980s. London. If you were a woman looking to meet other women for sex or romance, this meant opening doors that were only half open, entering strange rooms and small worlds. For some women, this happened through politics. For the rest of us, it meant chains of acquaintances, small ads in the classified sections, rooms above bars in backstreets, first names only. In 1985 I was newly graduated, and newly single. My attempt at heterosexuality was over and I was stepping into the unknown because there appeared to be no other choice.

June 1985: The upstairs bar at the Barley Mow, Smithfield, on a Saturday night was busy, the room filled with middle-aged women and the smell of cigarette smoke and cider. Nearly everyone was a stranger to me.

I sipped orange juice and looked out through the window as the light faded and the music was turned up. I looked downwards to the wet cobble stones and across to the vast empty locked-up market, empty streets. Then I turned back to Carol who was a face I recognised, perhaps twenty years older than me, already drunk, determined to introduce me to everyone.

It was all new. Everyone else could have traced a pattern of intersecting lines across the busy dance floor. Who had slept with who. Who was single. Who had a drink problem. Who was hiding.

'Look, here's another person under thirty,' Carol said hopefully, and Suzy grinned at me and put her drink down and we danced. It was the first time in my life I had danced with someone I wanted to dance with.

We talked too. Almost three weeks later we met in The Grave Maurice, Whitechapel. The kind of place where the regulars are post office workers, hospital porters and nurses wanting a quiet drink. This might have been the first time I had ever dated anyone. Students did not date each other. They turned up at each other's rooms, talked, went to bed together, or more often did not. Here, now, I had come straight from work, dressed in a navy-blue skirt suit, looking as though I had been taken out of a filing cabinet for the evening. Suzy was impressive. Her work gear was remarkably similar to her dancing gear. She wore pale chino trousers and a crisp white open-necked shirt. Her skin was smooth and her short hair was sharply cut with a tendency to spikes on top. She was putting away the stethoscope that had been draped round her neck when I first spotted her coming through the door. She paused when she saw me in my civil service disguise. We were not on safe ground. She was reserved.

Suzy had tickets for the Regent's Park Open Air Theatre – *A Midsummer Night's Dream* – and drove us there. It was the 1980s. There was no congestion charge, and parking was easy after six. No one else I knew owned a car. I was a Londoner but this was a part of London I had never been to. Suzy might as well have rolled out Regent's Park on a magic carpet – the white façades, the crescents, iron railings and rhododendron jungle.

It rained five times with short sharp showers during the performance, but this did not matter. It was an excuse to huddle together under Suzy's umbrella as the light faded and the temperature dropped, wrapped in a blanket. The fairies romped around the stage in very little, camp and flirtatious. There was a brief sense that the world was opening up.

Then Suzy drove me back to my family home. My mother was away. Our small house was empty. We sat in the austere living room on benches, staring at each other across the bare pine table. In the car, and in my home, Suzy told me about her mother's death the previous year. She mentioned previous girlfriends. She told me about the challenges of her work – the hard end of poverty and psychiatry. Suzy said I was frowning. I was listening hard. We were both exhausted, I can see now.

We met again at The Barley Mow the following night. Suzy had been at work and was late. I was waiting for her and we danced to the usual smoochy music. Suzy told me more about Carol – a few warning notes – Carol 'who's into monogamy at the moment. She was trying to seduce me, but she changed her mind halfway through because she was falling in love with Julie.' I turned and could see them on the other side of the room. They were pleasantly mellow and I was feeling mellow too on too-sweet cider. Suzy and I danced very close. Something new for me. In the middle of a slow dance, Suzy put her lips to mine and we danced, kissing. An eternity in which my mind revolved around her lips and body.

Again, Suzy took me home to the empty house. This time I took her to bed with me. It was a shock to find her body opening up to mine. As if we were half way through a film at the cinema and suddenly everything switched to colour and 3D. I had never been inside a woman before. A first time, after a long prelude of a heterosexual relationship when I had always expected the film to be black and white, blurred and flat.

I must have done something right. I must have reached some dark recess of Suzy's emotions. When I came home on Friday night, my mother said there had been a call for me. Then the phone rang again. No mobiles. No texting. No knowing whether you were being cold-shouldered or someone was simply out or at work. No bleep unless you were a doctor.

Suzy was tentative. There was a party tonight in the doctors' tower at the hospital. Would I come? It was last minute. It was someone's birthday. I pulled myself into some jeans. I packed a bag and took a bottle.

It was a trek from my home to Whitechapel. No Docklands Light Railway. Trundling, infrequent district line trains and a walk through the dusk and the rain along a main road. The hospital when I reached it was essentially deserted and behind locked doors, a psychiatric institution. But I was on the list of people allowed in. The security guard gave me his first knowing look; there were to be many over the coming months.

The tower where the doctors on call slept and ate stood high above the corridors where medicine was practised and patients were behind locked doors. Suzy was waiting for me and led me through corridors of linoleum and chipped cream paint walls, up concrete stairs, through pass-coded entry-points.

The party was improvised in squalor. What could have been a doctors' mess was furnished with the rejects of hospital furniture from different phases of modernisation. Plastic upholstery was sticky with the grime of people passing through. An unloved shared space, and a zero budget for cleaning. The best thing about the tower was the view from the windows. From here, custodians would have been able to look out and see every wall and gate. Now, we could watch the sun going down behind Whitechapel's tower blocks. We could see uninterrupted across the East End. The only regeneration had been the slow filling in with tower blocks of the holes left by the bombing, night after night, of London's dockers.

Looking at the psychiatrists and nurses at the party, a leaving party, it was hard not to feel that I was examining the results of some kind of social sifting. There was one token white male heterosexual doctor, bearded, in a suit, leaning against the fridge, in deep conversation with a female doctor he was having an affair with. There was a definite gay contingent, at a time when homosexuality was still on the official list of psychiatric disorders, part of a diagnosis. Sitting on a randomly raised platform on the floor, was a young woman who had made it to the rank of registrar despite being female, gay and having one wasted leg shorter than the other.

Later in the evening, when I was stroking Suzy's neck, I saw one of the male Indian doctors glance away, trying not to look out of his depth. There was a quiet African man in his fifties, a psychiatrist too. Suzy told me he lived in the tower. He was, otherwise, essentially homeless and rootless. Months later, she told me he had died in the tower too, overcome with a bout of pneumonia. The tower was the kind of place where you could die, alone, in a borrowed bed in a room with no other furniture. My colleagues, privileged government officials, were in contrast white, better-fed, taller, male, polished.

Suzy was six years older than me. She, like me, was finding her feet in a profession that her family did not begin to understand. She had made the kind of social leap that Margaret Thatcher would have given a nod to. She, like me, was heady with the shock of a salary and the freedom to spend. I had two work suits, but was still playing catch-up with the idea that I could walk into a shop and buy clothes. We went out to restaurants. We jumped in Suzy's car at the weekend and, if her bleep did not go off, we could walk round art galleries.

Some weekends, we would make it back to the outskirts of west London, away from the bleep, back to the council house she shared with dad and her brother, on a cottage garden estate, where her father grew vegetables. Suzy told me about the fine, egg-laying hen that Suzy had hatched as part of biology class.

Everything was new. We went with Suzy's brother and his girlfriend to a Dire Straits concert in Wembley Arena. When ten thousand people murmured, it was the sea roaring. Suzy had brought cotton wool from an NHS store cupboard. She handed it out for us to put in our ears. The music when it came, thrummed bass straight through my chest. Lights circled purple, changing, sweeping the audience. We were standing and singing. Suzy and I had our arms round each other. 'You don't think anyone cares about us, do you? They've got other things to think about,' Suzy said, and we felt invisible and free. Afterwards, my eyes ached with the sound. It was a long drive back to their home. Suzy was buoyed by adrenalin, drove determinedly, but collapsed in bed asleep when we got back. We scarcely had the energy to put our arms round each other.

Increasingly, Suzy was anxious as well as tired. She had more exams to do the following spring, the next hurdle to jump, and she had to do it exhausted on long working hours, juggling life with work, trying to find her feet. She had failed exams before. Her pride and sense of self was hanging in the balance. In bed, she told me about the drama of being in the hospital crash team as a house doctor, sprinting down corridors, fighting to drag people back to life from cardiac arrest. She used to be glamorous. Once, she had run barefoot down a corridor in her tights, high heels clasped in her hands.

She wanted to impress. But instead, I found myself spending hours alone in the high hospital tower at the weekends. The police would bring in a succession of distressed and suicidal people. The hospital was open for business all hours; schizophrenics could walk through the door any time. Once, the police brought in a man who did not speak, because he had been 'acting strangely'. She stopped the police leaving. She handed the man paper and a pencil. He wrote on it that he was deaf mute and had got lost when out walking.

The tower became grimmer the more you knew it. It was pre-vandalised; nothing remained. When I brought the ingredients for supper, spaghetti bolognese, we had to cook it in the only two metal containers Suzy had been able to find in the hospital – a baking tray and a kettle. It was worse if you stepped outside – a bare road and a cemetery. There was a newsagent's – offering out of date snacks to hospital staff.

At times that summer, we were optimistic. We would set out in Suzy's car from the far west of London in the early hours. As the sun rose higher, we would belt along the Westway, above the terraces of sleepy streets, blasting out Capital Radio and its traffic news. We would play a game of how far we could get before the traffic snarled to stationary. We would crawl along bumper to bumper and talk, sip coffee from a shared flask. There was a particular traffic jam almost at Parliament Square, at the end of St James', where I would leap out with my holdall and walk early into work.

One morning, at that corner, I kissed her exuberantly goodbye before the traffic lights changed to green. Everyone could see us. No one was looking. Apart from the woman on the pavement, waiting to cross, who saw where I put my hand and was visibly shocked.

Too often though, Suzy was withdrawn into herself. She said our relationship was bound to be transient. She felt the pain of the age gap – it was too tiring that for me everything was new. She was bored with an overgrown kitten.

Suzy bought a new car. She was in love with the car she wanted to buy. It had a sun roof. She wanted to feel the breeze through her hair on the Westway. She dressed Biggles-style in scarf and leather jacket, and took the car for a test run. She was in love with speed. I felt, seeing her enthusiasm for the car, her lack of enthusiasm for me. She said I was too dismissive. That she had grown up without things, took pleasure in having things. That I laughed at the pleasure she took in having a car, having her freedom. I said that I had grown up learning not to want things, had still not learned to want things. She accused me of having money in my bank account. That's freedom too, I said.

One long evening that turned into night, Suzy tried to tell me more about her mother. We had made love, in between bleeps. We were less tense. We had opened up. But we were exhausted.

Her mother had only been in her late fifties when she died of cancer. Suzy had scarcely been out of adolescent rebellion. Had still been finding her real friendship with her. Her mother read books, was the kind of woman who in a later generation would have had an education, and would have done more than cleaning and shop work. She had seen Suzy go to medical school. Her mother had been losing her, just as Suzy had been losing her mother.

I was too young. It was not a grief I understood. I held her. I felt her anger at her mother's death direct itself against me. I felt blank. I was not able to explain what I felt. Someone with more experience would have comforted Suzy better. The only way I reached her was to make love to her, and that was her only release.

Autumn ran into winter in a succession of hurried weekends where too often Suzy was on call or on the wards.

She would return to me waiting in the tower and give me flash summaries of the afternoon's drama. A young woman dying of a brain tumour who had just wanted to talk about her sexuality because it was important to her. A colleague who had had an abortion and needed a hug. A depressed, hospitalised nurse who she had talked round from discharging herself. It reminded me of the way my mother would come home from teaching and tell me which small child had been beaten, which one stayed up all night to watch pornographic films with his mother and her boyfriend.

One evening, we were crossing the busy Whitechapel Road at the beginning of one of these weekends. We were stranded on a traffic island, waiting for the opportunity to dash across, when on the wide pavement ahead of us, we witnessed something dreadful.

Six young men, tall and black, chasing two small, fat Asian men in shirt sleeves. What I noticed was their faces. The Asian men were terrified. They had been run a long way down the straight length of road and their speed was failing. The younger men were running light and fast, chasing them into the ground, smiling, hunting, and going in for the kill. They brought them both down on the pavement almost in front of us. Suzy said one had a stick. I saw only a tall boy kicking a man's head again and again as he lay on the ground. And then the boys were gone; they had sprinted off, and Suzy was on the pavement beside the man with a bleeding head, who had lifted himself off the paving stones. Who seemed dizzy. Who needed to stay still, very still. Suzy was saying, 'No, he should not lie down, I am a doctor.' I sprinted to The Grave Maurice to ring 999. The woman behind the bar made me pay ten pence for the bar phone, not believing my breathlessness, until another man ran in a minute later.

I got back. The police were already there, relieved they did not have to be in charge. Suzy had quiet authority. She was talking to the men, very near, so no one could hear. She was checking a pulse. They were not strangers here. The shop keeper knew them but they were not his friends. I do not know what the argument was – drugs, protection money, vengeance. The ambulance sidled in.

Afterwards, Suzy said she had been afraid one of them would have a heart attack. That was why he needed not to move. Blood poured down his white shirt from his skull. We went over it again and again afterwards, the different things we had each seen, our varying witness statements given in the street.

Months went by – we threw ourselves round London. My hours were long. Hers were longer. We would grab small pockets of time and go in Suzy's car to an art gallery or park or Indian restaurant. The bleep would be on Suzy's belt.

Or we would hide ourselves in the tower's bleak bedroom and caress, fully clothed, ever mindful of interruption.

Christmas was coming and we went to a party. It was in the Porchester Hall in Bayswater. It was huge. Polished wood, yellow-glowing chandeliers and a dance floor. Imagine a lesbian version of the Women's Institute throwing a Christmas extravaganza with disco and too much alcohol. Imagine that for most of those there, the room contained past lovers, past rivals, romantic opportunities, jealousies.

I was under-dressed in jeans. Suzy had bought a yellow bow tie with polka dots to go with her crisp white shirt. Everyone had turned out. The room was arranged 'cabaret style' as they say in conference brochures, six to a table. Women I knew, women I did not know, walked up to Suzy, spoke into her ear against the noise of the sound system. We had pushed away the world outside. The security guards were bribed to disappear.

A middle-aged woman from Suzy's work, a sister on a ward, Pat, came and put her arms round Suzy's shoulders mid-evening and they danced. They talked a great deal. Pat's partner looked on jealously. 'I'm glad someone can cheer Pat up!' she commented. I too was watching, watching Suzy laugh and come alive. As the evening wore on and the crowd decided to surge into a conga dance, Suzy pulled me into the snaking line of women singing.

We argued. Suzy thought I was naïve. In the depths of winter, just after the new year, we went into town after Suzy had come off shift, and saw 'The Life and Times of

Harvey Milk' at the National Film Theatre. Not a good rap that he got assassinated. But he was a machine politician in the way that the GLC and Ken Livingstone aspired to, building a rainbow coalition of minorities, handing out grants to different minorities. Vote for me. He faced the other machine politicians – white, working class, supported by the police and fire brigade's unions. And he was assassinated by that kind of politician. Gunned down with his mayor.

Suzy was angry. Suzy was pessimistic. What you have to remember, looking back, is that we did not know what direction we were all going in. It looked like things were getting worse. Our generation was just as homophobic as the older ones. AIDS had made people question liberalism. At work, our Ministers' agenda was to attack just this kind of 'Loonie Left' politics. The Conservative government pointed to funding for gays, Irish centres, nuclear-free zones. Look, this is how they are spending your money – not on you! They were in the middle of dismantling the Greater London Council and its rainbow politics and cheap tube fares.

At work, I felt little protection. Suzy felt she was accepted so long as she kept her mouth shut and said nothing in front of the senior consultant. Don't ask, don't tell, don't get political. The film was optimistic despite everything. We were not. I hated feeling I had to hide, hated the difficulty of answering simple questions about my life. Suzy said the film hadn't told us how many people were being beaten up in the streets while politicians argued there was a gay takeover of San Francisco.

'You're too innocent,' she said. 'Don't you know you're a second-class citizen?'

We said goodbye to each other in a dark, rain-sodden corner of the South Bank complex and went our different directions home. Suzy wanted more time to be with her family, more time to study. I kissed Suzy on the cheek. She said I looked miserable.

We experienced a growing sense of separateness. We would fall asleep after too long days, tiring out the evening with talking. We would wake and make love. We would start again.

Once, when my house was empty at the weekend, we were making love mid-afternoon. Around us, the world was busy. Next door, the couple who lived there were arguing. We could hear no precise words, only rising bitterness. We paid no heed. He shouted. She shouted. Suzy was rising to a climax, and groaned. As if a switch had flicked, the voices next door turned off, to silence as Suzy gasped and cried out. We looked at each other and giggled silently. We held our breath. Next door stayed silent, holding its breath too. We held each other, and felt a blissful pause.

When I came to join Suzy for another weekend in the bleak hospital tower, I found her sitting slumped on one of the few soft chairs, her expression blank, unapproachable. I tried conversation, but faltered. 'Sometimes I feel like water being repelled by greased metal. The water breaks into tiny droplets and I can't touch you. I feel like hugging you, but I can't.' She stirred, and hugged me instead.

The more I showed affection, the more Suzy pushed me away that winter. Then we would fall back together, sexually, pulled together by gravity. We would touch each other slowly, an electric emotion between us, our screams stifled by pillows.

Suzy was still grieving. I was not sure she could have said how much she was grieving for her mother, or for the grim reality and long hours of the profession she had chosen. We were drained.

Survival in the NHS was all about friends. Friends who would take over your shift, your bleep, when you were too ill to stand. Friends who would spot your hangover errors before you made them. Friends who would rush to your side when one of the patients had a cardiac arrest.

Suzy had friends among the nurses as well as the doctors. They would try and share shifts together. Box and cox, help each other out through long hours of lost causes, elderly confused patients, schizophrenics failing to take medication, young women with such a history of abuse that mental illness seemed a healthy shut-down response.

Then they would fall back on each other's sofas and drink when a long shift came to an end and they had a few days spare. The gay women all knew each other, even if they were invisible to others. 'I have my spies,' Suzy said.

One night after one of those long shifts, we gathered in the living room of a small flat that looked out over more tower blocks. The two nurses who lived there said they wanted to buy their flat. I shook my head. I knew about the repair bills. They knew about the drugs problems, the failed locks on the staircase doors. It is difficult to remember that mid-80s dream of self-improvement.

The music was mellow. There were pizzas, red wine. I was the only one there who didn't work for one of the hospitals. I curled up on the sofa, collapsed, warm against Suzy's body. Suzy squeezed in against Pat, and Pat put her arm round her. I think I slept.

Suzy told me about Pat. She told me about Pat when I said, 'I don't like being lied to.' I took it quite calmly. I cried. It was a car crash that had already happened. Pat had the stronger cards. She knew what Suzy was up against. She had a depth of experience. When Suzy talked about her grief, Pat was there. If Suzy wanted mothering, and perhaps she did, Pat was used to mothering. Pat said that when she saw Suzy in the corridor, she would be about to rush up to her and embrace her, and then realise she had to say good morning instead.

On the last day of the Greater London Council, the last day of March 1986, everything was due to go up in smoke. The government could tick a box, work done. County Hall would no longer be across the river reproaching Parliament with a giant roof-top display of the number of London unemployed. The other side could at least go out with a bang, a giant firework party. Afterwards, the government claimed that the South Bank firework display and concert cost a quarter of a million. The BBC managed to mention that a quarter of a million people had attended.

We went to the party, for old times' sake. And to celebrate the fact that Suzy had passed her exams. It felt like everyone we knew had turned out, just because. On one stage there was Hank Wangford, Smiley Culture, and the Mint Juleps, periodically drowned out by the trains thundering over the iron of Hungerford Bridge.

We were smiling. Suzy peeled off with me for the afternoon. It felt like the kind of funeral where the corpse wanted to say goodbye with a heavy metal band and threatened to rise again like a bat out of hell.

I was told I had been well behaved. I was not told that we would stay friends. This afternoon together was my consolation prize. Pat's jealous partner had flipped. She had pulled a knife from the kitchen drawer. Then departed shouting obscenities, and in the morning Pat's car was found spray-painted blue on white, 'Lesbian Trash', indelible. It was ancient and a write-off and Pat could not afford another. The phone still rang at Suzy's in the middle of the night, and went silent when her father answered it.

As evening turned to night, we waited in the crowd for the fireworks. We had made our way onto the raised walkway in front of the huge tower of the Shell buildings by the river. We were surrounded on three sides by the walls of high buildings, and from our vantage point we could see the dark barges in the river where the fireworks were ready. One rocket rushed up into the sky. The crowd hushed. Then six rockets launched simultaneously. Again, again, and again. Up in the sky, exploding rainbow fountains cascaded like a bombardment. The sound banged back in multiple echoes from the walls and windows around us, and pounded through our bodies.

We held on to each other as everything exploded.

Wonderbra

Before my bit of inner London became a forest of high density 'luxury' and student flats, it was low rise. In fact, mainly it was flattened. It was at that stage of regeneration where the landmarks you tell strangers directions by had been removed. The 'Duke of Cambridge' had disappeared, replaced by a bus station with multiple entrances next to a roundabout. So, it was difficult to tell anyone lost to turn left at the pub to the train station.

You could say, when you see the hand car wash on your right and the railway bridge ahead of you, just turn left up the narrow path in between the railway bridge and the two surviving huts with the dry-cleaners and the minicab firm. The path that looks unpromising, with cracks in the tarmac and substance-dependent rough sleepers sitting against the fence, who will say good morning.

I never went inside the minicab office. But we were regular customers at the dry-cleaners, because we wore suits and skirts to work, and the place was an ideal stop-off before the station.

Inside, the dry-cleaning lady had her palace, complete with leftover tinsel and a giant green lemon verbena that thrived in the chemical gloom. There was a sewing machine in the corner and large machines in the back, ventilated by the door that opened onto the security-fenced yard and scrubland that fell down towards the wall of an unloved urban stream. There was a constant hum. Light filtered through the plastic, corrugated roof. The machines may sometimes have been attended by her husband, but he was not referred to and largely kept out of the way. He may have been in the back yard contemplating the buddleia.

Her name was Sibel. 'Si-Be-ll' she repeated. 'Like Sybil but Better.'

She was about our age and she looked like she could see off trouble. No one would have been stupid enough to hold her up for the takings. She would have found out who they were.

She conformed to the important urban myth about south London dry-cleaners: they are all Turkish-Cypriot except where rents are silly. Sibel was not otherwise a conformist. Her parents may have escaped a war zone and dereliction may have been all around her, but Sibel was Queen of all she surveyed.

She rapidly worked out that Maddie and I were connected. Not too difficult. If Maddie was coming home late from work, I would take her ticket and collect her clean skirt or coat. Like the down-and-outs, she did, for about five minutes at least, assume we were sisters who shared each other's clothes. The down-and-outs called me Maddie. Maybe we were just one person. Maddie had said a cheery 'Hi!' to them once. Although she denied it, she had contributed to their drinks fund.

Sibel told us what school she had been to – 'I've got Maths GCSE, you know. I bet you didn't think that.'

I nodded. Fair point. 'You know what you're doing.'

'Running this place isn't just shoving things into machines. But if we're going to put up these trousers, we need to measure you in inches. We're Turkish, so it's inches.'

When Maddie switched to working for a more arty magazine and went for a new, less conventional, spikey hairstyle with putty, she asked Sibel what she thought before she asked me. 'Well, the dry-cleaning lady liked it!' she protested when I gave her my opinion.

My role was to be the shy one and nod. But after a year or so, I knew I was on the list of regular and serious customers when I got asked to help with a crossword. I didn't know the answer to the clue either.

'You were always hopeless at that,' said Maddie. 'I got right the one she asked me.'

But I had read *Jude the Obscure*. I came in and found her reading it, one quiet late morning. She'd managed the first fifty pages.

'It's weird,' she said. 'Why Greek?'

'It gets more depressing,' I said.

'Yeah, but it's good as well. 'Hey Jude, don't be afraid', and all that.'

One day I called by to find her leaning on the counter with a copy of a long official-looking form. I pretended to peek over it.

She raised herself to her full height. 'They're running a teacher-training access course at the College,' she announced. 'Like A' levels. But you can do it part-time.'

'What would you like to teach?' Good move, no messing with. Will they let you in?

'English. It was always my favourite subject at school. And they let you read novels and call it work.'

'My Mum taught primary,' I said.

'No. I prefer bigger kids. I have more fun with mine, now they're a bit older.'

'Bet you could deal with them, like stroppy customers. You going to put that on the form?'

'Oh yes. And running my own business and having to do the accounts.' She leant over and whispered, steering her eyes towards the back of the shop theatrically 'Because I don't trust him.' He was still invisible.

She got the place on the course – then was only at the shop some days, sometimes chewing a biro and taking notes. 'What do you think of Jane Eyre?' she said.

'Gothic?' I tried, and she wrote it down on a pad on the counter.

'I used to do my homework on this counter when I was at school,' she said. 'I had a big stool to sit on. My mum didn't know the answers, so I had to ask the customers.'

'Governess escape-fantasy with mad woman in attic?'
'I've got that one already.'
'Proto-feminist but ends with 'Reader, I married him'.'
'Yuck!' she said. 'Well, it was the nineteenth century.'
'Don't they give you anything fun to read?'
'It's called 'narratives of social advancement'. It's supposed to give you attitude.'
'Yeah, she's got attitude!' said a voice from the back. His face appeared from behind the clothes rails. He gave a conspirator's wink.

Sibel announced that spring that she was getting a divorce. 'You'd think there wasn't a world outside the dry-cleaning shop,' she said.

Outside, they had begun demolishing the bus station and moving it. Everything around the shop was even flatter than it had been and then hidden behind painted chip board. The developers glued ten-foot-high photos to the chipboard of smiling young people learning trades, and the photogenic, multicultural elderly on a sunny day shopping in the market. We weren't sure whether they were to cheer us up or the people who might move into the flats that hadn't been built.

'I'm getting out,' said Sibel.

But she was still there a few months later, as the summer holidays approached and the course ended. Her husband had become even less visible.

'I've got a teacher training place for the autumn,' she announced. 'Full time,' in a low voice. 'Even if he thinks that means I can work weekends and holidays and any old time he wants to bugger off.'

I gave her the thumbs up, and didn't say anything back that could be overheard.

Then a couple of weeks later, Maddie went into the shop and Sibel came out from behind the counter, unlocking the counter lid and the anti-intruder under-the-counter door with a firm click.

'She positively sashayed,' said Maddie, in the safety of our living room. Maddie did a re-enactment for me, to make her point. Shoulders back, bust out, hips swaying, 'Just like this!' And Maddie swayed up to me until her sharp breasts were almost pressing against mine. 'Super-flirty. And then she said 'Do you like my new Wonderbra?''

The big ads at the time, one just outside my office, had a cut-off shot of a blonde looking down rather than up, at the effect of her Wonderbra uplift, with the caption 'Hello Boys'. New bra, new you.

'And did you?'

'Oh yeah! I said 'Fabulous, darling!' Maddie looked me in the eye, close up. 'Maybe I should get one. Just look at your face! You're blushing. Or have I had a deeper impact?' she growled in mock sexy tones.

The next time I walked into the drycleaners, it was a few weeks later. The weather was warm and I had been wearing a hand-wash cotton dress. Everything was different.

Sibel, for the first time, was weeping. She had been weeping all afternoon, it looked from her face.

She came out from behind the counter again, but without any flourish. She sank her head onto my shoulder and she cried.

'I've had an abortion!' she wailed. 'I had to do it. To protect my two children. I need to be able to look after them.' She whimpered.

'You're brave,' I said.

'I was so stupid! I was like some fucking teenager going out on the town. I should have thought. I'm just a soggy mess. And they need their mummy.'

'You need to be there for them.'

'I need to be sensible. I need to be qualified. That bastard won't shift his arse for them.'

'My mum brought us up on her own,' I said, to avoid having to express an opinion.

'It's tough.'

'Yes. Teaching's a good job. But it's tough too. My Mum did it for thirty years.'

'I want to show them. Show them you can be something. And then I muck things up.' She grabbed a tissue from the counter box. It had been there all the time, perhaps for customers. She sniffed and dried her eyes. 'I didn't know what it was like being a teenager,' she confessed. 'Here all the time. Doing what my dad said. Carrying on the family business. Second adolescence, that's me.'

'Yes,' I said with some feeling. 'Like you can't let them down, because they've tried so hard.'

She went and got my clean navy suit, my office respectability. It was the nineties, so it was still a skirt suit.

'Good luck!' I said. 'You'll do it!'

'Do you think they really will divorce?' I asked Maddie.

'They don't even speak. She says she was eighteen when she married him and her dad bribed her with the dry-cleaning business.'

'Maybe they'll find her body in the river.'

'Or his,' Maddie retorted.

Maddie saw Sibel again that summer. 'She's determined,' she reported back. 'She's planned it all. She gets the money from the developers and she gets out with the kids.'

That was the last time either of us saw her.

Summer ended. The autumn term was due to start. When I went back to the dry-cleaners, she was not there, and the man who was her husband was front-of-house. He was silent. Maybe like me he thought there was no small talk possible. He was used to silent customers, the same customers Sibel had talked to, whose names she had known. I did not know his name.

Often, the shop was closed and shuttered. I took my suit to another cleaners.

A few months on, the shop was not there either. The chipboard had extended to surround the place where the huts had been, and the hidden walkway up to the station was being dismantled.

Where the dry-cleaners once stood, the buses now turn left onto a road up to the station, and the hoardings have been replaced by twenty-storey blocks of flats, opening onto the street by the new bus stops. If you want directions to the trains, the answers may be complicated. But the railway bridge is still there. You need to turn left before the bridge. Where the carwash used to be, is now a hotel.

Catherine Meads

When will they come for me?
after the original by Martin Niemöller

First they came for the environmentalists.
And I didn't speak out because
    I wasn't an environmentalist,
But I did admire them and thought they made good points.

Then they came for the women having miscarriages,
wrongly claiming they had done self-induced abortions,
and I didn't speak out as I had never had a child

Then they came for the trans people,
and I didn't speak out because I wasn't trans,
and I didn't know what to say, even if anyone would listen

Then they came for Black people in senior positions,
Saying they only got there because they were Black, and
    ignoring their multitude of skills and abilities,
And I didn't speak out because I wasn't Black.

Then they came for lesbians' children,
    saying that they were being harmed.
And I tried to speak out, with lots of research
    showing the children were fine,
But nobody would listen to the evidence

Then they came for the US academics and researchers,
cancelling all DEI projects and deleting the data
and I didn't speak out as I didn't live there

So when will they come for me?
And who will speak up when they do?
Can we please stop this before we get to the final solution?

Zekria Ibrahimi

With Jules

I talked with Jules, my rent-boy mate,
He said he'd been hiding – this thing.
He stuttered – it was night, real late –
He couldn't stop his trembling.

He whined about Karma and fate,
He'd got into a stupid fling,
A kid with whom the sex was great,
But, as always, there was a sting –

'What is it?' I asked; he replied
His secret was his HIV.
His tears increased, even I cried ...
Secrets are scorpions, just see,
Soho's full of them. At his side,
I wondered: Could it next be me?

On an empty Saturday in Soho
(May, 2020)

(i)

I was in Old Compton Street yet again,
Round midnight, for an empty Saturday.
The boards were up on every window pane.
I limped around, an old man, stooped and grey,

As if what I was seeing was insane –
No crowds, no disco down each alleyway,
No G-A-Y, but – how can I explain? –
A nothingness, to hold love's grace at bay –

A void, where once existed a heart,
A vacuum, instead of community.
All that is Soho has been sliced apart.
A cleaning truck was whirring close to me.
Is all Soho destined for the bin cart?
This place is scarcely well-scrubbed decency.

(ii)

It was eerie, to view such desolation,
Not the mad bustle that had seemed consoling.
The unhinged marvel of Soho's elation
Had been lost, far beyond any cajoling.

Old Compton Street, the hub of the gay nation,
Was a wasteland where a grim bell was tolling.
Down Oxford Street, round Tottenham Court Station,
The emptiness was callous and controlling.

I longed to conjure up what once had been,
To persuade Prowler, Clone Zone, G-A-Y,
To open again, bright, wild, and pristine,
With queer love as their crux, their reason why,
Their focus, their magic that, being seen,
Was like a thousand rainbows for the eye.

(iii)

The shadows increased, into Soho Square,
And absence spread its drab curse everywhere.

This Saturday night, down Old Compton Street,
The sweet crowds were gone that made it complete.

The people who came here have vanished now,
Remembered, and, as it were, mourned, somehow.

Soho, with the ambience of a tomb,
Was buried in such grief, and echoed doom.

The music, the lights, sex shops, wine and beer,
Were our life – baffling, potent, dangerous – here.

Soho Square, near to midnight, in late May,
Was deserted and spectral, mute and grey.

Queer love had turned to a ghoulish abyss,
No longer softened by a hug and kiss.

(iv)

Then, as if produced by life like some light,
There emerged, near an unsubtle streetlamp,
Its brash electric glow slapping the night
With a vigour that shadows could not cramp,

Two lads, holding each other's bodies tight,
Obviously timid. I, some ageing tramp,
Looked on at what was an inspiring sight ...
These two still had, on their faces, fear's stamp –

A terror of the usual straight norm ...
But, never hand in hand outside before,
They, at May's end – and it was rather warm –
Chose to show their cute love, which I then saw ...
Rainbows seemed everywhere, rainbows would swarm,
As both boys passed by Soho's every door.

Soho in autumn
November 13, 2022

Soho in autumn is a dream,
Tumbling like the hues of a leaf;
It has a gentle, poignant gleam,
A bit like joy, a bit like grief.

All these people, who jostle, teem,
Tarts, queers, are also sadly brief;
Transience has to be their theme;
Time's winds, like the hands of a thief,

Rip them away from all they knew –
The massage parlours, the sex shops,
The strip-shows, and the gay bars too ...
One leaf drops, then another drops.
Soho's streets are, as I traipse through,
The season of love – but love stops.

Not the fairest of fields

It won't be fields that are fair,
Gleaming under a wholesome dawn,
Gentle butterflies everywhere,
And never any need to mourn ...

It won't be hope beyond compare
Without a harsh jab from a thorn,
Hope like the decent morning air
That makes the lungs seem quite brand new ...

No, Soho, amidst this New Year,
Will be the same old mad morass,
A cruel miasma, far from clear,
As choking as thick chlorine gas –
Look, twenty twenty-five is near!
And cockroach sins resume, en masse.

I glimpse

I glimpse, across Soho's crammed mesh of streets,
A poem by John Donne
About crowds of kisses between the sheets.
Loud-mouthed rhymes, on and on
(Where many a tramp, or tart, or queer, meets)
Come, party, then are gone.

Glad metaphors as packed as G-A-Y
Are summoned up, I see.
Donne writes of the flesh, and its reason why,
Its risks, and ecstasy ...
In Soho, busy young fools, once so shy,
Grow strangely wise, and free.

Carpe Noctem
(Seize the Night)

'Seize the day,' Horace said.
I answer: 'Seize the night.'
Mere morning is like lead,
And noon has little light,

But, when dusk is ahead,
How Greek Street will look bright,
Unleashed, unlimited!
Soho sings: 'Seize the night.'

What is day but a shred,
A rag lacking in might,
Tatters that must be dead?
I answer: 'Seize the night.'

Love's near me in a bed;
Your gentle skin's in sight.
Why think of day instead?
I answer: 'Seize the night.'

Peter Scott-Presland

The Belt

It was a white shirt with a smart pair of short flannel trousers, and Lee was new to putting on his own clothes. He was proud of his recent mastery of sleeves and buttons, and pushed his mother away when she offered to help. After one mistake which left the bottom buttonhole dangling, he got everything aligned, and smoothed down his symmetrical shirt front, admiring himself in the full-length mirror. Then he pulled up the trousers, buttoned the flies with more confidence.

He realised that he had not threaded the belt through the loops. He looked in the mirror again and gave a big theatrical sigh. He was a born actor, and delighted in an audience, even if it was himself. He shook his head knowingly at his reflection, which agreed with him. What an idiot!

Removing his trousers, he pushed the end of the belt through to the left through the first loop. It was marginally too large, and Lee had to make an effort threading through each, until the belt came out through the last one, on the right-hand side. He gave himself a big smile, as if inviting applause and pulled up his trousers, buttoning the top button with improved dexterity. He fastened the lower ones in quick succession.

He hooked the belt through the buckle to the left, pulled it back on itself to tighten it, took an enormous breath to draw his waist in, and managed to slot the prong into a belt-hole which gave him a pronounced wasp waist. Not that he knew the concept, but he liked the curve over his hips.

His mother peeked round the door. 'Well done!' she enthused. 'Quite the little man.'

Then she looked a little closer, and her smile faded. 'No, no, I'm sorry, but you've got it the wrong way round, Lee. You've got the tongue to the left. That's not what I taught you. That's the girls' side. Boys point to the right. Here. Give it to me. We'll be late for school.'

So Lee had to surrender his new-found skill to his mother's superior competence. As he held his trousers up with his hand, she whisked the belt out and reversed it rather roughly the other way through the loops. To his chagrin, she took his hand and drew him out of the house.

That evening, Lee stood again in front of the mirror. Carefully he removed his trousers, unthreaded the belt, and put it back the way it had been in the first place. He smoothed his hands down his hips. He posed turning to left and right. He pouted his lips like a model off the telly. He smiled alluringly at his reflection. And as he looked at his reflection, she smiled back.

Age Concern

The neon sign hummed over the café, like a mosquito buzzing somewhere in the background. The windows of the exclusive shops dripped gold into the puddles on the pavement. The crowd window-shopped on its leisurely evening *passagio*.

The laid-back mood was infectious. Josh stretched and yawned at his table, pleasantly conscious of having nothing to do, and three more days to do it in.

For the last week or so, he had spoken to no-one, except to order food and drink, and to wish *'buon giorno'* to the landlady of his pensione. She was a tiny, fierce woman in black who went to church twice a day and almost certainly thought that people like him, *gli omosessuali*, would feature among the damned on the Day of Judgement. Well, fuck her.

He'd been to the Uffizi, walking smugly past the queues because he'd remembered to book in advance; he'd rubber-necked at Michaelangelo's David in the Academia (huge workman's hands, shame about the dick); he'd ventured as far afield as Fiesole up on the hill. But mostly he'd sat at café tables such as this.

From this vantage point, he'd watched the tourists and the good wealthy *signori* of Florence go their separate ways. He always felt faintly superior to this intense non-activity around him. He played God with these little people, he imagined the fabric of their lives, these bouncy brash Australian and American girls, the sullen Italian schoolboys scowling through their acne as they trailed behind their teachers to another improving museum. He felt the sameness of their emotions, and allowed himself to pity them. He never bothered to speak to them, because he had convinced himself he knew them all too well. Besides, he could barely scrape a dozen words of Italian, which in some ways helped him maintain his sense of superiority.

He had been to one queer bar; a bar listed in Spartacus as both 'Cruisy' and 'Young Crowd'. Outside he found a canopy, a red carpet and a silk rope. Inside, a load of prissy Italian queens mostly in couples with too much jewellery and vicuña, and a taste for tacky Europop. Stuck-up bastards. They looked down their noses at his leather jacket, but at least the other tourists fancied him, and the Italian chicken he'd picked up eventually wasn't half bad, even if he wouldn't come back to the hotel. He'd shagged the boy up on the Belvedere, looking over the city, and really it was just as well he ran off back to his mamma when he did, because they couldn't speak much and Josh was starting to get bored already.

But at least it broke the spell. He'd had a run of bad luck, these last few months. And OK, maybe he'd made a bit of a fool of himself, but it wasn't his fault Steven had turned out to be such a cunt. You can't tell a book by its cover, and you never know someone till you live under the same roof.

It seemed a good idea at the time, inviting Steven to take the upstairs flat. Steven, be it noted, and never Steve. As Josh reminded him, 'It's cheap, and you are on a student grant.'

And, after all, they were fuck buddies. And when they got together, boy, did these buddies fuck. On one occasion, he'd looked at the bedside clock and realised that he'd had his dick inside Steven without break and without coming for five solid hours. Not bad at 35.

So it seemed reasonable when Steven moved in that their occasional sex would be put on a more regular footing.

But Steven was not to be ordered. Closer proximity meant that Josh had witnessed in silent misery a series of men climbing the communal stair past his door and up to Steven's. And that door was now increasingly shut to him. Josh had listened sleeplessly to the noise of talk and laughter above him; to bedsprings creaking that would creak with his weight no more.

Josh fought back. He brought guys home from discos. When he did so, he made a point of broadcasting his enjoyment. He fantasised about paying a very attractive escort to visit him. The Adonis would arrive after Steven got home from college; he would ring the wrong bell as arranged, so Steven had to answer the door and direct him to 172a rather than 172b. Adonis would then dutifully and convincingly project his ecstasy through the ceiling to the flat above. In Josh's best fantasies, Adonis didn't have to project. But he rejected the idea of paying for sex as too humiliating, even in a good cause.

There were rows, of course, though never about the real points of conflict. Always about not cleaning the stairs, wasting electricity, noise. There was even Josh's absurd, unconvincing suicide attempt, after he saw a picture of what he recognised as Steven's body – 'Always Horny' – in the 'Escorts' section of a popular gay magazine. After three months of this gut-churning treatment, Steven had left, and Josh had arrived in Florence exhausted.

More than exhausted, he felt profoundly old. Felt old? Hell, he was 35, he was old, compared to the Stevens of this world. And yet he envied them. He struggled to remember and distinguish dance tracks, assiduously read *GQ* and noted trends in masculine toiletries. Keeping up with Steven had been a strain. For a few weeks, when George Michael was back in the news for some retro reason, Josh had hopes that beards might make a come-back. A beard might suit him. But it was not to be – a wisp at the chin was all that the Follicle Fairy allowed. Da Yoof were such self-centred little bastards.

And yet here in the company of the corrupt, canny Florentines, Josh felt these traumatic events were all starting to fall into perspective. He counted his blessings as assiduously as Julie Andrews her raindrops on roses. He had a new job to look forward to, in a new city, and just before the old one's redundancy pay-off ran out. All his money had gone on clothes, CDs, clubs. And as a last splurge, this holiday. But now he'd be able to get real things – a non-stick frying pan, a full-size duvet that fitted his bed, bookshelves that weren't milk crates.

So what if it wasn't the most exciting job in the world? It would end five months of featureless idleness. His days would have shape again. He wouldn't have to fawn at any more job interviews, at least not for the moment. And Manchester could be good – sure, why not? He'd watched *Queer as Folk* like everybody else back in the day. He thought about Nathan in that, the shaggable one. He felt a stirring in his Calvin Kleins, against the crotch of his jeans, and smiled. Yeah, he was ready for Manchester.

For the first time in ages Josh felt a burst of energy. He turned and looked at his reflection in the Art Nouveau glass of the Café Florian. He studied it dispassionately. The eyes were the greatest asset, certainly. Hazel and soft, equally adept at pain and sympathy. He should use them more often. Since he'd lost weight, the chin had become decisive, the figure pleasingly lanky. The heavy leather jacket gave him broad shoulders. There was an urchin quality worth cultivating – he was glad he'd let his hair grow, since he showed no sign of losing it. 35? In this light, he could pass for 28 easily.

He was suddenly aware that he was being watched. In the mirror of the window, he could see a chunky figure, shadowy under a peaked cap, standing under the streetlamp in the middle of the square. He turned and looked. It stood motionless. The two men held their gaze between drifting knots of people for fully three minutes, before the figure broke off and walked off in the opposite direction, into the voluble crowd.

A few moments later it was back, leaning against a scraggy tree a few yards away from the café. Josh smiled at its nervousness. The man's emotions were as transparent as a child's. Josh returned the stare, put on his most engaging boyish grin, and gestured with his eyes to the seat opposite him at the table. The man hesitated, then joined him with a little sideways dart, sitting down heavily.

'Drink?' asked Josh, evenly, inwardly admiring his own assurance.

'Beer.' Almost inaudible. 'Please.'

The English was heavily accented, the face large and unattractive. Knobbly features, deep pits from childhood acne. Josh's heart sank as he beckoned the waiter, who took in the situation with an amused, knowing glance.

Silence stood between them as they waited for the drink to arrive. Josh studied the bulky figure opposite him, hunched, fiddling with a twist of sugar on the table.

He could have been any age between sixteen and twenty-five. His uncertainty and inexperience made him seem younger, his bulk and pitted face, older. And I thought Italians were meant to have this fantastic sense of style, Josh smiled to himself. This one certainly didn't, in his shapeless donkey jacket, large dirty work boots, hair chopped anyhow, probably in front of a mirror. Josh guessed his nervousness was only partly a result of the situation; the whole city was strange to him.

'Do you speak English?' He dropped the obvious into the silence.

'A little.' The reply was almost lost in the noise around them.

'You are not from Florence?'

'No.' Josh congratulated himself on his powers of observation.

The boy thought for a minute. 'You are English?' Josh could almost hear him thumbing through his mental phrase book.

'Yes.'

'Do you stay long?'

'Three more days. I've been here a week already.' This one was going to be hard work.

'Do you like Florence?'

'Yes. Very much.'

'I hate it.' The remark was surprisingly vehement.

'Why?'

The boy shrugged. 'The people. They are like this.' He laid a finger under his nose and pushed it into the air. It was a universal gesture, and Josh laughed. The boy laughed as well. He set the twist of sugar down on the white oilcloth. For the first time, their eyes met at close quarters. The irises of the youngster were a melting honey brown, as simply appealing as a baby calf. He drew breath, as if reaching an important decision. He grabbed Josh by the arm across the table and drew him into the middle.

'How much?' He whispered.

'What?' Josh couldn't believe the words he could scarcely hear.

'You sleep with me. How much?'

Suddenly the customers around him, the to-ings and fro-ings of the square, took on a different significance.

It was the first time Josh had ever been offered money for sex, and he found it something of a turn-on. He remembered Steven's ad: Always Horny. Now he'd show Steven. Why not? He didn't fancy the boy, but he seemed almost desperate. It was probably his first time. The only way he knew to meet anybody. Or maybe he was just frightened of going into a bar on his own in a strange city. Better me, Josh thought, than some of the café's other customers. I'm abroad. Between lives. Nobody'll ever know.

The boy's eyes were still fixed on him.

'What's your name?' Josh asked.

'Stefan,' said the boy. Stefan ... Steven ... Suddenly Josh noticed his heart beating faster. Strange, they didn't look at all similar. But it had to be an omen. His manner softened.

He'd treat this boy well. With tenderness. He'd give him a seeing-to he wouldn't forget in a hurry.

'You don't need money,' said Josh, softly.

'Oh, yes. I must. I must.' Stefan was most serious and emphatic, as if the rules of some vital game must not be broken. The Need to Distance Oneself, Josh diagnosed it confidently. OK, play it your way, Stefano mio.

He made a quick calculation. He scarcely knew the current prices in England, let alone Italy. Then there was the exchange rate, the strong pound against the Euro ....

'A hundred and twenty Euro?' he suggested tentatively. Stefan smiled broadly. Obviously sex was expensive in Italy. I should have said a hundred and fifty, Josh thought.

There was a pause. Josh realised he would have to take the initiative. Fine by him. He hated being passive. And whatever the customer wanted ...

'Do you want to go to a club first?' he asked, casually, but hoping the answer would be no. He didn't want any more prissy queens.

'No. No people, please.' Then, quickly: 'But if you wish ...'

Josh liked the deference. 'Another drink?' he asked.

The boy shook his head.

'Do you have a room?' asked Josh.

'No. I stay a hostel – the youth hostel.'

'I have a hotel room. It's a bit small but they don't mind what I do.' He tried to make it sound as if this was an everyday experience.

They downed their drinks. Josh paid for the beers; Stefan didn't try to stop him. The air still smelt fresh from the earlier shower, and there was a surprisingly chilly wind. They walked briskly, carefully apart.

The streets were narrow and ill lit. They crossed the river, heading south. The Arno was hissing, swollen. It seemed deafening. And still they didn't speak.

Five minutes later, they climbed the five flights to the pensione. Josh prayed that Signora Dragon would be off guard; he had an idea she might put a serious curse on him if she caught him bringing a strange man back. But his luck held. The hall was empty, and from her tiny quarters he could hear the sound of a television. Signora was glued to *Chi vuol essere milionario?* He tiptoed past, and thankfully Stefan was quiet too.

His room was adorned a heavy nineteenth century crucifix over the bed, a poster for Fiesole, and a cheap reproduction of the Lippi Annunciation. Stefan drew a breath when he saw the cross, so Josh hastily took it down and put it in his clothes cupboard. He pulled back the blankets on the bed. With typical Italian restraint, the landlady had given him a pink flowery pillow, bright yellow striped sheets, and a paisley-pattern shawl on top of everything. Just the thing for a rent boy – not! thought Josh.

On the bedside table there was a quarter-full bottle of duty-free Scotch, left over from his first lonely nights.

'Drink?' he asked.

'Please.'

Josh filled his tooth mug. Stefan took it and drained it quickly, gratefully. As Josh watched him, he realised he still had no idea of what was expected of him. The lad probably didn't know what he wanted either, so, hell, Josh would do what he himself wanted, until Stefan told him to stop.

He took off his jacket, hung it on the door. Sat down on the bed behind the boy, put his arms round him and nibbled his ear. Stefan's body stiffened and pulled away. So that's how you want to play it, thought Josh. He turned the boy round by the shoulders, pressed him flat to the bed. In a second he was on top of him.

'No,' cried Stefan. 'Ssh!' soothed Josh, his finger on Stefan's lips.

'Put off the light.' There was no politeness in Stefan's voice, only panic, and Josh knew he'd never get anywhere till he plunged them into dark. In the blackness he drew the ungainly body towards him. The muscles tensed under the boy's skin. Josh brushed the down on his cheek.

'Get into bed,' he ordered, adding. 'It'll be all right. You'll see.'

Stefan trembled as they lay together. Face upwards, his whole body was rigid. The skin flinched as Josh ran his fingers down the chest and stomach. Out of its baggy clothes, it was really quite a pleasing body: smooth, soft-skinned but barrel-chested, with firm working muscles. Josh felt his own cock grow satisfyingly hard.

A few moments told him that he'd have more trouble getting the boy to an equal state of excitement. Neither fingers nor mouth seemed to make any progress. He tried to plan it as he paused for breath.

As if reading his mind, Stefan said, 'Please not to disturb for me. Do what you want.' Josh needed no second telling. He lifted the right shoulder and turned him onto his stomach. As he did so, his hand rested briefly on some tiny soft bumps under the skin at the top of the shoulder blade. Acne scars again. He really was very young. As young as – as Josh's fingers slid over the clenched buttocks and he brought his weight down on the broad back, he murmured in his ear, 'Steven.'

He pushed the boy's legs apart with his knee, pulled the end off his little *Rubberstuffers* sachet of gel with his teeth, eased a slippery finger into the puckered sphincter. Stefan drew breath through his teeth. Jesus, this boy was tight. For a second Josh thought about using a rubber, but decided against it. It would take too long, he needed to seize the moment. And besides, the boy was obviously a virgin, so he wasn't in danger of catching anything.

He thrust in, and the boy called out in pain. Josh whispered in his ear, 'Don't worry, don't worry,' all the while grinding his hips to work Stefan's arse looser. He'd show him there was nothing to it. Relax, relax. Josh plunged in. I said relax, you bastard. Oh, Steven, Steven, Steven.

It was coming towards the false dawn when Stefan started to dress. As Josh woke and became aware of the figure moving in the grey shadows, he remembered. His skin was hyper-sensitive to the flannelette sheet, and his dick ached pleasantly. Just as with Steven. Suddenly he was wide awake, remembering the 120 Euros. Stefan was putting his donkey jacket on.

'Hell,' thought Josh. 'If it's that important, he'll leave it somewhere.' He'd wanted to see what it felt like, being a whore like Steven was, but now it had all got confused. And he'd never liked talking about money.

Stefan stood by the door uneasily. Josh pretended to be asleep. 'The money,' said Stefan, the words trailing away ...

'Thank God,' thought Josh. 'He hasn't got any. It was just an excuse, a way in.' He turned over in bed. 'It's all right,' he smiled. 'I don't mind.'

'Where is my money, please?'

'Your money?'

'A hundred twenty Euros.' Stefan was getting excited, loud. Josh shushed him, thinking of the Dragon. 'A hundred twenty,' he repeated, obstinate.

'But I – '

'Please. I need money. I want to go home.' He crouched by the bedside, turned the full force of those honey eyes on Josh. Josh could smell the sweat on the boy, feel his heat.

'I want to return Rumania. We are poor family. Bucharest, Timişoara, Iashu, no work. I think here will be work. We can come now, many Rumanians have come since the EC. I think Italy is rich. But it is not rich. Only work in restaurante, bar. I am not good, I do not know this work, I am not quick. They think I am stupid; I am not stupid. I want to go home. I want the fields, the flowers.' It all came out in a rush. He was near tears.

Without a word, Josh indicated the leather jacket on the door. Stefan handed it to him. He took out his wallet, took out a hundred Euro note, then a twenty. He hesitated a second, and then took out another twenty. Hell, he'd be earning again soon. He handed the notes to Stefan, who stuffed them in his jacket pocket without looking at them. He looked as if Josh had been giving him a reprimand. His eyes on the floor, he groped behind him for the door handle, opened the door, and was gone.

Josh stared at the ceiling for a long time. The leather jacket felt warm and heavy on the bed. Slowly he started to drift back to sleep. 'When I get to Manchester,' he thought as he turned over, 'I might try a beard.'

The leather jacket slid off the bed to the floor, as if the bed was a snake shedding its skin.

Truant

McMurdoe's may not be the oldest boys' college in Edinburgh, but it is certainly the fiercest. From its hillside eyrie near the Botanical Gardens, its sandstone façade glowers disapprovingly over the back of the New Town to the Castle beyond.

Fiercely it had fought to keep its Grammar School status, and when defeat loomed, it had neatly side-stepped by going independent. So everything could go on exactly as before.

Fiercely McMurdoe's urged its charges over the hurdles of examinations, leading inexorably to places at St Andrew's and Heriot-Watt Universities. Any other destination was unthinkable. If you had muttered anything about privilege or class, the headmaster would have fiercely denied it. Instead he would have urged the virtues of continence, thrift, hard work and self-discipline, which were fiercely beaten into all pupils – metaphorically, of course. And for the most part its pupils said they were grateful for it in later life, and would fiercely resist any liberalising moves, preferring to rely instead for sticks and carrots on the various tourniquets of guilt.

Even the school motto had a fierce air about it. 'Per Dedicationem ad Victoriam'. As if sheer perseverance could overcome all inequalities, either innate or man-made. The Calvinist democracy of toil. This in turn was emphasised by the crossed swords on the school coat of arms, which was devised like the motto by some dedicated pseudo-medievalist towards the end of the nineteenth century. From this period too dated McMurdoe's massive arches and gables, its pinnacles and turrets. And though the architect had tried to soften it by the addition of a couple of cupolas nicked from a chateau on the Loire, the effect was overwhelmingly and alarmingly martial.

One Wednesday afternoon in early July, the sun was beating down on the tarmac of the quadrangle in front of the school. A radio somewhere in the college servants' quarters incongruously played Abba's *Super Trouper* on a Top Ten countdown programme. A boy, perhaps fifteen though he looked younger, stepped out of the shadow of the Science Block and into the glare of the sun. The nylon shirt beneath his grey flannel blazer prickled against his skin, and the battered black briefcase – his late grandfather's – seemed enormous, funereal, in his hand.

He flicked a blond forelock out of his eyes. The only concessions to modern fashion the unturned collar and loosened tie of the Tom Robinson Band.

Slowly he walked through the ornamental wrought-iron gates which formed the school entrance onto Inverleith Place. As he went along the edge of the playing fields, his hunched shoulders and downward gaze seemed to be willing people not to notice him.

Behind him, from the school, he heard the sound of a large hand bell. The lunch break was over, the first period of the afternoon would start in five minutes. Boys who were playing or sunbathing on the grass slopes raised their heads and looked towards the school like so many sheepdogs. They grumbled to themselves, collected balls, books or blazers, and ambled in chatty groups back towards the gates. But the boy whom we are following kept walking in the opposite direction, head down, eyes on the pavement.

There was something curiously self-contained about him. Studious, you would have said, until you saw that the briefcase contained only a copy of a cheap paperback, *The Front Runner*, by Patricia Neal Warren, with a picture of two men on the front cover; one young, wearing glasses, in running gear, the other, behind the first, older, suntanned, muscular, clad only in a towel. Not studious then – withdrawn. When spoken to, his eyes took on a slightly pained look of surprise; surprise that anyone should find him worth speaking to, pain at having to speak back. His slight frame seemed to shrink into his blazer at such times, to the point of invisibility. His mother had carefully chosen the blazer two sizes too large, so he would 'grow into it'. He was a scholarship boy, and scholarships, which had remained unchanged for fifty years, certainly took no account of adolescent growth rates when it came to clothes.

But he was the kind of boy who would withdraw naturally into his clothes, however well they fitted.

As he turned into Arboretum Place, Mr. Malleson, his maths master, came up the hill in the opposite direction. It took an absurdly long time for them to meet, like two gunfighters in a Spaghetti Western. Mr. Malleson walked, as he did everything, with an intense energy, but he combined it with a curious absent-mindedness. The boys thought of him as a very old and rickety engine, liable to emit a cloud of scalding steam in your face at any moment.

'Playing truant?' he shouted as he came into view. The boy didn't answer until they were nearly level.

'Dentist, sir,' he muttered, not looking up.

'Got a note?'

'Yes, sir.'

'Marked your homework last night. Not bad. Well, if the note's a forgery I hope for your sake it's a good one.'

The teacher had not paused in his stride, and threw his parting shot back over his shoulder. The boy was left alone with his thoughts by the steaming playing fields.

At the bottom of Arboretum Place he wound down a cobbled street by the Water of Leith. Birds sang overhead. The little artisan houses gave him a welcome cloak of shade.

At Stockbridge, a main road into the city. Car tyres crunched over the cobbles. A parade of shops. A stringy woman called out, 'Good day, William!' to a fat baker in a striped apron and straw hat, and the baker gallantly raised his boater to her. The boy stopped and looked at the pies, bridies and pasties in the window. The baker looked at the boy. Then slowly, solemnly raised his hat again, to him.

In the Royal Circus, the private garden in the middle looked cool and inviting. In the garden a madwoman – resident and keyholder, presumably, since she was inside the palings – was sitting on a bench and talking to a wholly imaginary dog. The boy crossed to the other side of the Circus, went up some steps to the door of an impressive Regency house. A heavy brass nameplate bore the words, 'Commercial Development Agency'. Through the window in the front parlour he could see some dark oil paintings in heavy gilt frames.

He rang the bell and waited. The madwoman shouted something, but he couldn't tell if she was shouting at him. The door opened and a man of about sixty in a morning coat admitted him to the hall. He had a large bald skull with a shoulder-length fringe of lank ginger hair. It was impossible to tell whether he was a particularly dishevelled servant, or an eccentric with a fancy for quaint dress. He put out his hand for the briefcase like a butler, and laid it on the hallstand.

'Is Alasdair here?' the boy asked.

'Yes, but he's busy.' The man's voice was as flat and grey as the Leith mudflats. 'Can I take your blazer?'

The boy removed his blazer and his McMurdoe's tie, with its crest and broad, subdued stripes. It was a quick, confident, practised motion, and the action gave him a sudden maturity. Under the shirt his body was unexpectedly trim, compact.

'Come upstairs, please,' the man was saying. 'There's someone who particularly wants to meet you. I'm glad you got here; I was going to have to give him Gavin instead.'

They climbed the elegant Georgian stairs. Bundles of glossy magazines stood on each landing, soft-faced youths grinning from the cover. Some lay prone, naked, buttocks to camera, smiling invitingly over their shoulders. As he climbed, the boy's walk turned imperceptibly into a swagger.

All afternoon the traffic roared in the distance along Princes Street. The madwoman dozed on her bench, and the square was at peace. Every so often a taxi drew up discreetly to the door of the CDA. A man in a dark suit would get out, and the front door would open for him as he paid the cab driver. An alert observer could have spotted a junior minister from the Scottish Office, come from St Andrews House, a senior producer from BBC Scotland, a director of the Port Authority. The shadows lengthened. By late afternoon, they spread across the whole square.

Inside the house, the boy went along the first-floor corridor to an elaborate old-fashioned bathroom. He soaked in the freestanding zinc tub with brass taps, which the man in the morning coat had run for him. The water, at room temperature, was silky and cool to his sweaty skin. As he soaked his body, hairless save for a small clump of golden moss, he inspected himself for any bruises. A slight discolouration on the upper arms, where he had been gripped too tight. He dressed. He looked in the full-length mirror set in the tiles, with some satisfaction, then came downstairs. He walked a little stiffly, as if in some discomfort.

'I suppose you'll be wanting to see Alasdair,' said the Butler, as the boy always thought of him. He had never learnt his name. The boy's face lit up. 'I'll get him for you. But you can't have long, he's very busy. Sit yourself down, have a smoke.'

He was ushered into a pleasant drawing room looking on the square. He sank into a deep leather Chesterfield. There was a mahogany coffee table in front of it, with a bowl of hand-rolled cigarettes. A second's thought, and he was on his feet again and closing the huge wooden shutters. The room felt stuffy in the half-light. He flicked through the pages of a magazine, looked at the naked boys without seeing them. Pop stars. Pages of small print, listings, personal ads. The magazine was a complete world, and it was going to be his.

Quietly the door opened again. A lanky older boy stood in the doorway. He had a perfect olive complexion, high cheekbones and the smile of a friendly Alsatian. His long smooth neck disappeared into a white towelling dressing gown.

'Alasdair,' the boy whispered. As always, he was in awe of his beauty. The chasm of the three years' age gap yawned in front of him. It was inconceivable that this god, this glowing alien creature, could love him. But he did.

He hugged Alasdair close to him, buried his face in the dressing gown. The towelling felt rough and warm on his cheek. He found his eyes were filling with tears.

The older boy stroked his hair. 'Are you ready?' he asked.

The reply was muffled in Alasdair's chest.

'Waverley Station, 8.30 tomorrow. I've got the tickets. How much cash have you got?'

'About seven hundred pounds, I think. I've been saving.'

'Me too.'

'Plus today, of course. I don't know how much I'll get for today.'

'How many did you do?'

'Three.'

'Was it all right?'

The boy shrugged his shoulders.

'Well, that's at least eighty. ... Are you scared?'

'Not – not with you.'

They held each other tight, not speaking for several minutes. Alasdair kissed the boy gently, then urgently. He seemed to suck the inner core out of him.

There was a knock on the door. It was a command. 'Georgio, you're wanted upstairs,' called the Butler.

'I must go,' said Alasdair, brushing his lips against the boy's forehead. 'Just think, this time tomorrow we'll be in London.' And with a little encouraging wave he was out of the room.

A few seconds later the man came back. He looked at the bowl. 'You've no' had a spliff?' The boy shook his head. 'Do you want to take one for later? You're very welcome.'

'No ... thank you.'

'Please yourself.' The man took out a fat wallet and counted out seven ten-pound notes, paused, and then added another ten.

'That's from Mr. Burns. He was very pleased, ... Never let it be said that we're not on the level with you.' I'd better be off then.'

'I suppose you had. You'll be wanting your tea.' The Butler fetched his blazer. The boy put it on, took the tie from his pocket, put it round his neck. He turned up the shirt collar. As he did so, he seemed to shrink again into the uniform. He rolled the money into a wad, and put it into the top pocket, emblazoned with the McMurdoe coat of arms.

In the hall the Butler handed him the briefcase with a little nod which might have been deference or satire. 'No doubt we'll be seeing you again,' he said as he opened the door. The boy looked up and down the street, and, seeing no one, slipped out.

He sat on the top of the 29 bus, at the front. The briefcase, upright on his knees, almost dwarfed him. They passed grimy Roman-style villas with pillars in front of them; anonymous little shops; a housing estate in cracked ochre. As the bus lurched along Ferry Road, the branches of the plane trees whipped and crashed into the window in front of him. He was oblivious to the onslaught. Instead he stared at some point of concentration far away, known only to himself.

He got out at Silverknowes. On his right, the golf course stretched away to the Forth estuary. He looked out across the expanse of water, dark blue in the dying rays of the sun. Golfers were driving hard and free along the fairway, and overhead a skylark was still hovering and trilling. A cool breeze blew in off the water.

Tomorrow, he thought, we'll away from all this. There'll just be the two of us. We'll disappear in the big city and they'll never find us. There were arcades near Piccadilly where there were boys just like him. Alasdair had told him he'd met a man there who would help them. We'll get a room somewhere and then we can be together for ever. There would be places they could go. He would buy the magazine and find them.

And there'll be no more flannel blazers, no more McMurdoe's; no more trying to be clever to please his parents all the time; no more bullying, no more preaching; no more of the Kirk; no more knowing smirking looks and name-calling; no more face ground into the tarmac or head down the toilet; no more tell-tale carpet burns. Most of all, no more lying.

Suddenly he whirled round and round like a shot-putter, with the briefcase for a shot. He hurled it high across the grass, and it fell with a satisfying thump. Then a frown flickered across his face, and he went to pick it up again. It was too soon.

He walked past bungalows and trim gardens with miniature spruce trees. On the streets, Cortinas and Vauxhall Vivas, lovingly polished at weekends, and saved, like Sunday suits, 'for best'.

The garden gate clicked shut behind him. Cradling the briefcase in his arms, he walked up a path of crazy paving. Behind the leaded glass of the bay window, he could see distorted and fragmented images of his mother as she hoovered in the lounge. He pulled his key out of his pocket on a long key-chain. Quietly he let himself in. He shut the front door very softly, hoping she wouldn't hear him, but as usual she had a sixth sense.

'Is that you, Davie?' she called.

'Yes, mum,' he mumbled as he put the case down.

'You're very late. The drama again, was it?'

He didn't answer, but started upstairs.

'Never mind, hen. Your tea won't be long. Did you have a good day at school?'

'Not bad,' he called down. And shut the door of his room behind him.

John Dixon

Growing Up

Grandma died
and Grandpa came to live with us.
He said he never wanted to.
For company he presented me a tortoise.
'That won't hurt him,'
he assured my parents
'and more to the point he can't hurt that.'
And I knew then they'd told him
about the budgie I'd let out the cage.
'And it won't cost much to keep.'
That pleased them even more.
Their heads nodded like the tortoise's,
its skin resembling Grandpa's.
'Don't let it get near the lettuce patch.'
I asked, 'It is a boy or girl?'
'That,' Grandpa said, 'I do not know.'
And I called the tortoise That.

One day when They were out
and Grandpa was in the shed asleep
I fed That the outer leaves
from full-grown lettuce plants.
Its tooth-line clean-cut the fleshy ribs.
Grandpa woke and held That above my reach
its splayed-out claws swam helplessly
its back legs treading water.
'Don't smash it!' I cried.
'That didn't eat the lettuce heart.
Tell Them it was me.'

Grandpa took That into the shed.
I heard a rattle.

He held the tortoise above my head.
'Can do no harm now.'
He'd drilled a hole in the overlap of shell
and knotted in a length of flex.

Grandpa died.
My parents talked of money,
of moving to a flat in town. No garden.
'You realise That will have to go.'

I took That to the cemetery
where Grandpa had been cremated
Grandma too
and put it on a sunny slab
watched it hoist up like a hovercraft
and make off for the nearest plant.

Pit Stops

The further I travel
the more likely I am to encounter
what I've always tried to avoid.
And in versions
ever more picturesque and tempting.

Take Shakrisabz.
The statue of Lenin
has been replaced by Tamburlaine
'My Lord Timur', as he's known,
a rallying point for displays
of loyalty to the new regime.
Weddings are held in its shadow.
The celebrants must stand well back
to fit the whole statue in the lens.
That's when the presence
of the lone tourist is legitimised.
Am I really to be entrusted
with their brand new camera?
How photogenic the groom
in his long-sleeved,
high-necked waistcoat!
And the bride, too,
in colourful girdled silk.
And her entourage with sunshades.

In Amman
my hotel is hosting a wedding reception.
Food, music, and the withdrawal to bed.
The staircase is spiral,
a central pillar, handrail
and each tread made of glass.
The happy couple lean over
to touch the outstretched hands.

Musicians stamp and yelp
and play fortissimo on drums and cymbals.
And one over there by himself,
bent arms pumping his chest like bellows,
blows harmonics on an adenoidal instrument
someway between woodwind and brass.

In Aswan
the noticeboard behind Reception
recommends 'a guided tour'
that includes 'a typical Nubian wedding.'
I ask for details, and am told
'Already oversubscribed.'

So, in Siwa,
I make doubly sure
and ask outright
'Are there any traditional weddings?'
And the man behind the makeshift counter shrugs.
'No need for the wedding,' he gestures.
'Just listen. Join in.'
And he tries selling me a tape
he's made of Berber wedding music.
He gyrates to the rhythms.
I sense there probably is a wedding
and he doesn't want me to attend.
Perhaps he's not the marrying type himself,
some unofficial match-maker
who makes possible the event
then stands aside
and keeps his own sort safely at a distance.

Only One Thing For It

I'd been to all my bucket-list destinations.
This was the first time I'd been
to the middle of bloody nowhere.
I sat outside its only café
sipping a glass of wine
which like a visit to the dentists deadened sensitivity.

'Has this place,'
I mouthed into the hand mirror
I use for re-inserting contact lenses,
'any redeeming features?'

The waiter
was hardly worth a second glance.
He hung to the left.
He warned me that all transport
had stopped the moment I arrived.
And the driver who'd brought me here
was the star of week-long festivities
that would need a further week to sleep off.

'Not to worry, sir,
this café doubles as a guest-house.
Currently, there's no electric current.
You'd best see the room before the sun goes down.
Beyond those impassable mountains.'

At the top of the stairs I stamped my feet
to warn livestock of my imminent arrival.
'Would I be right,' I asked the waiter,
now acting as guide and porter,
'in assuming the hot tap doesn't work
and the cold tap's been dripping for years
and has left a rusty ski-slope to the plug-hole?'

'You have been here before?'
'In nightmares, many times.'

'And what time would you like your morning call?'

'Morning will be far too late.
Wait till the sun goes down
and the livestock come out to play
and their claws clatter on the bubbling lino
and my demons emerge and
I have no strength to ward them off.

Say in half an hour.

Knock twice.
Be naked.
With your dick
neither to right nor left.
Bolt Upright.'

Tarpaulin

A tarpaulin had been stretched over the back lawn of the Lodge. On the far side were chairs for the drummers, and either side benches for spectators. In front of the veranda were rows of small dining tables. A barbecue was tucked in one corner, with a cold buffet in the main dining hall. Many guests were confused by the new layout – The Saturday Night Special – and moved from seat to seat until they felt settled. Several moved inside because of the 'mosquitoes.' Sam and I choose to sit outside. It was our last night at the Lodge. We were waiting for the drummers to begin before we ate. There was a sudden cry from behind.

'Hello. Again. You Two.'

Without turning Sam and I knew who it was, the Mother of the family with whom we'd shared the Land Rover on the journey coming here. We hadn't seen them since arrival. Presumably they had rooms in an annex, different shifts for meals and had gone on other scheduled trips. The Mother had always looked at us askance and addressed us as 'You Two.'

'Thought we'd catch you here. We're staying inside. We'd like a late start tomorrow. The children have been missing out on sleep. They need to catch up for the long journey back.'

I paused. She had not in effect asked a question. I answered, 'And have you checked with David, the driver?'

'No, we haven't actually,' said the Father.

'Perhaps see what he says first.'

'But the children must have a good sleep,' the Mother persisted. 'They get over-excited. I do hope those drummers don't keep us awake.'

I blinked and asked unhurriedly 'At what time do we have to vacate the premises?'

'Oh! That's a factor,' the Father said. 'We'll come back to you.'

A waiter came round with the drinks. Sam put a serviette over the glasses. Hundreds of white water-flies were hovering round the candle on the table, even more round the spotlight over the tarpaulin.

A drummer gave a couple of 'stand-to-attention' thuds, and a rhythm emerged on a dozen or so drums of different types and sizes. There was some chanting as well. After ten minutes the drummers stopped and from the far end of the lawn, still in darkness, came the sound of bells, not in any rhythm, just as if shaken anyhow. The dancers entered, six women and six men, all barefoot, wearing little bells round their ankles. The men wore loincloths, and the women short-sleeved blouses and beaded skirts.

'They're from Ruwenzori,' Sam said, unimpressed, implying they were little more than tourist fodder. We were sitting quite close to them and on the same level and could not really judge the inventiveness of the dance formations. There was a lot of stomping and strutting and half-raising one bent leg. The 'curtain call' was a fast routine, the sound of the bells almost drowning the drummers. We clapped and they moved off in line for a break.

The Family re-appeared.
'All sorted,' the Mother said. 'We can go as late as we like. We were thinking eleven would be good.'
'Mm!' I replied. 'Perhaps make it half-past ten.'
'Oh.' She hesitated. 'All right, then. About half-past ten.'

Next morning, all packed, we waited in the foyer of the Lodge. The Family appeared just before ten-thirty. All five of them. Two parents, two daughters, a young son.
'Got here,' the Mother exclaimed. 'Just.'

'The children all had a good sleep' the Father said.
'We were the last ones down for breakfast.'
'Thank you for agreeing to a late start.'

The Mother packed their luggage in the boot of the Land Rover. She then took it all out again and rearranged it. We got in the van before her. At the front was David, the driver, and a new passenger, a man of Indian descent, who had been hurriedly called away on business. In the middle seats, same as on the outward journey, were Sam and I. The five seats at the back were for the Family.

We were soon in the savannah and passing herds of zebra and antelope. On the outward journey the children would have whooped and asked the driver to stop for photos. Mbarara was the only scheduled stop.

As it turned out there was to be one more.

It happened parallel to Chambura Gorge. We were leaving the scrub vegetation and getting into more rocky terrain with dangerous hairpin bends when a frantic cry came from the Father.
    'Stop. Please stop. My daughter's been sick.'
    'Can't stop here,' said David. 'It's too dangerous.'
    'Pull over. Please.'
    'I can't at the moment.'
    'Don't you understand? My daughter, my younger daughter's been sick.'
    'I'm sorry,' said David, 'but ...'
    The Indian gentleman added, 'We really can't park on a corner.'

The embankments of the Gorge came down to the roadside. There were no lay-bys. Round a bend on the right was the entrance to a campsite called The Jacana. We slowed, veered over and stopped along the grass track leading to the encampment. Just by an enormous Welcome sign.

Sam and I could not help a quick glance behind as we got out the van. The Mother must have been cradling her daughter when the latter puked up a hearty cooked breakfast, trimmings and all, plum tomatoes in particular. It was all down the Mother's neck, down her arm, all over her hands, in her lap. The liquid element fanned out as it was absorbed into her clothes. Slowly she got out the van, put down her daughter and she held out an arm and shook off the multi-coloured macédoine.

The Father unpacked the boot of the van. Out came towels, tissues and changes of clothing. Surplus bottles of water intended for drinking were used for cleaning.

He called over to us. 'I'm so sorry. I really am.'

The Indian gentleman shrugged and said, 'We've all had children.'

Sam and I looked at each other. 'We've all had children.' We hadn't. But … what a splendid and placatory remark given the situation! We smiled back knowingly.

Passers-by, wheeling their bikes up the incline, looked askance as the younger daughter was given a stand-up strip-wash. David tried cleaning the back seat of the van with a toilet roll. The elder daughter took her young brother to pee.

When it was the Mother's turn to change she crouched the far side of the van. She took an inordinate time, and emerged wearing an outfit suitable for an evening meal.

We all avoided eye contact. The rubbish was thrown into a bin just by the Welcome sign. The Family got into the van. We followed. The Asian gentleman got out his laptop.

David turned on an air vent and left his window full open. Sam and I hardly dared swig at our bottles of water.

Very little was said. There were no shared remembrances of the short safari break.

Nairobi

The station master was on the platform. He smiled and remembered my name. He pointed to the sleeper carriage. I was in a central compartment this time, which should prove much quieter. In the dining carriage, as with the outward journey, the waiter seated all the sleeping car passengers together. I was placed opposite a doctor of Indian descent. Across the aisle were two young couples. All seemed set for an unremarkable return journey.

Then, at the threshold of the carriage I noticed a slightly dishevelled and bewildered-looking man, mid-aged, well-built, but with greying hair, tired eyes and trousers popping at the knees. He seemed uncertain where to sit and was escorted to our table. He glared at the free seats further down the carriage, then sat opposite me and lowered his eyes. We were at the stage when the orders for food had gone in, and the staff were bringing the drinks. The man was offered a Tusker Lager. He pointedly refused. I wondered from his rather vacant stare if he might not have had some alcohol already. There was a long silence, as if he was seeking ways of putting himself at ease by attacking the object nearest at hand – this was the waiter hovering to take the man's order.

'Why ask? There's no choice. Bring whatever you've got left.' He turned to the doctor and said, 'Always the same, isn't it? That's why I usually fly. Couldn't get a seat this time. Had to settle for second best. Have to go to Nairobi regularly. Hate the place. So bloody cold.' That was almost certainly true, Nairobi was higher and less humid than Mombasa. The man added challengingly, 'Been here before?' The doctor did not reply. I was about to say it was my first time when the plates were laid out and the food arrived.

'See what I mean?'

It didn't look particularly appetising. Plain white rice, stewed meat and diced vegetables. It was edible, though the meat was chewy. The man didn't start to eat till we had half-finished, and then ate fitfully. He wolfed a few mouthfuls, put down the fork, took it up later for a taster, followed by a large mouthful, pushed the plate away, out-stared it, stabbed his fork into a bit of meat and spooned the gravy over the rice and mixed it all up. Eventually, grudgingly his plate was emptied.

After the perfunctory sweet we were offered an extra Tusker. The man barked at the waiter, 'I already said no. Don't you understand English?' When the waiter had gone he added, 'What's to be done with them, eh? You can take them out the jungle, but you can't take the jungle out of them.'

He seemed surprised that what he had said should even raise an eyebrow. Perhaps it wouldn't have done in the circles he usually moved in. I broke the silence. 'That's just a form of words. It may sound mildly catchy on the surface, but it's really very objectionable.'

He focused his eyes on me and shrugged. 'It's what my wife says. And she's black. I go by what she says. Wouldn't dare cross her.'

He seemed to think he'd gained the advantage and continued in the same vein. 'You should hear the way she goes on at weekends when they all go down the beach. She says it's like an oil slick. Black and shiny. That's what she says. And she's as black as they come.'

It wasn't worth pursuing the conversation. I'd like to have stayed on in the spacious dining car before returning to the cramped sleeping compartment. But it was impossible to remain while he was there. He had begun to tell his life story, his failure as a sheep farmer in the Welsh borders, his time on oil rigs and his near-death experience as a trainee diver.

Next morning – after a far quieter night than on the outward journey – I was the first in the dining car. I took a window seat facing the engine. The doctor arrived a little later and sat opposite. We got chatting.

He worked in the Paediatrics Department of Mombasa Hospital, and every so often he and colleagues from hospitals in other parts of Kenya get together to tour remote villages and perform minor operations. One of the most common – and indeed the purpose of this particular expedition – was to repair hare lips and cleft palates. 'Not a major operation,' he said. 'Re-constructive surgery. To be carried out as early as possible to get the best results. And prevent negative effects. Problems with breast-feeding. And psychological. Some parents reject children with any 'imperfection', and the children become progressively alienated.'

'Actually ... reject them?' I queried.

'Yes. It's often taken to be a form of divine punishment, a visitation. They're ashamed of the child. Keep it separate, abandon it, or let some village matron bring it up.'

'That's awful.'

The doctor shrugged. 'The situation's changing.'

'So ... what actually causes a hare lip?'

'A lot of factors. The roof of the mouth doesn't fuse during the early stages of pregnancy. It's nothing you can foretell from a scan. It can affect hearing.' He paused and went on, 'Our transport and equipment are arranged in Nairobi. We have to 'rough it' for a week. I don't mind. It's all to the good. We do follow-ups on the children we operated on last time. The parents have come to see the advantages. But,' he added, 'it does mean I have to leave my hospital patients. I've one very worrying case at the moment.' He pointed to his mobile.

I was full of admiration. I ran out of questions. The doctor asked, 'And where's 'Our Friend' this morning?' We smiled, but hardly a minute later as if on cue I felt someone plump into the seat next to me. It was 'Our Friend'. He seemed cheerful, as if nothing had happened the night before. Almost at once he took up the narrative where he had left off. It had been so cold, he said, on the Welsh borders. He liked the heat. The oil rigs weren't much better.

'And,' the doctor queried, 'you say you were a diver?'

'You remember? Fancy that. Yes, I trained to be. But didn't finish the ... ' he tailed off.

'Did you ever get the bends?'

The man paused, taken aback. 'No, but a friend of mine did. Why do you ask? You a doctor?'

'My speciality is paediatrics.'

'Paediatrics? That's to do with children, isn't it? Too many of them born. I know what I'd do.' He paused and bellowed his solution at the dining car staff, 'Cut off their balls.'

There was a long silence and the man said, 'Doctor, eh?' Another pause and he added, 'Actually I've been under the weather a bit myself recently.'

'Oh, dear,' the doctor said, looking out the window.

'It's depression.'

In other circumstances this word might have elicited a modicum of sympathy. In his case it didn't.

The doctor asked, 'And is that where you're off to in Nairobi?'

'Not treatment. No. I've come to renew my papers. For another three years.'

Aha! Interesting. The man's drifting may not be over yet!

The doctor's phone rang. He gave detailed advice for the treatment of a patient. He apologised for the call. 'One of my patients has taken a turn for the worse.'

The train was approaching the outskirts of Nairobi. The doctor pointed to a complex of buildings. 'That's the school my eldest daughter goes to. I hope to fit in a visit, time permitting.'

The steward passed through and announced that the dining car was about to close. The doctor left, but the man stayed seated, trapping me in the inside seat. I said, 'Time to go,' and he let me pass.

Inscription

I can no longer travel abroad, or even out of town. This is not a travel restriction imposed by a hostile government. Just age, health, mobility. Not as yet, poverty.

However, I am still able to go round the world! In food. No longer as a tourist in some latter-day exodus and exploitation – which is all I now feel holidaying ever was – but on a day-out basis to enjoy the efforts that immigrants who have come to this country for whatever reason have made in maintaining the food customs of their former homeland.

It's said London is a collection of villages. Estate Agent talk. Far more interesting are unmarked but distinctive enclaves. You'll sense their approach from a few out-rider shops with names, lettering and window displays that differ mildly from the general pattern. A growing concentration highlights the differences. Then comes a row of shopfronts, almost a parade – and parade in the sense of 'on show'; shops with no window frontage, just retractable grilles, totally opening to view the range of unusual produce; shops with a frontage but plus a stall narrowing the pavement; and small but noisy delivery vans hopping from one shop to another, everyone seeming to know each other. This is certainly true of the South London enclave known as Little Portugal.

And just look at the range of places to eat! The smaller cafés – all licensed – open early morning and close late afternoon. The larger ones winch up their shutters and put out the odd table and chair just prior to lunch, and stay open late in the evening.

I much prefer the smaller family-run cafés. They give a better idea of day-to-day life. My favourite is tucked around the corner from the main parade. It has a large notice outside – Cakes For All Occasions. Inside at the counter is a display of palmiers, custard tarts, rice-cakes and Madeira cake. I asked for a black coffee, a glass of Portuguese brandy and a slice of Madeira cake. Proper Madeira cake, that is, flavoured with orange zest, a sizeable wedge, not the mass-produced slab that tastes wet, sickly and sticks to the roof of your mouth.

Cakes For All Occasions! It took me some time to work out the motto. Which occasions? Feast Days, Saints Days, Name Days, religious holidays, coming of age, weddings, births, birthdays, national independence? Or special days that celebrated a particular town or region, the local saint or football team? Endless possibilities.

But where were the cakes? They weren't cooked on the premises. There was no smell of baking. I felt rather let down. Then a delivery man arrived, with a trolley piled high with boxes. He was met by – the owner of the café or possibly the manager, a man always in evidence, ever eager to please, the main man surely – let's call him Pedro. They greeted each other like brothers and went to the far end of the shop, beyond the seating area, to a glass-fronted cabinet. They began unpacking and re-stocking the shelves.

When the delivery man had left, I casually approached the cabinet. It was temperature-controlled and contained a range of large cakes. Some were heart-shaped or cross-shaped, most were round, with a diameter of at least twelve inches. All were fully iced and edged, but the icing on top was left blank as if waiting for an inscription. Aha, I thought, the occasion is decided by the purchaser, and an appropriate inscription is added.

I could quite understand a cake as the centre-piece of a celebration, and the cutting of the first slice as an act of almost sacrificial significance. The baking, the icing, the decorating, these were all acknowledged arts, but ones where mistakes could perhaps be rectified. Not so with an inscription. One error there and the whole cake would be ruined. How, I pondered, was it done?

Almost as if to answer my query three customers came in and walked straight down to the glass cabinet. They were taken aback by the choice and noisily began discussing which cake to purchase. They called over to Pedro. I could not catch much of what was said. Pedro seemed happy enough to sell the cake but shook his head when one of the customers pulled out a piece of paper with writing on it. They all gestured from the writing to the top of the cake. Pedro nodded that he understood perfectly. He pointed to an empty chair at the far end of the counter, implying that the usual inscriber was absent. The customers were insistent and threatened to leave without making a purchase. Pedro shrugged and reluctantly looked at the writing on the piece of paper. He spent a few minutes mixing up something behind the counter. He filled an icing bag and tested the nozzle. He held the bag above the iced surface of the cake. He asked the customers to stand back. He took a deep breath.

How I felt for the man. He was taking his life into his hands. Any hesitation, distraction, or loss of concentration could spoil the whole cake. Blots, smudges and misspellings were obvious pitfalls. But joined-up writing must be particularly hazardous. Should the 'nib' of the icing bag leave the surface? Were the straight lines of letters in capitals any easier?

How I wish I could have seen!

Pedro paused, perhaps at a name, a greeting or a well-wish. He looked tense, dissociated from his place of work. He grew more confident and finished with a flourish. He breathed out as if he had been holding his breath all the time. He called over the three customers. They looked at the inscription on the cake and grudgingly gave a nod. He shrugged as if to say 'Best I can do' and called on a counter hand to pack the cake and settle the bill. He went to sit in the empty chair and leaned forward, his head in his hands.

A week passed before I went back to that café. I had been pondering which country or continent to visit next on my world food tour. This café was as good as anywhere to relax and gather my thoughts. I'd got to know the busy times, lunch and the late afternoon school run. I felt at ease. I could almost become a permanent fixture.

This time a young man was sitting in the chair that had been empty, the one at the far end of the counter. He was wearing a pale-yellow shirt with long floppy sleeves and a wide collar, and a bright red bolero. An arresting combination, almost a mascot. He was in his early twenties, good-looking and economical in movement. I wondered vaguely if he was part of the family set-up, even closely related to Pedro. Occasionally one of the counter staff would pop by and speak to him. He shook his head or nodded emphatically. If a customer called across the café he would wave exaggeratedly and smile ear to ear. Then he'd revert to his usual immobile, frozen position. I began to wonder if he was … what are those dreadful phrases people use? Not quite right. Something wrong? Or missing? Not the brightest bulb in the chandelier. And of course, the concomitant – a cheap analysis of why the person was 'Like That.'

Two elderly customers came in and hovered round the glass-fronted cabinet containing the celebration cakes. They made a choice and Pedro was called over for further discussion. A cake was taken out and the customers wrote the required inscription on a piece of paper. This time Pedro was not hesitant. He nodded gratefully and beckoned over the young man – let's call him João – and introduced him to the customers, who seemed rather taken aback.

João was handed the slip of paper with the legend to be transcribed. He stared at it, fixedly, intently, clenching his teeth and screwing up his eyes and forehead. Then, without double-checking the writing he picked up the icing-bag and inscribed the cake in one continuous movement, as if he was ironing a crumpled shirt.

Pedro beamed ear to ear, and looked at the customers as much as to say, 'You see?' The customers applauded as if the result exceeded their wildest dreams.

How I wish I could have seen!

I watched João go back to the chair and sit down. His smile faded. He'd been mute throughout. Did he understand what he'd copied? Did he have a photographic memory? Was he a savant? Could he have copied at a glance lettering in Arabic or Chinese?

It was nearing 3 o'clock. Several mothers dropped by for a brief purchase and chat before going off to collect their children from a nearby school. Others came in later with their children. João moved awkwardly and scowled. I wondered if he felt threatened by children. He got up and left through the door marked Staff Only.

It was time for me to go too. I never returned to that café. I recommended it to friends, without telling them of the near miracle I had distantly witnessed.

Kevin Crowe

The Bench

In the warm spring sunshine, John sits on the bench, gently rubbing its nameplate and hoping he'll live to see the end of the cricket season. Regardless, he knows it won't be long before he is, he hopes, reunited with his beloved Geoff.

His mind goes back all those years to when he first met him, shortly after joining his local cricket club as a scorer.

As a kid, all he'd ever wanted to do was to play cricket. He had no idea where his love of the game came from: his parents hated it and it wasn't played at school, but he had his transistor tuned to Test Match Special, listening to the dulcet tones of John Arlott, even getting detention at school for listening to the commentary in the classroom. When he could, he watched it on TV.

He was fourteen when he began to watch his local town amateurs and, after a few weeks, was asked if he wanted to help score the matches. He jumped at the chance and the official scorer taught him how to record every ball. He was fond of telling anyone who would listen that he learnt more about maths from cricket than he ever did at school.

The scorer's grandson, Geoff, a stylish left-hander, opened the batting for the team. John could hardly take his eyes off him, so when Geoff suggested he take up the game and offered to coach him, John jumped at the chance.

It soon became obvious that he was never going to be anything more than a mediocre batter. He did however discover he could bowl and bowl fast. Geoff encouraged him, even after one net practice when a fast bouncer from John hit him in the balls.

Geoff collapsed on the ground, rolling in agony, tears rolling down his face. John dashed over and asked if he was okay.

'Of course I'm not bloody okay,' Geoff yelled.

Other players came from their own nets to see what was going on. When they were told what had happened, they all started laughing, which made Geoff all the angrier, and the more annoyed he got, the louder they laughed. Eventually, after several jokes about losing the family jewels, Geoff himself saw the funny side.

The captain was so impressed with John's bowling, he picked him for their next game. He became a regular and was one of the team's most feared players.

Not everyone was happy about the team's success since John joined. One in particular, Stephen, was angry at losing his place and vowed to get his revenge.

John and Geoff were inseparable, even after the season finished. One night in the autumn, they ended up near some allotments, drinking beer and smoking cigarettes stolen from Geoff's dad. As time wore on and the beer loosened their inhibitions, they both realised they felt more than just friendship for each other. They tried to pretend it wasn't happening and to ease the tension began wrestling. The wrestling turned into love making.

Afterwards they were embarrassed and for a few moments couldn't look at each other, then Geoff joked: 'Well, it seems you've bowled a maiden over' and they both burst out laughing at the weak pun.

Then they became serious, agreeing they couldn't tell anyone. Less than ten years earlier it had still been a crime to engage in homosexual behaviour, and as they were both under 21, it was still against the law for them. But they were less concerned about the law than they were about losing their places in the side.

Secrets can be difficult to keep. At the start of the next season, Stephen told John he would reveal what he knew about their relationship unless he gave up his place in the team. So John faked an injury and went back to scoring.

Geoff was furious. 'There's nothing wrong with you,' he said, 'so why are you pretending you can't play?'

Unable to look at his lover, John said: 'It's Stephen, he knows about us. Giving up my place in the side was the only way I could get him to keep quiet.'

This made Geoff's anger even more incandescent. 'The bastard can't be allowed to get away with this. I'm going to tell the captain what he's done.' He stormed out of the door.

John ran after him, urging him not to, telling him it would end up in them both being dropped from the team. Geoff shrugged his shoulders, as if to say 'so what'. Eventually, John calmed him down and Geoff agreed to leave things are they were. 'But he's not going to get away with it.' he said.

He didn't play again that year. Before the start of the next season, on John's seventeenth birthday, Geoff told him it had been sorted and that Stephen had left the club.

When John asked what had happened, Geoff grinned and said: 'He was given a stark choice: either leave the club or be reported to the police.'

John stared wide-eyed at Geoff. 'Why? I haven't heard anything.'

'Oh, it's been hushed up,' Geoff said, his grin growing wider. 'Some property went missing from the dressing room and it was found in the back of his car.'

'Bloody hell! I know he's a nasty piece of work, but I never thought he was a thief.'

'He isn't as far as I know. But hey, the stuff was found in his car. I wonder how it got there.' Geoff winked.

For years, Geoff opened the batting, John opened the bowling and they remained lovers. They both got jobs locally, earned enough to rent a flat together, began saving for the deposit on a place of their own and eventually they were able to buy a small house.

Then Geoff died. One winter evening, they were walking along the river bank when he slipped on some ice, fell in the water and drowned. It was no-one's fault, but despite him being told this time and again, John continued to blame himself.

'If only I had learned to swim, if I hadn't panicked, if I'd got help earlier,' he would say. On one occasion he added wryly: 'So many ifs. If wishes were rainbows, we'd all have our pots of gold.'

In accordance with his wishes, Geoff's ashes were spread at the ground. The team had a collection and bought a bench engraved with his name as a memorial. It was placed outside the pavilion and it became a custom, almost a superstition, for anyone waiting to bat to sit there and to tap the metal plate with Geoff's name before going on to the field.

Although he continued to play and take part in the social life of the club, John was never the same after Geoff's death. He became morose and introspective and began to drink heavily. Some days, he was so hungover he didn't get up for work and eventually his boss lost patience and sacked him. That just meant he had more time to drink. He was okay during the cricket season: he was still so keen on playing, he made sure he was sober most of the time and kept himself reasonably fit. However, in the winter he locked himself away with only bottles for company. Not being able to talk about his grief made it worse.

Everyone at the club was devastated when they lost the ground, but no-one more than John: cricket was the only thing keeping him sane. The club had rented it for years from a local businessman who was a fanatical cricket fan and only charged a peppercorn rent. When he died, his son wanted to make money out of what was prime building land, even though his father had left him enough to live comfortably for the rest of his life. He had obtained outline planning permission for houses before he evicted the team. When the club offered to pay a higher rent, he shook his head.

They tried everything they could: legal action, petitions, lobbying the council, they even had the support of the local paper and radio station, but it was all to no avail. They looked for suitable land elsewhere, but without success. So, after over a century, the club closed down.

It was the club secretary who suggested that Geoff's memorial bench should go to John. 'After all,' he said, 'John was closer to him than anyone.'

Everyone agreed. John blushed as he thanked them, close to tears. He wondered if, after all, people knew he and Geoff were lovers.

John's drinking got worse. Once building work began on the former cricket ground, he would often be seen, can or bottle in hand, shouting abuse at the site workers. Many of his former team-mates did their best to help him, but one by one they gave up.

One day he met a stranger in a local pub and got chatting to him. Keith had only recently moved to the town to start a new job, didn't know anything about the one-time cricket ground and had no interest in and less knowledge of the sport. When he told John that he'd rather watch paint dry, John had burst out laughing.

They became friends and proved to be good for each other: John showed Keith around and Keith helped John to sober up and recommended him for a job operating a press cutter, a tedious and heavy but reasonably well-paid job, particularly as he was a quick worker and so was able to supplement his basic income with piece-rates. Keith was an engineer, employed to maintain and repair the machinery.

They remained firm friends, but nothing more: although they attempted a relationship, it didn't work out, partly because John couldn't imagine living with anyone other than Geoff. When Keith moved on to a better paid job in another town, they kept in touch.

Now, sitting on the bench in his garden, looking at the nesting birds gathering food for their young and facing death from his terminal liver cancer, he wonders if he will be reunited with Geoff or if his death really will be the end for him. His one hope is that the process of dying will not be too painful or prolonged.

He is wakened by the creaking of the garden gate. He looks up and sees Keith. 'Hope I didn't scare you. I rang the front door, but no-one answered. I got your letter and wanted to see you again before it's too late.'

John struggles to his feet and hugs his friend as tears roll down his face.

The Platform

Brian

This wasn't the way he expected things to be. He was the one with multiple chronic conditions who needed two sticks to move more than a few feet. Yet it was his husband, James, who had died. James, who was as strong as an ox, walked everywhere and went to the gym three times a week; James, who was to all intents and purposes Brian's carer; James, who without warning collapsed one day, dead within seconds from a heart attack.

For over a year, Brian felt unable to move on. He often forgot to take his medication, only realising when the pain in his joints became almost unbearable and his mobility got even worse. He rarely showered, only occasionally shaved, allowed the bungalow to get into the sort of mess that would have shocked James, couldn't be bothered to do the exercises he was supposed to and lived mainly on delivered take-aways. At first friends visited him regularly, but gradually they stopped coming, put off by the state of his home and irritated by his circular monologues, punctuated with uncomfortable silences.

Then one morning he looked in the mirror and was disgusted by what he saw. He cleaned himself and his bungalow, threw out all the detritus and vowed to begin living again. He knew he would never forget James, but he didn't think his dead husband would want him existing like this.

He met Michael online. It had taken weeks for him to make himself known on the gay dating site, and even then he'd provided only minimal information. As he added to his profile, he found fewer people interested in him. His age put off those who were seeking youngsters and as soon as he found the courage to include his disability, his followers dropped off like lemmings over a cliff. There were a few weirdos who claimed to be turned on by the thought of sex with what one of them called a 'cripple'. But it soon became apparent that these sickos didn't consider him disabled enough for their fantasies. No-one seemed interested in anything other than what they could do to his body. Back in the 1980s when the internet was little more than a technophile's wet dream, he knew clubs that were little more than meat markets, where clones and leather queens displayed their steroid enhanced bodies, hoping to attract effeminate chickens, all the better if they were virgins.

Now the meat markets were as likely to be online as in the real world, but what was the point of being able to see all that beef steak if you couldn't touch?

He recalled he'd met James at one such club back in the late 1980s and that memory was the reason he persevered with the site. It seemed he'd made the right decision when one day he logged on and saw a new message which, after he opened it, pleasantly surprised him. Free of the usual emojis and irritating text speak where vowels were missing and parts of words replaced by numbers, the message was easy to read and understand. Not only that, but it also lacked the tedious innuendos common on the site. Instead, Michael gave some basic information about himself, a photograph that didn't look like it had been touched-up and the suggestion that they talk online.

After exchanging messages for a couple of weeks, they agreed to meet on Zoom. Beforehand Brian showered and dressed as if he were going on a first date and when they saw each other, it was clear that Michael had done the same. At first there was some awkwardness, but gradually they became more confident and they could have talked for a lot longer than the hour they had booked. Over the next few weeks, they met regularly on Zoom until the day they agreed to meet in person. They both thought it would be better to meet on neutral ground for the first real-world date and Michael suggested a pub in a village about halfway between their two homes.

Michael said: 'It's called the 'Railway Hotel' and there's plenty of parking. It's near the station, hence the name.'

The day they were due to meet, his Motability car wouldn't start and he knew from experience that it could be hours before the rescue service would get to him. He didn't want to cancel the date, so he checked the train times and discovered one of the few that stopped at the station arrived about half an hour before he was to meet Michael. He hoped he would be staying the night, but in case anything went wrong he could return on the last train back to his home town.

He rang for a taxi and packed a few essentials – a book, a change of clothes, his toothbrush and his daily medications. When the cab arrived, he put the rucksack on his back, leaving his arms free for his walking sticks.

For once the train was on time and 40 minutes later he disembarked onto the platform, noting that the station was unmanned.

It was then his problems began.

At first, he couldn't see the exit: there was an unbroken fence the length of the platform and it continued as far as he could see. When he stared across the rail lines, he saw the exit on the other platform. Looking to his left, he spotted the bridge that would take him to the exit. As he walked towards it, he realised it wasn't a ramp, but steep steps he knew he couldn't manage. Nonetheless he tried, with the only result being that he fell back down, his two walking sticks clattering on top of him. His legs weren't strong enough to get him upright, so he crawled to the bridge, dragging his sticks behind him. Then, holding on to the bridge, he forced himself up on his feet.

He hobbled to the only bench on the platform, sat down and retrieved his phone from his rucksack, intending to call Michael and explain the problem.

There was no signal.

No problem, he thought. He'd read online that even if there was no signal, you could still call the emergency services. When he tried calling 999, he realised that was another internet myth.

He made his way to the Information Board to check when the next train was due, only to discover that there were no trains leaving from this platform until the next day. He knew there was one that could take him back home due later in the evening, but he had no way of crossing the line.

He realised he could be stuck where he was, without food or shelter, until the morning.

Michael

Michael spent so long deciding what to wear for his first real date for years, he was in danger of being late. He eventually decided on what might be called smart casual: white shirt open at the collar, denim trousers and suede waistcoat. He'd already booked a ground floor twin room at the Railway Hotel, just in case. He had decided it would be presumptuous to book a double room and a twin would keep their options open. And if Brian said he had to get home, well that would be up to him. But he hoped he would stay. After all, neither of them would want to fall foul of the drink/drive laws.

By dint of breaking the speed limit, he arrived at the pub in time. He saw Brian was not there yet, so he got the key to his room and dumped his overnight bag, before going back to the bar and ordering a pint of IPA. When half an hour later, Brian still hadn't arrived, he began to worry. Over a second pint, he thought about all the reasons why Brian was late or wasn't even coming. When his phone calls went straight to voicemail, he became even more concerned. Perhaps he'd had an accident on the way here.

Perhaps his fragile health had taken a turn for the worse. But if that were the case, wouldn't he have phoned? Perhaps he couldn't phone because of an accident.

By the time he had finished his third pint, he was cursing Brian.

Hastie Salih

A girl at last

It was that time of the year when people flocked around gigantic Christmas trees, with artificial boughs and flashing baubles, stuffing themselves with mince pies and Christmas puddings that I hated. I preferred the roasting chestnuts.

The festive period just led to putting on weight, bouts of gastritis and yuletide lies. Last Christmas was horrific but I have a plan about what to do this year when visiting family...

On Boxing Day last year, my girlfriend and I decided to visit my mother and grandmother. Jenny encouraged me to come out to my mother. I tried telling her that it wasn't a good idea. But she batted her eyelids, stroked my hair and begged me to finally talk frankly to my mother. Jenny had already come out to hers. But then her mother was a hippie and couldn't care less whether she went out with a girl or a boy. Jenny didn't know my mother like I did.

I had to fulfil her wishes of coming out to my mother. Bah, Humbug! Whatever next? Would my girlfriend want me to dance with elves? I'm not much of a dancer and I don't believe in elves.

As I gingerly entered my mother's cottage last year, my mother and grandmother hugged my 'lady companion' and myself and asked who she was. I opened my mouth, then closed it again. I couldn't say that Jenny was my girlfriend, could I? So, I said she was my beautician and tried pouting my lips to make them look fuller. Jenny gasped at my Yuletide lie and prodded me in the ribs causing me to cry out in pain.

My mother glanced disbelievingly at Jenny's torn jeans and shabby white shirt. She then turned to glare at me, obviously waiting for a proper explanation as Jenny didn't look like a beautician.

So, I whispered 'Mum, I ... I like ... girls.'

My deaf grandmother, standing next to my mother shrieked 'She's having a girl. At last! She's pregnant!'

My mother's face turned grey as she stepped towards me and slapped me on the cheek. My face felt hot and stung. I felt my eyes welling up with tears.

'What did I teach you?' My mother glared at me and added, 'I always told you to use a condom ... You haven't even finished college yet!'

My girlfriend rushed towards me and squeezed me so tightly that I couldn't breathe. She started sobbing. I extricated myself from her and said loudly,

'Mum, I'm not having a girl. ... I *like* girls.'

My mother started tearing her hair out and rushed towards Jenny. That's when Jenny and I turned towards the front door and ran out without exchanging any words.

Now, I did promise you that I had a plan for this year's Christmas celebration with my mother. My plan is to tell her that I'm officially pregnant – with the help of my girlfriend and ... a sperm donor.

And the baby is going to be a girl. At least my demented grandmother will be happy – A girl at last!

Afterlife

I've been flitting through the British Museum for decades, mad ghost that I am, hoping to find the soul of the divine Queen Hathor whom I served when I was a mere mortal in ancient Egypt thousands of years ago.

Thote, our scribe, should have written a story about my beloved goddess Hathor and myself. Now that's a relic that should have been pinched and put into this museum.

I could weep whilst watching the visitors of the British Museum surround and celebrate the Rosetta Stone and its mundane tale. Is my story, my love, not worth applause?

I lived in Deir el Medinat, a village not far from Thebes, the name we used to give for Luxor.

My whole life was dedicated to making my goddess Hathor happy. I was her seamstress and followed her everywhere, yearning for a glance in my direction, to finally embrace me with gratitude and yes, with love.

She was the goddess of the sky, of women, of fertility and love three thousand years ago. I remember dancing with her, twirling to the flute and music she adored. But it wasn't enough for me. I craved her closeness, her admiration and more.

She crossed boundaries between Egypt and foreign lands, and also helped the spirits of deceased humans enter the realms of the dead.

But I can't find her soul and so I keep darting through this overcrowded museum, trapped in this Netherworld.

I will not rest until I find her.

Hathor's role as a sky goddess was linked to the afterlife, of which I am now an unwilling part. Ha! The afterlife is anything but blissful. All the food, the wine, the make-up, the skin products and utensils that were put into the pyramids with the pretentious pharaohs were useless. I should know as I live in the afterlife, in the twilight.

I can't taste or smell anything, I have no skin and therefore no use for make-up. You may laugh at my sarcasm, but you too, one day will understand how it feels to be confined to a floating afterlife, entombed and entrapped like ancient pharaohs' bones.

My goddess Hathor was depicted on statues as a lioness and a domestic cat. I loved both those parts of her; she could be ferocious and tame at different times, a hybrid.

My goddess was an icon and her most common form was as a woman wearing the headdress of horns and sun disk, with a red or turquoise sheath dress. And who, may you ask, embroidered her dress with these beautiful colours? Yes, it was me, her seamstress, the one she ignored when she went to render services to her love Horus.

The king loved her menat necklace, made up of many strands of beads. Little did he know that it was me who slaved away connecting those straying beads. Indeed, I was a slave to the rhythm of her feet, listening carefully to catch her stride into the palace.

My goddess Hathor was like a lotus flower floating on the Nile. How I miss those days when we would wander on the shores of our great river, plucking reeds, lying on our backs, tickling each other and watching the cows graze nearby. Hathor would lean on my arm lightly when we climbed the rocks and threw pebbles into the Nile. We would avoid the river during the flood season, even though she was the goddess of the afterlife.

I know she loved her human life more because she used to dance merrily, drunk with happiness. I didn't need wine to make me high with longing and despair when I was so close to her, yet so far in her esteem.

In my eyes, Hathor's fine features and luscious mouth were more beautiful than Nefertari's, Ramessus II's wife. He may have built a temple for his favourite wife Nefertari in Abu Simbel. But the fool had two hundred wives and concubines and over a hundred children.

Thank goodness, my goddess Hathor didn't fall into his greedy hands. I would have killed him and not allowed my goddess to assist him into the afterlife.

This morning, I watched some schoolchildren flock around the Rosetta Stone. Their teacher explained that the stone was found in Egypt two hundred years ago. The story on the stone was written in Greek, Demotic script and Hieroglyphics. As the scribes could read Greek and Demotic, they were finally able to decode the Hieroglyphics.

But let me tell you what this story on the stone was about. It was merely a decree issued by some Egyptian priests on the anniversary of Ptolemy's coronation. What a boring story. And yet, the visitors flock around this stone that the British carted in after they defeated the French.

Once upon a time, our Egyptian civilization was powerful and we kept track of our wealth using hieroglyphics thousands of years ago until the ghastly Romans annexed it.

But from what I hear when I roam the museum, land grabbing is still happening even now in 'modern' times. Why should I leave this museum?

I was shocked this morning when I heard a boy compare our hieroglyphics to Emojis. The impertinence. I felt like shaking the child, but then, as a ghost in the afterlife, my arms would have gone straight through him. If all mortals are like this today, maybe I'm better off where I am.

Anyway, back to the point, I'm still hoping to gain a glimpse of Hathor's soul. Even a statue of her would appease me, would remind me of our days on the shores of the Nile and nights dancing with each other in her palace.

I long to feel the flame of a candle, even if it burns me, or to sink my teeth into a sweet clementine, like I used to with Hathor on the shores of the Nile. But, alas, I have no tastebuds now and no feelings in my fingers. I'm as lonely as a light feather of an ostrich.

Tomorrow, I will visit the sculpture of King Ramesses II again. It's one of the biggest statues of this museum that I'm confined to. He was the king of kings, who reigned through most of the thirteenth century BCE. But like I said, I'm disgusted by his harem of two hundred women and over a hundred children. How could Nefertari tolerate all that?

At least my goddess Hathor only had one love – Horus. But maybe one day she would have succumbed to my devotion and admiration, my lingering glances.

A few days ago, I was gliding behind the Amenhotep statue when I heard someone mention Hathor's name. My heart, if I had one, would have been pounding with excitement.

A statue of my love is apparently in the Egyptian Museum in Turin. That's in Italy, halfway back to Egypt. The curator was whispering to his companion that the British museum was trying to loan the statue of Hathor from Turin.

Since then, I live in renewed hope. If the curator manages to obtain my mistress' Hathor's statue from Italy, then maybe, just maybe, her soul will reach out to touch it, here in the British Museum, where I will spend the rest of my afterlife.

I breathe in, count to three, then breathe out. I need to stay calm for the day my love comes floating back, into my arms and into my life.

Immortality need not be a curse. It could be a blessing. *If only my Queen glides into it.*

The Journey

I was perched on the highest mountain,
Yet lost in the deepest valley.
My thoughts were like bubbles emerging from a foaming fountain,
Yet they were too entangled to carry.

I hope you find me.

My words are like spirals of wind spraying out of my soul.
In this eternity, what is our goal?
Adrift on a lonely cloud
Is this the threshold to a discovery?

I hope you find me.

Is it not our every aim to be free?
Yet we are imprisoned
By conformity and configurations,
Spurned sensations.

I hope you find me.

In the stream of silence,
There is a scent of hope.
You beckoned me, acceptance – a healing remedy.
Inviting me to understand, showing me how to cope.

You found me.

You carried the shadows of my soul.
Light illuminating my role.
Like rivers, your soft rays reach out, transcending the roughest surface.
You plant seeds of love; I can almost feel a kiss.

You found me.

Between the bitter and the sweet
Our gentle ripples meet.

I have found you.

Twisted apple tree

Little apple tree
In the shadow of the moon

They say your twisted branches are too frail
To carry the weight of a fruit family.
They say your baby apples will leave a staining trail
When they break away from you, their mother tree.

Little apple tree
In the half-hidden path of the moon

They say your fruits are withered and sour
Your tortuous branches are queer.
Day after day, hour by hour
The scent that emanates from you is – fear.

Little apple tree
In the closeted path of the moon
Branches bending in turmoil
Defying gravity
That feeling of being on foreign soil.
Listless leaves swaying in the wind helplessly.

Mother Earth pulls Ying and Yang towards you
Closer and closer to the core
Tighter and tighter
Till it squeezes open a fictive door

Towards a path in the sun
Away from the maze
Of false assumptions and conceptions
Towards the shining fingers of the sun's rays.

Magnificent apple tree
Under the glowing path of the sun

Throw away your sound of silence.
Set yourself free.
You deserve respectability.
You have a right to be!

Stunning apple tree
Golden russets you bear.
For your budding family you do care
And even if in an unconventional way
Your beautiful path is here to stay.

Twilight

My love, your small, limp body, confined to this strange cot,
   is as fragile as a fawn.
Your bouncing, brown locks defy the paleness of your face.
I can't bear to think of our final embrace.
Your soft lips linger quietly in your bitter-sweet fight
Against this disease, this injustice of life.
You are waiting to be torn.

In a place between darkness and light.

The sun was a sea of brightness the day you were born,
A silvery-red lining appeared on the horizon, that dawn.
But soon the decision will be made, whether your life
   should be erased.
A Court of Justice will preside and decide
the price of your life, the timing of your death.
Solidified grief has come by stealth.

In a place between darkness and light.

I will talk to your doctor; I will plead for your life.
I will not let you go without a fight,
In this endeavour, we will be together.
From the sidelines
I see past the maze of your twisted tubes and failed
   lifelines.

Am I the only one to see your soul's searchlights in the
   twilight?

Your spirit will soon flutter away
Like a butterfly escaping darkness and decay,
Giving way to a jolt of lightning in my weary heart
Tearing us apart.

But this cannot be just a lament, a mere capitulation.
My tears give way to an appreciation
Of your tenderness, of your fleeting life
Of our love before twilight.

My Mother's journey

My love, you shiver, trying to escape your mind's descending mist,
And jolt like a startled antelope, trapped in a confusing maze
Then, a flicker of recognition as I touch your silver-birch skin and give you a tender kiss.
You hold me tight and let out fearful cries as I meet your wavering gaze.

I yearn to hold this moment, capture it before it dies,
I hold my breath; I don't want to leave your bedside.

Your eyes are moist but the tears will not tumble
Long lost is the familiar, unswerving flame,
It has been extinguished and relinquished, making me feel small and humble
As I call out your forsaken name.

You used to brush my tangled hair
Now I comb yours, dry from the lack of care
You'd cook biriyani, bamya and fragrant red rice,
Then, suddenly, you'd keep away from the kitchen, your trembling hands cold as ice.

You live in a time warp, memories reduced to your happy childhood in a faraway country.
The words I try to console you with lie senseless, floating in your brain's wild sea.
You're locked up in your mind's tiny room as I frantically search for a releasing key
But I realise, your cruel illness refuses to set you free.

I thank you for your proud retelling of Newroz in the jagged mountains, the safekeeping of your soft Sorani language.
But then I remember with a shock, the bitter challenge –
Your disappointment about my newfound freedom and unconventional love
Your anger and incomprehension instead of embracing your daughter's desire to live as unrestrained as a soaring dove.

The pastures of your mind are overgrown with cobwebs,
But I recall you as an oak tree, spreading your roots in the earth,
Cradling and guiding me since birth.
I try and brush aside my fear that one day, my own memory will also ebb.

David Flybury
A Clearer Idea of Everything

Buxton Morning

We are now in the Peak District. It is quite cold. The heating is rudimentary; a fireplace and an electric radiator cannot compete with the fresh air seeping like a miasma through the pores of the plastic framed double-glazing.

Tomasz huddles in a blanket.

Visible from far off, brazenly exposed, our whitewashed cottage is a lone tooth set in green gums, overlooking the valley of one of the River Dove's nascent tributaries. Close by, there's time-worn, hope-chucked and charity-shopped spa-town Buxton, its profitable waters choking and broken by post-industrial despair; but we are isolated at the tip of a filament split from a long single track off the main road, the A53 to Leek. There is no mobile, no Internet. This means that arguments about the precise meaning and etymology of the word 'bucolic' (Pastoral. What's that? Pertaining to spaghetti?) can persist untruncated by Wikipedian intervention – literally, until the sheep grazing all about are summoned by shepherds of merry youth to return with their tripping lambs to the warm safety of the gentle night-time bower, there to sleep in quiet ignorance ... an eclogue.

Our bedroom has a four-poster entitled 'The Love Nest' (there is a plaque) and is decorated like a boudoir in the style decreed of the French Parisian Montmartre (if you get my meaning ...) It was quite intimidating to my time-worn libido, or would have been had I packed my time-worn libido – but I had not, thinking I'd have no occasion for it; I don't see the point in schlepping my time-worn libido about if it isn't even going to get unpacked!

The other bedroom is in similar style but has twin beds – a kind of celebration in amour-less terms of the coldness that sweeps across the arching landscape outside, cold beneath the touch and filigree brilliance of the lonely sun, where cows lounge like pubic lice amongst the rudely verdant hedgerows, and lambs trip unaware that heat is something you make by rubbing two bodies together.

Kneeling in front of the open-hearthed fire, which I built, I try like a child (how many decades is it since I did this?) to perceive in its palatial embers the structures and strategies of future time – difficult not to believe that this same flaming instant might represent both decided fate and the book of means to defeat it. Know-all fire seems to summon its own spells and can't be built without kneeling, heaping coals like prayers. It mocks the time I've burnt as well – disdaining its own short-lived glory: but what can a hearth fire teach me about time (what has time not already taught me?) except that it burns, and hurts, and goes?

Next day, crouching again, my burning face reminds me: Why did gas and back-lit-plastic replace our real coal and its grate full of secrets?

So that *never again* would we have to coax fresh flames from morning ashes ...

Buxton

This morning I accompanied Tomasz to the railway station. He's off to Manchester for a conference. We parked the car and I said I'd walk home, I had nothing else to do, but first I dawdled through the empty morning streets of Buxton; morning, before the people; when any city is at its best.

In its street of pound shops, already open and heaped with inexpensive delights that boggled mine eyes! After much consideration, I bought a pack of sheep-shaped Buxton butter shortbread and some black-pudding, 'priced for quick sale!' They displayed a greater variety of competitively priced black-pudding than I had ever before seen in my life, from fun-size up to super-mega.

Drifting past sad representations of lost Victorian grace with all its inbuilt resentments, class conceits, and envies – the Buxton Opera House, where an X-Factor winner stars in another revival of 'Joseph! (and his amazing etc.)' – I entered into the Pavilion Pleasure Gardens ('restored 1997–2004', yes, apparently it took that long) and all the slightly desperate amusements of a seaside town therein.

The bandstand ('rebuilt 1997–2004').

I sat by the lake ('extended 1997–2004') where dogs sniffed hopefully at my shortbread – the park is mainly used for dog-walking. Mallard couples and cancer-faced Muscovy ducks picnicked all around me, quacking and flapping, hissing, occasionally honking like old men who just couldn't help but laugh, and waddling unconsciously across the silent line of the Pavilion Gardens Miniature Railway (again, since 1997–2004) – a fun-sized celebration of that super-mega Engine of Northern Industrial Growth: The Railways.

We always say, 'the coming of the railways', like it was a new Jerusalem – but it was! It was a foundational moment. The railways entailed everything else, from the opera house to the Muscovy ducks. And they built miniature railways because they just couldn't get enough of them and they just couldn't believe their luck! They used to sit on the tiny unstable trucks like giants, dressed in their Sunday best, slightly scared, holding each other's waists naughtily, and laughing like they just couldn't help themselves.

After the park, I weaved back and visited the giant Doric St John's Church nearby. A lady who had come to arrange the flowers opened the door when I knocked and welcomed me in, greedily. The interior is absolutely splendid. She told me it was built for the Dukes of Devonshire, the local dukes, as a chapel of rest (whatever that is – If you're dead you're not resting are you? You're not asleep.) but, 'with the coming of the railways,' she said, it had to be extended and a gallery added. All the people suddenly arriving by train to take the Buxton waters – which you can now find in plastic bottles on supermarket shelves – also needed to go to church, and if the pleasures of the park gave out, it has one of the best organs in the North-West, and its acoustics continue to impress, she assured me.

This is when the spa town of Buxton really took off, 'with the coming of the railways', but it was teeming already, with the mills and engines of the industrial revolution all around. The area seethes with its archaeology; strolling through valley forests you'll find Georgian iron water-wheels, remarkably complete, like the ribcage bones of dinosaurs jutting out from beech overgrowth, flushed with foamy hillside water, set and silent, holding on, by massive rusty axle cogs, to empty dressed-limestone factories, still attached, like dead husbands.

Here a natural vernacular tendency predominates to build in limestone and iron, where Southerners, like me, reserving fancy materials for fancy places, built in wood and brick. Therefore the North, like Egypt in its decay, has such a feeling of permanence, and changelessness, that permanence, and nothing besides, remains.

In the modern world, of course as we all know only too well, permanence is a liability, a guarantee of repairs and costs. Constant change, constant renewal guarantees survivability. You've got to be quick on your feet. You've got to be like a London cabbie: Turn on a sixpence.

Up here, the people are by agility unimpressed, unturned by metropolitan constraints. The men are proper rugby men. Drinkers. Roofers. Toilers. Indifferent to seduction. Used to having their way pressed up against drystone walls. I saw a man climb from his van, struggling with his shirt, pulling it off over his back, a vibrant mass of thick tanned untrained muscularity. Wherever you go, there's men: Gorgeous, humping, railway-building men, men with shirts and without shirts, men of limestone and iron and water-wheels, men architecturally populating the history and the forests, men who go to the parks and look at the ducks and just-can't-help-but laughing, men who aren't in touch with their feelings and just want to get the job done, have a pint, die of prostate cancer and to hell with it.

I left the town and headed home along the busy A53 road to Leek. As it penetrated the National Park – limited to 50, though the Tarmac winds seductively across the empty hills and begs for speed – I watched sheep and lambs on either side take no notice of the human rush. What's all the fuss about? So that more and more people can make more and more people? They have, I murmured bitterly to myself, lives that are pleasant, tranquil, and mercifully brief. Who's the winner here? And then I saw a large sheep standing by the edge of the road. I waved my finger, 'Stay by the side! Don't go and get knocked over, you silly sheep!'

She waited until I was really close before running along the bank, and stopped quickly to turn and look at me. At my feet a lamb corpse lay on its side, tiny thoughtless brains oozing from behind one ear. Oh dear, I thought, Oh dear. You silly sheep.

I walked on and turned to watch the mother slowly re-approach her lamb and stand over it. She bent to coax it with her nose.

She doesn't know it's dead!
She doesn't know it's dead!
She thinks she'll stand and wait,
and guard it till it wakes,
the sleepy head.

That's just about the saddest thing I ever saw.

A Fresh Start

1. Fear

Though both are white, is it possible to tell the female from the male swan? That measure of modesty – demure-though-raped, wings flattened like a Victorian bodice – balancing and shaming the male's extravagantly posed, elegantly flourished, Elizabethan dandy advertisement of quills?

It was the day of the attack. Sirens filled the air. Helicopters fluttered menacingly. Police tape webbed the streets. We hid in a pub full of false antiquity and magical transportation; the kind of place one might imagine an old-style gay existence still persisting elsewhere, outside: the pavements, cottages and hangouts; a life of loneliness, self-hating delusions, faked masculinity, faked femininity, and faked everything: Fear. How would it be, liberated from the demands of freedom, once again to have to hide, to have to make everything up?

They were serving food. The waiter was tall and menacingly thin. 'Sorr-wee,' he said when I misunderstood, 'a'cnfoos me sewf!' He gave me a good hard stare like he knew what my secret was. Listing the day's specials, aware of their nuances and their cadences, his liquid voice rippled, soft-jazz batons across a xylophone you really needed to buy on vinyl to fully appreciate.

'So ... whar'sit ... t'be, Ssir?' he whispered. I told him, panicked that my choices might unmask a deficiency. He repeated my decisions. 'And ...?' continued the waiter, pointedly without comment, turning to my friend. My friend replied without intimidation, ordering a hefty roast. Why couldn't I be ... unintimidated by circumstances?

'Thhat'l bi al, no'deser'?'

'We might have coffee ... later ... or ... perhaps not,' I hesitated.

'Wait and see how we feel,' my friend said, nonchalantly. He allowed his menu to be whisked away whilst I, seemingly, had to fold mine meaningfully, proffer it some coded and correct way, before the jazz-voiced servant took his cue and relieved me of it.

'Wet an' see, Sirss,' he said, as if that was a joke only he and my friend would get and looking at us both now as if to say, we must be close and I was the feminised subordinate one, the foolish one, the idiot who had to be protected, his own ingénue folksy charm as much a liability as an attraction; the one who does the cooking and the cleaning, possibly, back at the flat, marked by bra straps, recognising himself in girls bearing impertinent masculine control. Mansplained. Dependent. This is what it feels like to be read out loud. He looked at me with a sad smile and said, 'Swee'cheeks'. I thought he was going to touch my face.

Walking away, I noticed his 'jazz hips'.

When he had completely gone, my friend said, 'You look worried.'

'Do I?'

'Yes. You do. Why are you worried?'

'I feel ... aimless.'

'Aim-less or un-aimed? No aims? Not even an aim-lette?'

And I said, 'Can you make an aim-lette without breaking ... erm ... something?'

We smiled at that.

Nothing can bring Michael back.

Outside, the signs gave assistance that was menacingly imperative: 'Bicycles Will Be Removed'; 'Caution'; 'Crossing'; 'Information'; 'Private Property'; 'Caution'; 'Keep Out'; 'Public Toilets'; 'Wait'; 'Help Point'; 'Warning' ... THIS is what it feels like to be led by fear, I thought, to feel like, I'll only ever be a small part of everything; eventually, feeling at ease in its embrace, coddled by its demanding habits, mindlessly capable of any inhumanity, I'd be, able to ... murder on behalf of the state! ... able to give up names ... acquiesce to its demanding indifference, drag my feet to its chambers, sweat, forgotten, as the creeping fumes fizzle ... oh lord.

We stood in the square and watched stupid dancing fountains, other people's kids deliberately getting wet. Someone let their dog shake its fur near someone else, laughing apologies. Is this what it looks like when nothing at all matters?

I miss him.
 I miss his heft.

2. 1957, September

Sodomy was criminalised in England and Wales in 1533. All sexual acts between men were outlawed in the UK and, via sections variously numbered 377 throughout the Empire, in 1885. The publication of the Wolfenden Report on 'Homosexual Offences and Prostitution' was published on 4th September 1957 and led to partial decriminalisation in England and Wales ten years later. Variants of Section 377 remain in place in many former colonies – our gift to the world!

Do you remember when you thought yourself incapable of love? Without music you would have found it difficult to survive. You wanted to hide. You wanted to put up your hands and say, 'Is this for real?'

You tried to believe great art would make a difference, but realised that's not its function: Art legitimises; it doesn't confront the power that imposes our crimes upon us, it courts the patron's condescension and caprice. Art shores up the very edifice which – with its walls – exhibits and restricts. Art preserves itself; that's its sole function. It has no other choice but to comply, to acquiesce, adorn, collude ... (you know the list).

That's where you slept, tickled by grasses; half awake in his arms, you noticed without mentioning, spiders spread their convoluted legs like whiskers, fall into your lap and sprint to their next precipice.

Later, by the seaside, playing at jumping on tide-drained boulders; when the sun went in it got so cold so quickly that you dressed and headed back. Walking with him through fields close to harvest, clothes still wet and uncomfortable rubbing sand and salt on your skin, you were reminded of the rocky beach when you observed, but did not mention, wheat growing out of stony ground. How like two lines of music you two walkers were: together and apart, holding hands, occasionally, sometimes not, weaving in and out of precedence until you came to rest with the same cadence.

When you met him you thought him a man of great sophistication, certainly intelligence; yet he came over with enormous simplicity and charm, like a spring wells from the ground with crystal clear though chilling purity, like finding sweet water. When you asked him, he said, 'We'll decide where we're going when we get there, sweets.'

Later in the cinema's bedroom darkness, you felt you were a pair under close scrutiny. Aware of the impossibility of him putting his arm around your shoulders except in the guise of matey-ness, when he did (also pressing his foot on your foot in a way painful but welcomed) you felt with excitement his thumbnail gently scratch against hairs on the ridge of muscle behind the lobe of your right ear. In a flare of screen brightness you could see he was smiling, looking straight forward exactly as if it was the film that he was enjoying. Fear of the consequences made you shake uncontrollably, watching without mentioning: ushers walk the aisles like they were the police. As your nervousness mounted, you hoped the film would end soon and you'd escape, fearing that when you left, assaulted by daylight, you'd be arrested. You wondered, if this would be your last day of freedom. You didn't want to be caught. You didn't want to face the humiliation. He was less bothered, even suggesting you put your hand in his pocket. He was blatant, and when you replied that he was asking for trouble, he said, 'I am asking for trouble, sweets.'

When you received word of the death of your father you had to catch a train home. You were alone when you noticed the roof of the station, light, filtering through dirty corrugated plastic sheets, appeared golden.

Afterwards, when you said you wanted a new direction in your life, and he replied, 'You're already going in the right direction, sweets,' you didn't believe him; you already believed that fear would be your life's main emotion. You wanted to hide; you wanted to put up your hands and say, 'Is this for real?'

Consider the Renaissance: Palestrina, how he willed the human voice to sound like angels. That huge, clean polyphonic space, in his day had no competing 'modal take'. Its history un-enacted provided no lens, held possibilities still to be encountered, and inventions 'perforce' unknowable (Baroque, Romanticism, Modernity ... you know the list) – but now, no-one can imagine what it must have been like: to have nothing else,

3. July 1967

27 July 1967, The Sexual Offences Act received Royal assent, partially decriminalising homosexual acts in England and Wales on the condition that they took place in a private home, and set the age of consent at 21. Nevertheless, many aspects of gay life remained criminal, police repression worsened and continued to destroy lives. The law was extended to Scotland and Northern Ireland in the 80s. Homosexuality was decriminalised in the UK in 2013, though our battle for equality continues.

A plant stood in the corner of the room, scarily motionless. You watched, from your bed, as the gloom of another night filled the air with darkness and the plant, assuming once more its character, frightening, horrible, terrifyingly embodying all your fears and isolation and loneliness, yet grew familiar, and a kindness, like the pity of an angel watching, seemed to animate its blackened static leaves; like a friend who has left but, forgetting some article of clothing, seems still to be with you, still capable of holding you, still capable of holding your hand, still capable of holding your breath, of holding your heartbeat, of finding you there.

You lived in a world in which your very existence was denied – which is to say, your ability to define yourself was denied, your ability to love yourself. This is the paternalism that punishes a child for what they cannot help but be.

See how architecture mocks the power of the State – its hierarchies, assumptions, expectations, collaborations and collusions built by stone on ludicrous sarcastic stone. You sat still in that great chapel's empty choir, spellbound by its great sound, enveloped more than listening; some pale organist, intellectual and serious, a whole man grappling with this instrument, its many stops and keyboards, practising diligently for his exam, repeatedly performing massively arpeggiated progressions of sharp espressivo quavers that ricocheted through deep implosions of shoe-quaking bass, made a shattering noise that sought, you felt, to test the bravado of the vaults, to convince by emphasis, with still faster spatial and still deeper subterranean reverberations, the delicacy of that coloured glass, the tracery, and the permanence of those ribbed pylons that, engineered like spreading plants, soared from the choir's darkly mocking misericords to strike, in fans that were elegantly broad, the roof, above your head.

But you had nothing to be proud of, for you were no use really. Moral compass all over the shop; you saw nothing clearly. Even your own self-interest was obscure, let alone the finer points of civil rights. You didn't believe in class war; you weren't a soldier! Nor socially responsible – that's for people, who 'through no fault of their own' are straight, conspire to marry and perpetuate. Your own parents were straight; who could you rely on? Who could you not despise? What stones could you take and build your own cathedral that was not filled with clanging empty meaningless noise? The sound of brass. The sound of tinkling cymbals. Christ.

Shocked by reverberation, bounded by emptiness, you felt safest in other people's clothes. The trousers you wore that day had been given to you by a boyfriend, and your shirt you'd found, early one morning in a cruising ground, wet from rain, hanging from the branches of a bush – you'd put it on, rejoicing in its freezing clinging, like it needed you, clinging to your skin, your breath, your heartbeat (capable of holding you). Again, as you walked along a city road, one morning early, confronted by an array of cranes motionless like preying insects on the horizon of your city; no longer caring if it was a disease or a crime you thought with relief, 'I know I never want this feeling I have to stop', and you turned into your street, your house, climbing your stair, arriving at your door, thought, 'This is my home,'

4. The Homo-Spectrum

The 1967 act was just a start.

When you walked into the toilet an auto movement detector in one of the cubicles triggered a flush; you felt like you were not alone until you realised what had happened. Relieved, in every way, you reapplied your lipstick, mascara, painting an incognito portrait on your face.

Do you recall when the earth was covered in darkness? That was the day of the eclipse. Funny day. All the cars had their headlamps on for a while. Did you sleep though it? Everyone was saying, 'Oh it's so cool', 'It's once in a lifetime' ... you were asleep, and dreaming you had strong arms; you woke wishing you could walk once more in that darkened forest ... Had you heard the birds fall silent?

You realised you had missed the show when you opened your eyes, momentarily blinded: Through threadbare curtains, rays of the reborn sun hit the carpet in blobs that were inexpressibly bright and cast a dim gleam throughout the tiny empty yellow room, excessively illuminating its featureless walls, building warmth, smouldering dust, until the dry oven of the air, burning your nostrils, suffocated your sleep.

Glowing in its own bright pool, on the floor a large translucent tortoiseshell plastic comb with which you had stroked your long dark hair, lay ignited like your memories. That much at least was real.

To think that kissing might be such a, thing ...

You lay on your back, blank minded, full of thought. The thin dark coverlet draped across your propped-up legs looked like a large brown sail at rest. Your skin was frosted with a sweat that felt thick and seemed almost to crawl through the spaceless space between the mattress and your back.

The light crept in tiny stages towards your nails, your glittering fingertips playing with the cascade of jewels about your neck; you lay wondering without interest, about the time, what the day might bring, and if it had indeed, as promised, renewed itself ...

A Fresh Start

When people asked what you thought of it all, what you'd seen, the 'oh-my-god-ness' of the eclipse, you had to make things up: 'Yeah it was really strange.' Then you started repeating the things other people said to you: 'Yeah, strange – how the birds reacted? That was odd.' Soon it was as if you actually had seen the eclipse, and really could remember it.

That feeling was strange also.

But gradually you came to resent the way your own particular experience had been obliterated. That sleep was a private moment, like the privacy of all experience. No telling what you felt, trapped in your own private eclipse. Whilst, it seemed as if, everyone else had a shared version of events, your version of it was blank, dreamt, or, now, invented.

But gradually you came to realise that the emerging story – holding up bits of black plastic to watch the diamond ring coalesce into its famous annulation, for example; saying, 'Wow,' and saying, 'Oh my god' – that was the result of a joint confabulation from which you were excluded, but no one person saw or experienced everything! and like it mattered; only sleep is truly shared.

Touching his lips. Tasting him. Finding him strong.

The light crept in tiny stages, and when it touched the jewels around your neck it shattered into a spectrum of a thousand different colours,

Jeffrey Doorn
A Traveller's Tale

Brandon emerged from the hotel before twilight faded to dusk. He'd had a shower to freshen up after a day of exploring, enjoyed an early dinner and now set out for an evening of adventure. He was glad to be free of his backpack, happy to stroll, now that the heat of the day had given way to more mellow warmth with a hint of freshness.

It wasn't that far to Mishkat, that sprawling scrubland popular for rambling during the day, but reputed to be a cruising ground after dark, classed AYOR, At Your Own Risk, by his trusty gay guide. Despite this warning, Brandon decided to throw caution to the wind. This holiday was a chance to experience a different culture with all that entailed. He was determined to meet men, and if that involved a bit of danger, so be it.

Friends back home were surprised when he said he was going to Bolustan. Some had never even heard of the country, others asked why he should want to go there of all places. His only reply was that it was as far away from Brexit Britain and Europe as he could get. It was his chance for a complete break between Uni and real life. He did not want to be a mere tourist, but saw himself as a traveller. The fact that gay sex was illegal here was a challenge, but he was sure he could get round it, and it would be all the more exciting for that.

There were a few benches on the gravel patch before the foliage began; on two or three of these men sat dangling keys. Brandon wasn't interested in any of them. He moved closer to the bushes and was about to venture further when he saw a slim, youngish man leaning against a tree. The man nodded, Brandon smiled and the man turned towards the undergrowth. Brandon followed.

In a moment he had caught up and took a closer look. He judged the man to be in his late twenties or early thirties, not bad looking, though he couldn't really say he found him attractive. The hair was a bit stringy and the day's growth was neither designer stubble nor the beginnings of a beard; the fellow was just unshaven. Surprisingly, he was wearing a light sports jacket; Brandon was still in short sleeves.

The man took his hand and led him further into the scrub. It was hilly, and Brandon wondered how far they would climb before stopping. 'English?' the man asked. Brandon nodded.

'You like Bolustan sex?' Another nod, not that he had tried any yet. 'Bolustan sex very nice,' the man stated, as if to assure him. He started to feel a stirring; perhaps it would be all right.

After some more scrambling, turning and climbing, they at last stopped in the midst of a thicket. 'Bolustan sex very nice,' the man repeated, unbuttoning his loose trousers and taking out a flaccid penis. Brandon hesitated; does he want me to touch it, suck it or what, he wondered. There was a musty smell; when had he last washed his clothes, or his penis for that matter?

Suddenly the man stuffed himself back into his trousers and pulled a large knife from his jacket pocket. 'Bolustan money,' he demanded.

'What? No,' Brandon stuttered, breaking into a cold sweat.

'Bolustan money!' the urgent demand was repeated, the knife waving in the air.

'All right, here,' Brandon dug out the few notes he had and thrust them at his assailant, who grabbed and pocketed them, urging 'more money, you give more.'

'That's all I have.'

'No, you give more.'

Brandon was shaking now. He began to shout. 'I told you I don't have more, why don't you believe me?' On the words WHY and BELIEVE, he let fly with hard punches. The man fell flat on his back and Brandon started running. He couldn't think which way they'd come and it took a long time before he found a path which led down to the gravel patch.

Out of breath, he made his way back to the hotel. Safe in his room, he took a long drink from his water bottle, wishing it were something stronger, then sat on the bed trying to calm down. 'Why did I go with him,' he thought. Then, 'I shouldn't have run away; I'd knocked him out, I should have taken my money back, got his knife away from him, tied his shoelaces together ... I shouldn't have panicked.'

After breakfast the next morning he started to perk up. Well, just chalk it up to experience. It could have been worse, much worse. He would not go back to Mishkat. Just concentrate on sightseeing and enjoy the country. The old town was endlessly fascinating, and other areas offered a wealth of galleries, shops, museums, monuments and intriguing architecture.

He occasionally saw two young men walking hand in hand, and realised it was just the custom with friends, not an indication of homosexuality. He liked people-watching and the feeling he was himself being watched, sometimes with curiosity, sometimes amusement, rarely with an expression of disdain or hostility. Once or twice someone at a distance would greet him with 'You are welcome.' Otherwise, people generally ignored him, except for those who accosted him with trinkets to sell, or wanting to shine his shoes, offering to be his guide or lure him into a shop. There seemed no escape from the almost constant irritating intrusion.

Once after visiting a mosque to escape the harassment, he sat in a nearby garden to savour a moment's peace. A lad of about his age came and sat next to him. 'What are you selling?' Brandon barked; 'Everyone in this town seems to be selling something.' The lad uttered a surprised 'Oh,' and went away. Shit, Brandon thought, he was probably just a nice boy looking for a friendly encounter with a foreigner, wanting to practice his English, maybe even the chance of a gay contact. And I sent him away, no doubt hurt his feelings. Damn, damn, damn.

The days soon assumed a pattern: breakfast at the hotel, a morning walk, some fruit from the marketplace for lunch, then either a museum or historical site, or perhaps a bus ride to a village or small town where he could amble about, observing and feeling part of the local scene. In such places no one bothered him or tried to foist unwanted goods or services on him. Back in the city he would take a refreshing shower before dinner, glad to have booked half board in this pleasant three-star hotel rather than risk holiday tummy after a meal in some dodgy eatery. Evenings were for strolling, relishing the changing colours, views revealed by the glow of street-lamps or lights behind windows.

Always as he walked he would discretely seek out faces of young men; but if he noticed an attractive one and glanced a bit more boldly, his look was not returned. One afternoon, passing through the main square a bearded chap approached saying, 'What you like, I get you; you want girl, boy?' Before Brandon could think of replying, the chap went over to his mates, laughing as he repeated the spiel, 'you want girl, boy?' Brandon scurried away, embarrassed.

Near the end of his stay, he spent an early afternoon wandering around the souk, which comprised several narrow streets, with a large covered bazaar at the centre. He wound up buying a cushion cover in a colourful pattern from a fabric stall, a small brass ornament and finally, a wooden flute, on which he might recreate the distinctive local sound. Everything fit nicely into his backpack, and he was pleased with his purchases as well as his haggling skills.

Then he made his way to the Palace, the one major sight he hadn't yet visited. Sitting on a low wall in view of the edifice, he began to read the history and architectural details given in his guidebook. Happily, the grand building was open late, so he would have plenty of time to explore it in detail.

'You read about palace?' So absorbed had Brandon been that he hadn't noticed the dark-haired man sitting a few feet away.

'Yes, I want to know what I'm looking at.'

'Much history. Sultan in old times had many wives. You can see harem next courtyard. Every day Sultan pick which he want to ... ' The man made a gesture indicating sexual intercourse. 'Sometimes he doesn't want woman, takes boy or eunuch to ... ' He repeated the gesture. 'Which you like?'

Recalling how he was mocked in the square, Brandon turned the question back: 'Which do you like?' The man gave a short laugh. 'What you think?' For a moment Brandon wondered whether he would get to visit the palace after all. Dark-hair was not unattractive, seemed genuinely friendly and did not appear to be concealing a knife. Was that enough to abandon his plans?

Brandon's companion pointed to the palace grounds. 'We walk?' Though there was a charge to enter the building, the gardens and courtyards were free. 'Okay.' They stood; Dark-hair was shorter than Brandon, a bit on the dumpy side, and walked with a slight limp. They ambled around the grounds, not speaking very much. After a while Dark-hair took out a mobile phone. 'I call my friend.' He spoke rapidly in Bolustani; Brandon picked up the word for Englishman, but didn't get anything else. They wound their way to the palace entrance.

'You go in; I wait for my friend.'

'Oh, okay; see you later.' He felt a slight let-down, but was happy to have had companionship for however short a time. He bought a ticket, deposited his backpack, having extracted his camera and binoculars, useful to check details of carvings, mosaic patterns and any ceiling paintings or decoration. It took nearly two hours to view the entire complex, and he forgot all about the dark-haired one.

On exiting, he was surprised to see his erstwhile companion, with a lighter-haired man, apparently waiting for him. They all shook hands and the pair led Brandon away. They didn't say where they were going, and Brandon thought it best not to ask, but rather drift along and see what happened.

Winding their way through back streets, they eventually came to a scruffy bit of parkland. It was twilight, and Brandon began to worry he wouldn't get back in time for dinner. They took a path, which soon petered out; continuing through dense woods until at last they came to a small clearing. The others sat on the ground, and Brandon followed suit.

'Now,' Dark-hair made the familiar hand-gesture. Light-hair said, 'I take him here' pointing to his mouth. They lay down, Dark-hair on the left, his right arm around Brandon. Light-hair unzipped Brandon's fly and took hold of his penis. After a moment, Dark-hair said, 'You don't get hard?'

'I'm a bit nervous.'

Suddenly, the arm around Brandon's neck tightened! He was pulled to his feet and Light-hair grabbed hold of his backpack. Then, allowing Brandon to zip up first, they marched him to a fork in the path where they stopped again and said that if he wanted his things returned he must meet them with money the next day – stating the place, time and amount. Then, telling him to wait five minutes and take the left-hand path, they turned right and ... disappeared.

On his way out of the woods, which he realised must be the far end of Mishkat, Brandon nearly burst into tears. He was shaking uncontrollably. Never had he felt so alone and miserable. He came to a street, not knowing where he was or how to get to the hotel. A shared taxi came into view, and he heard the destination called out; it was an area near his hotel. He had spent nearly all of the money he had today on the souvenirs and palace entrance, but found he had one coin left – it was just enough for the fare.

As expected, they had stopped serving dinner; so he just crept up to his room, had a good cry and went to bed. At breakfast, his usual waiter, a soft-spoken man of about 40, commented on his absence the previous evening. Had he had dinner elsewhere?

'No,' Brandon couldn't hold it in; 'I was mugged. Two men pretended to befriend me, then one got his arm around my neck like this and the other stole my backpack, with everything in it.'

'I am so sorry, sir. You must tell your representative; I hope he can help you.'

Brandon was touched by his kindly reaction. He felt ashamed to take it further, but realised the man was right. The rep was due to stop by about 10.00 a.m., and Brandon waited for him. When he told his story, leaving out the bit about the almost-sex, the rep advised him not to meet the thieves, who, if they turned up would only try to extort more money from him, but to report the incident to the police. Brandon hesitated, but the rep insisted, saying he wouldn't be able to make an insurance claim unless he had proof he had reported the crime.

The rep drove him to the station and explained the situation in Bolustani to the desk clerk, demonstrating the arm-lock Brandon had described. They found an English-speaking officer and went through the story again, arm-lock and all. The rest of the morning was taken up with filling in forms and trying to pinpoint where the theft had taken place. 'I don't know exactly; I met them near the palace and we walked around till we came to a dark place near that big park.'

As that area was in a different district, it came under the jurisdiction of another police station. Before going there, the rep took him back to the hotel. 'As you missed dinner yesterday, I've arranged for you to have lunch here.' Following that welcome respite, they moved on and had to go through the story yet again, the arm-lock gesture eliciting looks of sympathy from several officers.

Brandon had to enumerate what his backpack had contained. 'My camera, binoculars, sunglasses, a guidebook, water bottle, three souvenirs: cushion cover, brass ornament and flute, also a Swiss army knife, paper hankies, sunscreen ...' Listing his losses felt like losing them again, and he broke down.

After a cup of tea, he had to look through books of mugshots. Turning the pages, he was surprised the collection hadn't been digitised. It was depressing viewing hundreds of pictures of criminals or suspects. What had they all done, or been accused of? Some faces were hard, others frightened or defiant. There were many photographs taken long ago; young faces would have aged since then. Even if someone looked vaguely like one of his assailants, he would be afraid to point him out and have to face the suspect being called in and questioned, or having to confront him.

Later, he was driven around the area to see whether he could pinpoint the exact scene of the crime or perhaps spot the thieves lurking about. All he saw was city scenes in beautiful sunshine which he could not enjoy. Finally, the report was filed and he received a sheaf of papers duly stamped and signed. This was his sole souvenir, which he would send to the travel insurance company. Whatever he might receive would be no compensation or replacement for what he had lost, nor would it alleviate the feelings of shame and failure.

After dinner, he packed his suitcase ready to leave in the morning. He stepped out of the hotel only long enough to take a breath of evening air. There would be no final walk around town.

His waiter friend was particularly attentive at breakfast. When checking out, he felt all the staff eyeing him with pity. While waiting for the airport transfer, the waiter reappeared. He gave Brandon a loaf of bread and a bag of fruit for the journey. 'Please don't think badly of Bolustanis; we are good people. But as anywhere there are some evil ones who prey on tourists. You were unlucky,'

'Unlucky? No, I was foolish. Why did I go with them, why did I trust them?'

'You are, like all of us, lonely.' Brandon looked into his eyes and smiled. Why hadn't he recognised this kindred spirit earlier? They shook hands, and had to make a move, as the transport arrived.

Sitting in the plane, feeling empty, Brandon looked out the window at the country he was leaving behind and would never visit again. He closed his eyes, remembering how determined he had been not to be a mere tourist, but a traveller. Some traveller!

Ringing

Friday night. In the past, Keith would have been out clubbing. How he missed the excitement of choosing his outfit, checking himself in the mirror and sallying forth to dance the night away. Tinnitus put paid to that, this bloody ringing in his ears.

It crept up on him gradually. He would leave a club in the wee hours, his heart racing, his limbs tired from all the shaking about, his ears pounding from hours of heavy-beat music. He was usually fine again after a few hours' sleep, but he then began to notice a persistent whistling, sometimes changing pitch, lowering to be almost unnoticeable, then rising to a squealing sound.

His doctor diagnosed the condition as tinnitus, told him there was no cure, though there were treatments. She advised Keith to avoid loud noise where possible. That meant abandoning his beloved clubs. He looked through books in the local library, searched the Internet for help, but apart from advertising supposed remedies, there was little positive on offer. Oh, he did sample one or two concoctions, but without any appreciable result.

He tried to console himself with the thought that the clubs had been taken over by twinks. They seemed to form cliques with their own fashions, their drugs of choice, colonizing their corner of the dance floor, shutting him out. Still, he could always find someone to dance with, if not take home. Not that he was into pickups, not any more. He'd had his share of one-nighters, brief affairs, even a boyfriend or two when he himself was a twink – though he didn't use that term then.

Turning the radio on, keeping the volume low, he could almost forget about the irritating buzzing. He danced around the room, imagining he were back in his old haunts, eyeing up the guys, checking whose eyes were on him. Yes, he thought, I can still shake my booty like the best of them.

Not tired enough yet for bed, he decided to read for a while; but suddenly the light began flickering. Was it the bulb? No, the meter needed topping up. Where was that key? Oh, shit, he'd forgotten to recharge it. Why did these flats have such a cumbersome method to pay for electricity? Can't leave it, the food in the fridge-freezer might go off. It was 1.45 a.m., but there was nothing for it; he'd have to go to that all-night petrol station shop a mile or so away.

He hadn't been walking more than 10 minutes when he noticed a group of youths ahead. One of them shouted, 'Hey Pops, you all right?'

Pops?

He would have ignored them, but they came right up to him, so no escape. There were four of them, the tall gangly shouter, a thin spotty one, a short tubby one and a quite good-looking one.

'What you doin' out so late, Pops?' Keith thought he could ask them the same question.

'Just getting something I've run out of, if you must know.'

'You wanna be careful,' the tall one continued. 'It's dangerous at night, if you can't see that well, uneven pavements and all.'

'Yeah,' Spotty piped up, 'my Gran took a tumble the other day.'

'Your Gran.'

'Yeah, and it wasn't the first time. You old folks are always falling over.'

'That's right' Tubby chimed in, giggling, 'me Grandad keeps tripping over hisself'. The cute one remained silent. Keith caught his eye and the lad gave a small smile, or was it a smirk?

'Well, thanks, lads, I'll bear that in mind.'

They stepped aside and Keith moved on, hoping they wouldn't rush him and knock him over, just to prove the point. Nothing happened; perhaps they weren't queer-bashers or muggers. Genuinely concerned or just having a laugh? Whatever, once he reached the shop and put £20 on his key, he decided to go home by another route.

On the long walk back, he went over those youths' cheeky words: 'can't see that well' – my eyesight's fine; it's my ears that have a problem. And that crack about old people falling over. Come to think of it, he had measured his length on the pavement recently, but he'd been hurrying and lost his footing; it could happen to anyone.

Safely indoors, he sorted the meter out, then poured himself a whisky and took a book down to calm his nerves. After a few pages, he couldn't remember what he'd just read. I'm not old enough to be somebody's grandparent, am I? He peered into the mirror. Where was that fit, sexy young guy who danced his arse off in the clubs and often shagged the arse off a dancing partner later? The remnants of that carefree clubber stared back at him.

Ah well, it's gone 3.00. Might as well go to bed. He finished his drink, put the book away, undressed, switched off the light and got between the sheets. But sleep didn't come. He lay awake till dawn, 'Hey Pops' ringing in his ears.

Joshua Shepperton

Such a posh name for such an ordinary bloke. When he first started working in our office, we couldn't make him out. Quiet, reserved, soft-spoken to the point of inaudibility, he seemed almost a non-presence. Despite that, we made an effort to welcome him, tried to make him feel part of the team. But after a few refusals to join us for a lunchtime pint, there was no point taking it any further, and we more or less ignored him.

Pity, because we're a close-knit, sociable team, friends as well as colleagues. All men, as it happens. We did have a woman member, very bright and highly competent. She often talked about starting her own PR firm, but in the end, got a job in a big organization down in London. Joshua was her replacement.

Being such an unknown quantity, he was often the subject of conversation down the pub, or in the working men's café, which he never frequented. Don't know where he had his lunch, or for that matter, anything about his movements, interests or private life. That didn't stop us from speculating.

'With an Old Testament name like Joshua,' I posited, 'he might be Jewish.' Manny, who is Jewish, shook his head. 'I don't think so. When I've used Yiddish words in the office, he hasn't reacted or shown any sign of recognition. Plus, excuse the cliché, he doesn't look at all Jewish, and Shepperton is not a Jewish surname.'

'The family may have changed it,' I argued. Jerry disagreed. 'Joshua was probably just a popular name the year he was born. Dear me, as you know, I have an Old Testament name, Jeremiah, but my parents were Evangelical and wanted something biblical for me. There are all sorts of reasons people choose names for their kids.'

Jerry was brought up by very strict parents. He managed to escape and leave most of the rules and regulations behind. The only remnant of his restrictive upbringing is that he can't bring himself to swear. Where anyone else would use an expletive, the strongest oath to escape his lips is something like 'oh dear' or 'my goodness'.

Sometimes in the office, especially just before or after a weekend, we'd talk about our wives, girlfriends or lack of them, or in Trevor's case, his latest boyfriend. Joshua never joined in, and we wondered whether he had any sort of romantic or sexual relationship. Over a pre-lunch drink one day, I asked Trevor whether he thought Joshua might be gay.

'Why, because he seems rather passive?' Trevor laughed. 'No, he doesn't register on my gaydar, and there's no reaction from him when I mention a gay club, personality or similar reference. And I've never noticed him looking at me the way I look at cute guys passing by.'

'Maybe he just doesn't fancy you.'

'Give over. Not that I fancy him for that matter, though I suppose he might be considered somewhat attractive in a nondescript, subdued sort of way. No, I doubt he's homosexual or heterosexual either; he strikes me as asexual if anything.'

At that moment, Ashit, who'd been getting the next round, returned and, putting a glass in front of me, said, 'The other day you asked Manny if he thought Joshua was Jewish, and now you're asking Trevor whether the guy's gay. Before you go any further, I can tell you without your asking that he's definitely not Asian!' We all laughed. 'All right, all right,' I conceded, 'but he must be something.'

Each of us had other things to think about over the next few weeks, so we didn't spend any time discussing the non-communicative member of our office. My final divorce papers came though; Trevor acquired a new boyfriend who he said was definitely the one; Ashit took some time off to deal with family matters, Jerry shared plans for an autumn holiday break and Manny went to spend Rosh Hashanah with relatives.

When Manny returned, he spoke of the tradition at the Jewish New Year of blowing the shofar, or ram's horn. 'By the way,' he added, the biblical Joshua famously used the shofar in the battle of Jerico.' I vaguely remembered something about the story. 'Wasn't there a song about that?'

'Indeed,' Jerry chimed in, 'it goes 'Joshua fit the battle of Jerico and the walls came tumbling down'. Joshua took charge when Moses died and led the tribes to conquer Canaan and take the Promised Land.'

Trevor looked thoughtful. 'I can't picture our Joshua 'fitting' any battle, much less making walls tumble down.'

'Neither can I,' Manny laughed, 'not Joshua Shepperton.'

'Shepperton,' I chimed in, 'that's a town somewhere down south, isn't it?'

Jerry nodded, 'In Surrey, I think. Perhaps his ancestors came from there.'

Ashit smiled. 'Big film studios there. The Bollywood of England, isn't it.'

The weather was getting decidedly cooler and new jobs were coming in, so we had our heads down much of the time. I was shocked, and not a little pissed, that Joshua landed a particularly juicy contract. The gang discussed it at lunch and were still talking about it when we got back. Joshua had stayed behind to take his lunch later than the rest of us, and was still out.

'I can't get over it,' I grumbled. That's a fucking major campaign for a top company, very demanding.'

'Damn straight,' Manny agreed. They want a real dynamo, a ball of fire.'

Ashit chuckled, 'Ball of fire? Joshua's more like a bucket of water!'

We all laughed loudly and I was about to say more, but heard the door handle turn, and then the man himself came in. We moved to our desks and kept schtum the rest of the afternoon.

That was a Friday. I had a lot of sorting to do over the weekend, so didn't think of office matters. On Monday morning, Joshua arrived a few minutes late, unusual for him. He was wearing a sharp new suit, coordinated shirt and tie, even shiny new shoes. He still looked like a wimp, but a well-dressed wimp.

Naturally, our lunchtime conversation centred around Joshua's sudden sartorial splendour. Was he hoping to make an impression on his new clients? Perhaps, but there seemed to be something different in his facial expression as well, not quite a smirk, but rather a self-satisfied, secret smile. He was no more talkative than before, but there was something about him I couldn't put my finger on. The others noticed it, too, but had no idea what it meant.

It wasn't long before we were travelling to and from the office in darkness. Christmas lights went up in the town centre and the ground level unit in our building, which had been empty for months, opened as a charity card shop. Sadly, we heard the start-up on the floor above us, which had been floundering since the lockdowns, was going out of business. Once they moved out, it would just be us and the temporary card shop, though the letting agent said another small firm might be taking a lease upstairs in the New Year.

I wasn't really looking forward to the 'festive season' except as a break from routine. In the office, the guys chatted about their various plans for whichever holiday they celebrated. All except Joshua, who sat there with a smug expression. Perhaps he was an atheist, but even so, he must do something to celebrate the end of year festivities, mustn't he?

The days wound down to the last before the break. The evening before, we'd gone out for a few jars. I did try to include Joshua, saying 'I know you don't normally come to the pub with us, but just this once, why not join in for some seasonal cheer, eh, how about it?' He barely lifted his head. 'I don't think so.' Did I detect a note of hostility in his low-voice response?

On that final afternoon, most of the others left early to catch trains or do some last-minute Christmas shopping. I remained to finish off my work, then closed down my computer. Joshua was still apparently working, head down. I couldn't just walk out without saying anything.

'Hey, Joshua, it's holiday time; you can bunk off, you know.'

'Don't patronize me,' he sneered.

'What? I'm just trying to be sociable.'

'Save it; I know what you think of me.' I didn't know what to say; but he continued. 'I heard you that time I was late back from lunch. You were all talking about me, about my getting that big contract and how I wasn't up to it. I waited outside the door and heard every word, Someone said I was a bucket of water, and you all laughed like drains. A bucket of water. At that moment I decided to show you how wrong you are.'

'Oh, sorry. Was that behind your getting all those smart new clothes?'

'That weekend I worked out a plan. The clothes were just part of it.'

'What else is in your plan?'

'You'll see. Now run along, I've got to sort out my files. Go on, I'll lock up.'

All I could do was mumble, 'All right.' I buttoned my coat and went to the door, then turned and started to say 'Happy ...' but he looked at me with such disdain I swallowed the rest and left.

It's not healthy to carry a grudge into a new year, and I hoped Joshua would reflect and get over it. As for me, Christmas was pretty grim. My relatives were too distant and it was too late to attempt to arrange a visit. Friends were all dispersed, or else too wrapped up in their own families for me to intrude. At one point I drafted a text to my ex-wife, but deleted it. I couldn't face Christmas dinner in a restaurant, even if I could have got into one; so I just ordered a take-away and downed a bottle of wine and half a bottle of port. As New Year approached, I got in touch with an old girlfriend I hadn't seen in years, and surprisingly, she agreed to meet for dinner and catch up.

Having been drinking every night through the break, I overslept the morning I was due back at work. As I approached the turning for the office I smelled smoke, and when I got there I saw the crowds, vehicles and spraying hoses. Our building was on fire.

In the confusion I sought and found my colleagues, all but Joshua. I asked if anyone knew what happened. Jerry said, 'They think it started hours ago, around dawn. It appears to have begun in our office and spread through the building. Oh dear, oh dear.' The others were equally distressed, though they expressed it in more forceful language, lamenting the loss of their files, personal papers and other items. I suggested we go round the corner and see if the café was open. Thankfully it was. We found a table and ordered.

When our coffees arrived we were wondering how the disaster could have happened. Suddenly I remembered my conversation with Joshua and relayed it to the others. Responses ranged from remorse to outrage. Jerry thought a moment and asked, 'Do you mean you think Joshua burned down the office just to prove he wasn't a bucket of water?'

'It looks that way.'

'Goodness gracious!'

Ian Everton
by kind permission of Sydney Leaf

Sam

Sam was always singing. And very nice it was too. From ancient folk to classical opera, Sam could sing anything so perfectly, you'd think it had been written with him alone in mind. Sam sang in the bath, while he was doing chores, on his way to the shops, everywhere. And people noticed. He was really appreciated. They would stop whatever it was that they were doing – slightly puzzled at first, wondering if they had left the radio on; then they would look up, and finally smile, and they realised the melody was coming from the good-natured Sam.

Neighbours would turn off their television sets in deference to Sam's singing and listen into the early hours. Relatives came round on the least excuse – or even on no excuse at all. They all wanted him to live with them, so that they wouldn't have to come all the way to hear him. So they moved nearer until, in the early days, much of the street was full of Sam's relatives. He began to make lots of friends. Young, old, all types. With a 'Give us ... ' Sam could cater for all tastes. Then it was suggested: why didn't he do it professionally, instead of being on the dole? He could teach, or perform, or even tour the country, and, eventually, sign a record contract for any company that he wished. Sam was bashful. Instead of the dole? Well, it might pay for a nice holiday in Torquay, he supposed. And he did need a new suit. The bedroom could do with a new layer of wallpaper.

So Sam, at first egged on by sundry friends, sang in working people's clubs, at large parties, even in the open air. There was no doubt in anyone's mind – Sam had to go professional. And it wasn't long before the talent spotters were there in the audience, thinking in terms of lucre.

He was asked to go on a talent show on television. Sam won every week. People said he should stop that and go pro. The Social Security had cut his money off, saying that technically he was working, even if he wasn't actually being paid for it. There were plenty of people around, of course, who could lend Sam some money until better times. It became every night. Sam was either live on television, taking part in a film, or touring Britain, never to forget his Northern working-class origins, of course. He always tried to give one free show a month in the working people's club where he had given his very first performance.

Sam got quite rich. He bought a house in the suburbs. He didn't have to work so often now. He was seen rubbing shoulders with opera performers, popular musicians, and wasn't without his admirers who could put their admiration for him into physical love-making.

And one night Sam was about to go to bed. He got a strange feeling as he looked at himself in the mirror. 'La, la, la, la, la, la, la, la,' he sang.

'Are you coming to bed?' his companion said.

'I'm packing it in,' Sam said.

'Whatever for?'

'I don't like it. I never did. It was only a hobby at first. No one ever asked me what I thought of it. I was only trying to please other people.'

His friend was on the phone. 'I think Sam's having a turn.'

Early the next day they were round. Relatives, friends, business people waving their contracts. There were crowds round the house. And, according to the media, there were several suicides, above the seasonal average which, some reckoned, were a direct result of Sam's decision. But that can easily be put down to fancy. Anyway, they were having a field day.

After a day, a week, a month, Sam still refused to sing a single note. Fewer people now came to the house. Then it was suddenly sold. Sam was said to wander round bars in disguise. Or, predictably, that he had gone to South America. Or that he would start again – this time in London, where he might be more appreciated. But it never happened.

A year later Sam was completely forgotten – though there were, by then, several very poor imitations. They just didn't have what it took. Sam was signing on because he'd spent it all – given most of it away, in fact.

'What sort of work are you looking for?' a junior clerk would say.

'When the economy starts to pick up,' said Sam, looking shyly at the floor, 'I'd like to do something with my hands.

People Just Don't Understand

'I'll tell you what happened,' Peter said. 'I'd only known him a week. We met at the Gay Soc. He came straight over to me, introduced himself, gave a big smile, and chatted to me right through the meeting. Some of the members didn't like that.'

'People need to talk,' Michael said.

'Yes,' Peter continued. 'We went over to the pub as usual. He didn't leave my side. I bought him two pints. Then I realised he must have been poor, so I bought him a third and then it was closing time.'

'Perhaps he was waiting for pay day,' Michael said.

'Yes. Anyway, I asked him back for a coffee ...'

'Oh yes ...?'

'Well, people do.' Peter and Michael looked at each other. 'He stopped outside the door, said he had to be up early, but he'd call in the week. Then he asked me to lend him five pounds.'

'I often have to borrow money,' Michael said.

'Yes. Anyway, I did have five pounds. So I lent it to him, thinking – "You'll regret this." '

'You'd already made your mind up?' Michael said.

'If you like,' Peter said. 'So I waited in. He came the next night. I thought it was too early to ask for the money. I was cooking a meal and he asked if he could have some. I couldn't refuse.'

'Why should you refuse?' Michael said.

'Some people would,' Peter said. 'Anyway, he came round every night. And he wanted feeding. So I thought I'd act it out and tell you – to get a second opinion.'

'Yes.' Michael nodded for Peter to go on. Peter had done the right thing, seeking Michael's advice.

'It was the night before the next Gay Soc meeting. He came round. I'd prepared a meal – spent all day on it. And he said he'd just eaten. I have to admit – I gave him a peck when he came in.'

'You were after sex?' Michael said.

'I gave him a peck.'

'Yes, but you'd gone through all that trouble to make him a meal – you were only after sex,' Michael said.

'Even if that were true, is that a crime?' Peter said.

'Certainly, if you're trying to force your attentions on to someone who doesn't want you,' Michael said.

'And if they say "yes" – then it isn't a crime?' Peter said.

Michael didn't answer Peter.

'Anyway – he said he had to dash down to London. Could I lend him ten pounds? I said I'd already lent him five pounds.'

'That was callous of you,' Michael said. 'For all you know, his mother might have been dying.'

'Well, he didn't say she was. It was the way he asked me. I couldn't possibly ask what he wanted it for. His eyes were huge, red, and watery like a lunatic,' Peter said.

'You imagined it,' Michael said.

'You weren't there,' Peter said.

Pause.

'I said I didn't have ten pounds,' Peter said.

'Did you?' Michael said.

Another pause.

'No,' Peter said. 'Then he stormed out of the room saying: 'You can keep your fucking Gay Soc – I thought you were all supposed to be communists.' I was going to explain that we weren't communists ...'

'You should have,' Michael said.

'Yeah,' Peter said. 'Anyway, it doesn't matter about the five pounds. I mean, it doesn't really matter, does it?'

'You shouldn't have treated him like that,' Michael said.

'Like what?' Peter said.

'Well – you were obviously after sex. When you didn't get it you threw him out.'

'I didn't throw him out,' Peter said. 'He's quite welcome to come back ...'

'As long as it's for sex,' Michael said. Peter went quiet.

'You have a duty to introduce him to Gay Soc,' Michael said.

'Yes?' Peter said.

'You obviously don't know how to handle people. What's his address?'

'65 Ash Grove,' Peter said.

'I'll go round and see him,' Michael said.

'You will?'

'Yes. He is the one with blond hair, blue eyes, nice complexion, nice figure, eighteen?'

'Yes, that's the one,' Peter said.

'I'll have to go round. And you'll have to apologise to him,' Michael said. 'You've obviously got a chip on your shoulder. And the Gay Soc will never get off the ground with people like you in it.'

Michael got up and left.

The Fly in the Ointment

After Yusuf's visa had run out, he had to return to his own country. Tim knew that Yusuf would never come back – his country had been involved in a war for over a year now.

Tim was an ordinary man in an ordinary town. The town had a radical gay group, a conservative gay group, one night club, and three bars. After Yusuf had gone home Tim attended none of these on a regular basis. He had the occasional look at one, then another, and he grew tired of seeing the same faces. But these places had to pass the nights, the weeks, the months.

One Friday night Tim went to the conservative group. He noticed a new face (to him) sitting in the corner. Jack was as shy as Tim – although Tim was on nodding terms with most of the people in the group.

Everyone had had to listen to an hour's dialogue between Stephen and Bill. Tim had heard the same anecdotes on his previous visit, and the one before. He had determined not to come again. But seeing this newcomer had somehow changed that outlook.

After the meeting the group went to a pub, and Tim noticed that Jack had tagged on behind, although not speaking to anyone. In the bar Tim found himself sitting at Jack's side. Both of them were brooding over something known only to themselves. It mattered little. The regulars from the group were having their usual conversations about the usual things that interested that sort of person. There was nothing wrong with sitting quietly. But what was Tim going to do next time? How long could he bear it?

Suddenly Tim plucked up the courage and offered to buy Jack a drink. This naturally started a conversation between them. Soon they forgot about the other people they had come with.

When it was closing time Tim and Jack headed for the night club, as though it had all been prearranged, as though the two of them had done this together many times before. Where the others from the group had gone, they didn't know or care

That night was the fastest Tim had known in months. He didn't know how much he drank. He and Jack danced while the night club filled, until it emptied again and closed. He and Jack walked back to Tim's place intoxicated by something quite different from music or alcohol.

Tim and Jack laughed their heads off, sitting in bed, from three o'clock to dawn.

'I don't vote,' Jack said. 'Both parties are too extreme. They'll never do anything for me.'

Jack was right – neither party did anything for Tim either. Tim thought next time he wouldn't even bother filling in the electoral form. He was glad that Jack wasn't political. All too often Tim got stuck with a left – or right-wing fanatic. Or rather 'bore' would be a more apt word.

Jack and Tim must have fallen asleep eventually, because at noon they woke up to find themselves in each other's arms.

Jack came round to Tim's that night. They went out to one of the other bars, then the night club. It was packed. Some of the people from the CHE group were there. Would Tim and Jack be at the next meeting? Tim grinned. The man was definitely joking. After much dancing, each step Tim took with Jack was like the beginning of a new world. They went back to Tim's place; as if there was any question that they might do something else.

'I bought this jar of ointment,' Jack said, revealing his well-kept secret from a leather pocket. 'I'm full of surprises. It's better than the stuff you have.'

'Are you?' Tim said. 'Is that a promise?' and they both quickly got undressed.

As the days ticked by the ointment in the jar went down until it was nearly empty.

'I'll buy the next jar,' Tim said. 'It's only fair.'

'Oh, it's only fair,' Jack agreed. 'You'll find I'm a very fair person – anyone would tell you that, just ask them.'

That same day Tim went to the chemist's.

'Have you got some ... Dr White's, er, skin ...?'

'What's it for?' the assistant asked.

'Er ... chaps,' Tim said.

'Oh yes, I know the one you mean. We've been selling a lot of that lately.'

'Lately?' Tim asked – he didn't know why.

'Since nineteen sixty-seven,' she said quite casually.

After some searching the assistant had to bring the pharmacist into the main part of the shop. A queue was forming behind Tim, which he did his best to ignore. The pharmacist asked Tim what it was he wanted.

The pharmacist then went into the back room where he did all his pharming. For some minutes Tim could hear the clinking of jars, the opening and shutting of drawers, the sound of conversation between the pharmacist and other members of staff. Meanwhile one assistant had to take care of the queue with her: 'Can I help you?'

Tim felt himself going quite red.

The pharmacist came back into the shop.

'I'm sorry – we seem to be out of Dr White's. I can order you a jar – it'll be two weeks.'

'But I can't wait that long,' Tim said, feeling the eyes of other customers who tuned into this fascinating conversation as one would automatically look at a television screen on entering a room. Whatever did he want that particular ointment for, that was so pressing?

'Would you like to try another type?' the pharmacist said. 'It's basically the same thing.' The pharmacist offered Tim a tiny jar with a label – £2.

Underneath the larger label it said: WARNING – MAY IRRITATE SOME PEOPLE.

'No. That's no good,' Tim said, and left the shop, glad to be out in the fresh air again.

Tim caught the bus into town and tried every chemist he could find, including the well-known one. Somehow – and why not? – the ointment itself was symbolic of his new relationship with Jack. After all, he had said he would buy the next jar, it was only fair. And so far, a jar seemed to last a whole week.

Tim went home feeling downhearted. Perhaps Jack had managed to buy some of the ointment himself. But Jack had said 'It's only fair.' He also said that he was full of surprises. But since Jack was a very fair person, he might not mind Tim's letting him down on such a small matter.

That night Tim was quiet; he didn't really know why. Jack didn't seem to mind. Then Jack started to be jolly and that made Tim jolly as well, and they drank more than usual, danced more than usual until the night-club closed.

When they finally got to bed they had to manage with cooking oil. There was still a bit of ointment in the jar which had remained on the table at the side of the bed but not enough. Jack didn't comment on the fact that Tim had forgotten his promise to buy the next jar of ointment.

In the morning the world seemed fine again. As Jack was getting ready to go, he said: 'They always sell that ointment in the wog-shop – but they overcharge.'

'The what?' Tim had never – in a whole week – heard Jack use a word like that.

'The Paki shop,' Jack clarified his meaning.

'I didn't know you were a racist,' Tim said. Tim tried to make the remark sound like a joke, but he had to know exactly what Jack was getting at.

'Of course I am,' Jack said. 'I'm sick of the sight of them. When I was a boy, you could walk through town and you'd be lucky if you saw one. Look at it now!' Jack grinned at his terribly amusing joke.

Tim couldn't speak.

'See you tonight?' Jack said. It wasn't a question, it was ... more like an order.

Jack had gone. The slam of the door had an eerie ring to it. The sound of Jack's boots down the stairs seemed to go – left, right, left, right, ten-SHUN! They echoed again and again in Tim's head.

Tim had an internal picture of Afghanistan. The tribesmen – devout Muslims – fighting first the British, now the Russians. He wondered where Yusuf was now – if anywhere. If only he would write.

Tim had the feeling that he wouldn't be going out that night. ... He went into his bedroom and looked at the bottle of cooking oil. In the bottom of the ointment jar lay a dead fly stuck to the last of the white stuff which had now become very slimy. Tim lay on the bed and wept.

Bodicea Iceni

Bereft

Hope exchanged for despair
Warm summer days
Replaced by bitter winter

New paths once visible
Creating endless possibilities
Have all but vanished

The promise of life
Transformed into
icy treacherous tracks
That lead into oblivion

Agony replaced by sorrow
Endless tears cleansing lenses
Now offer unobstructed views
Views of the void
Views into the void

Stark, vast expanses
Of emptiness
Bleak vacuous futures
Bereft of life

Desire for blindness
Forming a daily mantra
Clear vision inescapable
Expiration forever calling

Death an ending
An absolute certainty

Blue

The joy of awakening
On a midwinters day
To stark blue skies

Baby blue
Cornflower blue
Azure blue
A divine hue

Beams of orange gold
Streaming in
Caressing my heart
Strengthening each beat
Enhancing my spirit,
Enlivening my mood

Through murky speckled
Window panes
Each band of refracted light
Emerging through
A multitude of prisms

Promising energy
Promising warmth
Promising change
Promising life,

Another day
A new beginning
Renewal, hope

Second Daughter

I was never first
First in my mother's heart
That role was held for my sister.
The golden one, the chosen one

She loved my sister
Like no other existed
She loved her like
Only a mother could

I was forever in the shadows
Seemingly unloved but really unnoticed
Subsequent children came along
Sons, sons and then more sons

My mother died
With her daughter next to her
Not me of course but my sister
I watched them both silently
As my mother passed

I grieved for her
Like all daughters should
But my grief was less for a death
And more for an absence

She'd never been available
Not to me
So, she died without us
Ever forming a connection

So here I am
Grieving the loss of a parent
But really the absence of a mother

The impact of that non relationship
Has yet to be fully realised,
Fully acknowledged

But my feelings
Of non existence persist
Never quite good enough
Never really very special
To anyone

Eleanor (Nor) Dow
Ways of Belonging

We were lying in the dark, in a small cabin room. There was a single bunk bed, I was sleeping on top, you below. We were on our way to visit your Da, not knowing whether he would still be there when we arrived. Your feet touched the ends, your toes cold from the steel rails of the bed board. Of course, I had plenty of room, but it didn't help me sleep. The ferry was not made for sleeping. The sea jeered at you, mocking you like a sleepless parent. I had never slept on these ferries, even though I pretended to. I longed to sit up all night, clamber up on deck and look out at the vast dark ocean spreading before us. To scream in a frenzy with the gulls and listen to the waves lap endlessly against solid steel, solid boat.

12 hours 33 minutes

I was sat staring at the blank ceiling thinking about you. Listening to your breathing. Wondering whether you were thinking about me, but never daring to ask if you were awake.

We arrived to a sky so vast. The contrast of this to the darkness of the ferry cabin shocked and excited me. I was drawn to the extremes of things; the deep darkness of an unpolluted night sky to bright clear blinding sun, my intense lows to manic highs, the bustling sound of city traffic to rhythmic bird song. Here we were, in what felt like the lightest place on Earth, whilst knowing that grief was round the corner. However, I didn't hang onto certainty. Instead, I inhabited transitions; seasonal, spiritual, political. It gave me a sense of hope, a belief that things could change. I held your hand as we exited the ferry.

He looked so much frailer than when you last saw him. You remembered him as utterly solid. How you could lean against him during the high winds. How, when you held his hand, you felt like he really held you. You used to ride on his shoulders when you were wee, so you could see out into the distance to the islands of Yell and Fetlar. His shoulders felt as tall as trees, as sturdy as peat bricks. He was solidity to you.

I had a feeling that your parents wondered why I was with you, why you'd brought a 'friend' all this way to witness an old man dying. I stood respectfully beside you, trying to exude comfort whilst resisting the urge to touch you. You introduced me just by my name and decided there was no need to explain. I was here, we were here and that was all that mattered.

Your Da was all bundled up in an armchair, despite the mild weather, wrapped from head to toe in Shetland yarn. He didn't seem too pleased about it, having been smothered in an array of colours and textures, whilst he stared rigidly at the door. His face looked haggard, and you could tell he had lost a lot of weight in a short period of time.

'Will you be staying long?' your Ma asked.

'As long as I can' you say.

'Hmm' your Ma was staring at me, a look of concern in her eyes, 'I'll put the kettle on.'

Your Da whispered over to you, his voice rasping, asking you to tell him one of your stories.

You reached out for your Da's hand, 'Of Course'.

You told the story of the selkie, or your version of it. The besotted woman on the shore wishing to join her lover in the sea, the discovery of a hidden sealskin, the transformation from woman to seal to woman again. You told it as if this undoing of boundaries, this shifting of edges, was vital to keep this woman alive. In some stories the selkie was cut off from her human form, to become a seal forever, however your selkie was an eternal shape shifter, allowing her to be her true self.

The next morning, I woke with the sound of starlings, a scattering of electronic morse code rebounding off the bothy walls. We had slept for almost 10 hours after a sleepless night the night before. We went walking along Skaw beach, on the Northeast tip of Unst. You told me how your Da had nurtured you in the ways of this land. Taking you out in the spring to collect peat for the winter. You loved examining the layers of the earth, imagining how many layers of heather, peat, grass, Viking bones, stood between you and the earth's core. Your favourite bit was slicing the peat with the Tushkar and piling it into bricks to stack onto the bank. You and your Da would never talk whilst doing this, as if talking took away from the sound of the work. The sensations of slicing, the thoughts that you could create, just by yourself in this place; connected. It was an intentional silence that made way for companionship.

Then you would go on long walks. He would take you to untrodden parts of the island. You would walk for hours by the sea, again in silence, every now and then pointing out an orca, a dolphin, a bonxie. He told you the land would look after you and would teach you more about yourself than he ever could. It was on one of those days that you told him the land had made you realise you were a woman. He looked at you, smiled, and said 'It told me that too'.

We walked up the coast to a babbling cliff edge. I saw your eyes light up, your whole body becoming alive when you discovered the cliff was full of nesting fulmars. We lay in the heather watching them soar above us, laughing at their dangling feet, their broad swoops, their bubbling squawks.

'Don't stand too close to the cliff edge!' you shouted.

'I won't,' I cried back, my arms outstretched for balance, my feet edging their way closer to the edge to try and peek at their beaks. The sea rushed against the cliffs below. A flash of memory clawed at my mind. My sister and I, scattering ashes over a cliff. Dazed, I stumbled backwards. You reached for my hand and I took it gladly. It felt right, to sit on the cliffs with someone you trusted, even though you didn't quite trust the cliffs not to fall, the clouds to engulf you.

'It feels strange, to connect so much of this land to a person,' you whispered, the same tone as the tide.

'I've had such personal experiences here, not necessarily connected to him ... but he feels like the source, you know? He feels like he guided me to what I know now, whilst also reinforcing who I was, and I don't know, I guess without him I'm worried I'll fade away.'

I held my arms around you and reached out to brush your fringe from in front of your eyes.

'You have so much to thank him for. I can see this Island loves you, whether he's here or not.'

'But will the people love me?'

'I love you.'

Peta was thinking of her Ma, and the extended family. The difficult relationship she had tried to cling onto, despite their differences.

But many people on the island accepted Peta for who she was. People had known the Inkster family for generations. Peta had been part of the local school at Baltasound, had volunteered at the post office from the age of 12, worked at the local pub at 16, the fact that she had transitioned couldn't be separated from her identity here. She was still Peta, and they knew that. They were used to transition, everything had a distinct sense of change here, and if you didn't keep up with it, the rising sea levels, the eroding coastline, the economic shifts, then you became isolated. The shifting of genders did not seem at odds with the changes this community was in rhythm with.

'But Morgan, you don't understand. For you, you can go anywhere, you can travel the world if you wanted to. I can't leave this island, I've tried, but I just can't. There's this bubbling feeling that swells up when I am far from home, even when I'm surrounded by queer community, trans people who share my experience, I can't relax until I am by this shore, on this soil, even though I can't talk to anyone here like I can talk to you.'

'I don't want to travel the world, and even if I did, there are still places that don't accept me. I envy you; you have roots, you have a place where people know who you are and who you used to be. For me, wherever I go I'll just be me, now, in the present. My past is buried in old acquaintances that no longer know me. It's hard for me too, I don't know where home is.'

Where does it come from though? Grief? You ask. I say it comes from the mountains. Starts high and heavy. Heaving, rushing fast down the mountain stream, too much at one time; in a hurry to fall. Then where does it go? It will soon be in the river. It will flow slower there, more at ease with itself, part of something bigger. And then, the sea will welcome it. Comfort it. Greet it with understanding.

We were sitting in your kitchen. Your Da was asleep in the other room, your Ma had just gone out to fetch a few more ingredients for supper. Our day had been long, mainly helping with washing, medication, lifting and carrying your Da to the bathroom and back. He was barely conscious now, receiving twice daily visits from the local nurse who adjusted pain medication, washed his wounds so he wasn't wincing with each touch. I was rubbing your knuckles as we talked about the inevitable, the what's next, the hows and the whys. Why now? How do we keep him comfortable? Where does he go when the time comes? And what does that mean for us?

The next evening, I went for a walk by myself. I was observing the light, the dimness, the grey light, and how it only showed its face for a few hours before shrinking into dusk, before dark enfolded the landscape and hid things from us. I was longing for the dawn, for that rising light, for the time the birds were most vocal; you could learn a lot from them then. When I was younger, I used to get up at dawn to witness the light changing, wishing it could stay dawn forever. I wanted things to begin and keep beginning. I was worried about things fading away.

I often wondered how these moments shaped us, held us, gave space for our queerness. I remember always feeling my most authentic self in the woods, like I didn't have to defend myself to the trees – they knew who I was and accepted me. You said you felt the most yourself whilst working the peatbog, being able to feel the soil in your fingers, the sea breeze on your cheeks – your body felt yours. For you, you needed the stillness to grow, the familiarity of a small community to anchor yourself on. For me, I needed to run away.

I loved autumn in particular – in autumn I could be any colour, I could become anything. Colours gave way to shapes, gave way to shapeshifting. By 'becoming' orange, or red, or green, or purple, or brown, I could embody so many parts of myself.

There were some days I would sneak off through the park and carry on running and running until I reached that mulchy hazel smell, reaching the track that led to the woods. I would dig my fingers into the leafy dirt and sit staring up into the branches. The woods were more than company. In the woods I was genderless, I was gender-full, I was ageless. Some days I felt as old as the oak that stood at the gate, other days I was as young as a new sapling springing up from the deep mud.

For me, coming to the island had made me realise how disconnected from myself I had become in the city. Despite being surrounded by queer community, I often felt alone. I longed for the woods, the river, the contours of hillside; the non-human world that I had first felt myself in.

On 28th February, Peta's Da took his last breath. That day we stopped the clocks. We built a wall of peat bricks. We burnt juniper. That day we wailed like strangled crows at the clouds. We drew circles and crosses in the dirt and poured whiskey on the ground. That day we gathered all the village yarn and Peta's Ma knitted a huge cloth and spread it over his body, wrapping it round 3 times, then 3 times again. As the word spread, a ripple settled over the town; that Ewan George Inkster had passed, had been received by God, had been lifted to the great unknown – people began to gather, began to flock towards the croft. Peta's 3 aunts were there, and multiple sets of cousins, a great uncle. The village shop keeper. Local fishermen. Graeme, Peta's storytelling mentor. Fiddle players, Pipers and Singers, who used to play with Ewan every week at the session.

Then Peta began to share a tale, sitting on a small rock, with crowds of relatives and locals surrounding her. Today, Peta was dressed in a long black dress, with purple and green bangles on her wrists, her white, blonde hair lying loosely around her cheeks, and her sea blue eyes outlined in gold and black.

'It was on a clear night, we were walking up near the Brae, Da and I, and there it came – the lights, the aurora. My Da was a huge believer in the power of these lights, and the symbolism behind them. It was once known that he knew the folklore around them, and a story about this in 23 different languages, each unique in its telling of mystery, in battle for power, in celebration of the unworldly. It was on this walk that we developed our own folklore about them, just me and him. I had always looked to these lights as a guiding force and was most inspired by the Nordic myth of the shields of Valkyries racing to Valhalla. I was caught up in the spectacular dress often given to these women on horseback. Of their long dresses, elaborate jewellery, and shields of armour, alongside their pivotal role in the battle, defying stereotypical gender roles. My Da knew my gender identity long before I plucked up the courage to tell him. After that we would conjure up the many ways gender non-conforming and trans folk were speckled throughout Shetlandic folklore. Often the characters were not explicitly depicted as so, but we soon began to realise this had been only a recent adaptation. We began to re-adapt and re-imagine these stories, and as we stared at the Aurora, we saw a celebration of not just the Valkyries, but the drag performers throughout history, showing off their marvellous colours. Another traditional view sees these lights as voices of the deceased, of those gone to be closer with God, with the Angels.

'My Da was so weak these last few months, but during this time he would speak of dancing in his new body with the drag queens up there, filled with joy and vigour. He said he couldn't wait to meet them, and that he would continue to speak wisdom from up there. And then he would speak of the trows, our favourite folklore characters. As you all know Ewan was a keen fiddle player. He liked to imagine himself going in the way of Sigurd, who first described the music of the trows, and formed a special relationship with them through learning their music and song. When Sigurd returned, no one believed his experiences, and yet when playing their tunes he turned to dust, there and then. Whenever you play a trow tune I'd like to think the dust of Da is floating around you, ready to spiral into the sky for the next Aurora.'

Adrian Risdon

Praed Street

I've no right at all to complain –
as I do on many occasions –
that my sex-life went on the wane
the moment I hit adolescence.

I strode north along Praed Street
and thought: 'This district's rubbish' –
attendance at King's, Canterbury
having made me instantly snobbish –

and there he was: David Bradley,
my former Paddington pal,
haranguing a bus-driver rudely,
attracting a crowd as well.

I daredn't align with that rabble.
Police might be called and what then?
(David once got me in trouble
at our Infants' School off Park Lane.)

He was handsome by now, however.
Only one thing seemed wrong:
his voice was quasi-falsetto,
undermining his 'manly' aplomb.

I'd long entertained suspicions
concerning his pubic parts:
one of our naughty traditions
involved him baring his arse.

'Poke me!' he'd commanded.
I'd thought (but daredn't say):

'I really don't need you wounded
by my sharp nails that way.'

I sought to enquire – but I daredn't –
'Let me see what you've got in front.'
My fingers 'said' what I couldn't;
my fumble 'told' him: 'I want ...'

'That,' David snarled, 'is my private!'
'This *isn't*?' I struggled to shout
(but somehow failed to heave it
up from my heart to my mouth).

And still I wouldn't say 'David!' –
instead I strode cowardly past:
threw a boyfriendly future away with
'Alack!' and a snobbish 'Alas !'

Diana Dors

(Harpoon Louie's 19th April 1984)

The pub's fool *compère* rows
with her accompanist ...
Diana, dear, you're missed ...
We wait. Impatience grows.

But here at last our High
Priestess of sleaze appears,
singing how the stars
also quit the sky:

'Love being here with you ...
I face the final curtain ...'
Though her notes are certain,
speaks the last line or two.

'70 films: in most
I come to a sticky end.'
Does the remark portend
a battle won or lost?

Invites enquiries from
her audience, but cuts
a bore's *ifs* and *buts*:
others are in the room

and this their last chance ...
Quick exit. One more wave.
(A fortnight. Then the grave.)
That fool's back to announce:

'I do apologize
for the *awful* Sound ...'

Awe's somewhere around
when Diana dies.

Patisserie: a Fairy Tale

But if I thought just one faux-pas sufficed
to see me safely through the whole weekend,
I was mistaken. Jane and Johnny iced
audibly when, at our journey's end,
I said: 'How LARGE a garden to defend!'
Apparently the point of their remove
was getting both their back-aches on the mend.
Compared to this, their last had been a grove.
What wicked fairy was it, that my story wove?! [1]

Now when, in 1980-something, I
composed that stanza, I sincerely thought
(a) I'd found at length my writer's 'voice';
and (b) the question at the end was mere
exasperation at my naffness. But
in 1990 my 'real' family
revealed there had in actual fact been such
a wicked fairy – Nanna Sugden, who
(frustrated by her lack of access to
both my siblings) moved right up to London,
living and working round the corner from
where I lived with middle-aged adopters.
The consequence? My 'parents' let their house,
rented a flat in Hove, sent me to board
at Cranbrook – then at Canterbury – in Kent.
Worse still, the holidays were spent abroad
(ostensibly to improve my French and German):
so I never had the 'village' each child needs
if (s)he's to acquire maturity.
No wonder that, at Cambridge, my few friends
recommended listening to *The Archers*;
excellent advice I never took.

---

[1] *extract from Risdon's Survey of Somerset*

In 1990 step-mother Ivy
showed me Nanna Sugden's photograph ...
Instantly I re-lived going with
my 'mother' to the little shop in Spring Street
(to this day the word *Patisserie*'s
visible within the glass) and meeting –
for one dramatic moment – shockingly –
the elderly assistant's anguished eyes.
In between that horror and the photo,
at Cambridge I had studied and enjoyed
Sir Gawain and The Green Knight, where the hero's
entire quest is undermined (N.B.
Spoiler Alert!) by his old aunt Le Fay;
'aunt' and 'aunture' – both are intertwined. [2]
Now that I'm retired and trapped in Hampshire,
a curious reversal's taken place.
Just as *wicked fairy* in my *Survey*
changed from wild guess to factual history,
so blackmail turned to blessing when I was
invited to join Stanza groups in So'ton.
They rank with GAW in my life:
Evil has conducted me to Good.
Plus – beyond 'The Adrian Risdon Story' –
there is, I hope, a general lesson here.
Poets may arrest, interrogate,
even condemn their offerings to death.
What you wrote some 40 years ago
may, in the light (or dark) of further knowledge,
acquire a whole new truth. Another *Survey* [3]
records my brother boasting to a friend
he'd known about my gayness but had chosen
not to let-on. The friend recoils, aghast:
'And so – before you'd even *met* – you knew?!' –

---

[2] *'aunture'* adventure
[3] extract from Risdon's *Survey of Shropshire*.

'We knew! We knew! How history repeats!
He didn't know we knew. Salt in the stew
is: not-so-saintly Cyril went-up-to-Pete's [4]
not knowing Leo knew his long deceits ...' [5]
But, when it mattered, Leo didn't know.
Since then my brother snapped up all my sweets,
just like that gay builder long ago.
These three witches changed my name to MacMalvolio.

---

[4] *Cyril' does duty for Cecil, my phoney father.*
[5] *Leo' does duty for Adrian the author.*

Safeguarding

Anxious to find a church where I could hear,
effortlessly, what the preacher said,
I asked a friend to recommend one such
and she – poor soul, she's died since – said at once:
'Try St John's: they've just renewed their Loop.'
I went along, next Sunday, to this church.
I sang the hymns: I prayed the prayers: no joy
at sermon-stage, however...
So I thought:
'I'll hover round the coffee-cups. Perhaps
some regular will confirm – or else deny –
what Wanda said.' I stood and simply waited.
No 'welcomer' accosted me. No one at all
paid the slightest heed that I was there.
Finally a student on his own
approached me, smiling. I was on the point
of asking about the Loop, when suddenly
the church police sprang into action – led him
off to the Youth Group (in a side-chapel),
then frog-marched me up to the Gallery, where
I was firmly deposited next a crone
(as resentful of this practice as myself).
She too was hard-of-hearing and therefore
no information about the Loop
was to be had from this enforced encounter.
All I learned from this unproductive visit
was: Wanda must have had some other St. John's
in mind when she responded to my question.
Also, I now know safeguarding's true name:
our old friend 'holy' homophobia.
I think I'll give up church-going, Mr Larkin.

Rainer King

What the Desert Keeps

Dust freckles the coach windows. Beyond, the desert stretches like skin pulled tight over bone – endless, empty, and waiting. The sky is bleached of mercy.

Alia's voice slices through the engine's low grumble – too bright, too fast.

'Hey – are you taking this coach too? Imagine seeing you here! I was meaning to message, ask if you were around for coffee or something, but ... well, here you are.' Her hands are knotted into her lap. A nervous tangle she presses down, as if to anchor herself.

Rowan hesitates. 'Erm. Yeah. I'm headed south.' She scans the rows for another seat – nothing free. Resigned, she slips into the one beside Alia, keeping her limbs as contained as possible. Alia watches as she stows her backpack and says, lightly, 'The hotel just before the border. Second to last stop.' Her voice softens. 'You?'

Rowan shrugs. 'Same.' Outside, the desert yawns. Rowan imagines it creeping through the coach vents – fine sand seeding itself inside her lungs, like the ruins of forgotten cities. Time here feels suspended. A vulture wheel in the heat. The kind of time that watches you, waits to strike.

Alia opens a bag of fruit pastilles, the crinkle oddly loud. A distraction tactic. She needs to slow down, not repeat last time. But it's already happening. 'Do you remember the film?' she asks. 'At the festival? Last summer. You were walking out, and the wind caught your hair and you turned around and smiled – like properly smiled. Then you laughed in my direction and I ...' She trails off.

Rowan blinks. 'I wasn't smiling at you.'

'I know,' Alia says, too quickly. 'But it felt like you were. And it hit me. That – pull. That first recognition. From then on, it just ... it grew.'

Rowan scrolls through old messages on her phone. Anything to avoid eye contact. 'You didn't say anything. Not the next two times we met.'

'I thought it would be more – organic. I didn't expect to see you again. Least of all here.'

Rowan slides her phone back into her pocket, leans her head against the headrest. The memory unspools, whether she wants it to or not. She didn't want to test the waters then, she wanted to loose herself to the heat of the city summer, scramble from monument to monument, proclaim them as hers.

Alia shifts slightly toward her. 'I was glad to talk that day. We really talked, didn't we? About the film, about how it showed something real. You even messaged me afterwards. I still have them.'

Rowan opens her eyes. 'Yeah. The film spoke to both of us. But I didn't realise you were reading more into it.'

'Well,' Alia says, smiling faintly, 'that was my deliberate mistake.'

Rowan pops open a can of juice. Sips. Silent. She can feel Alia watching her.

'Have you ever been drawn to someone like this?'

'No,' Rowan says. *Lie.* The truth is a scorpion curled beneath her tongue. She studies Alia from the corner of her eye – the laugh lines, the brow creased with hope or habit.

Part of her wants to reach out, peel back the layers. Another part wants to press the emergency exit and let the desert scour her new.

'I couldn't stop thinking about you,' Alia says. 'It wasn't just the film. It was everything. I wondered if you thought of me, too.'

Rowan replies carefully. 'I don't see the point of responding to your feelings.'

'I'm not asking for a response. I'm not saying you owe me anything.'

'Good. Because I haven't done anything to earn this.'

A pause.

'Would it be so awful to just ... get to know me more?'

'I don't want to.'

A beat.

'You don't even find me a little desirable?' Alia asks. 'You held me, after the film.'

Rowan says nothing. Sips her drink slowly.

Alia leans forward. 'Are you flattered by my attention? Even now? Was that it?'

Still, Rowan says nothing.

'I'll get off before the hotel,' Alia says. 'Better that way. I'll ask the driver to let me off early.'

'You'll be in the middle of nowhere,' Rowan replies. 'There's just dust for miles.'

'I'll walk. Someone will come by – truck or something. I'll figure it out.'

'That's dangerous,' Rowan says. 'Light's going.'

The coach jolts. Alia stumbles – and falls, graceless and burning, into Rowan's arms. For one breathless moment, they are one creature: heat, bone, breath. Rowan's hands tighten on her shoulders, leaving ghost-prints. It's the same as that night at the cinema.

Let go, the desert whispers.

Alia does.

At the next stop, the sky opens its throat – crimson, mauve, rust, bruised orange. A performance only the land will witness. Alia stands framed by it. A silhouette carved from light. Rowan watches her silhouette, backlit by fire and dust, and something inside her stirs – a wanting, or maybe just the memory of it.

Rowan steps off the coach. The dust muffles her footsteps, as if the land itself is holding its breath. 'Come stand with me,' she says.

Alia turns, surprised. The coach exhales and pulls away. Dust swallows the road behind it. Their shadows overlap on the dirt. Almost touching. Almost whole. A stranger, curious, snaps their photo. Rowan's arm settles lightly around Alia's waist – not quite a claim. Not quite not.

'For the memory book,' Rowan murmurs.
She thinks of fossils.
Of the pressure it takes to preserve a moment.
How even the softest things can calcify.
The shutter clicks.
And there they are:
Two in the desert's amber breath.
Forever almost.
Forever undone.

The Island

Floating face-down, saltwater cradling her like a tired argument, Jayshree opens her eyes. The world beneath the surface is blurred green-gold, streaked with sunlight. Her goggles pinch her nose – a small pain to tether her. She could stay this way forever, suspended between sinking and rising.

But memory is a hook in her ribs.

Lena.

She jerks upright, gasping, seawater stinging her throat. For a moment, she tastes tears – or maybe it's the ocean. 'How firmly shut I am,' Lena had said last year, her voice brittle through the crackling phone line. A photo arrived weeks later: Lena in red silk, her smile carefully placed. A man – *introduced by family* – stood beside her, his hand resting on her waist like a placeholder. 'Stick pins in my arm,' she'd said. 'I feel nothing at all.'

Jayshree wipes her face. The horizon wavers.

Ten years ago, the storm

The boat pitched sideways, tourists shrieking as spray lashed the deck. The locals sat silent, their faces carved from the same stone as the island cliffs. A pipe-smoking man glared at Lena's phone – that ridiculous pink-and-green furry case – and snorted.

'Don't expect to use that out there.'

Lena tugged Jayshree's sleeve. Forward seats, away from him.

Jayshree clutched the bench, knuckles straining. Lena rested her head on her shoulder, snapping photos of the boat's rusted rivets, the frayed lifebuoys. 'How quaint,' she murmured, 'how sweet,' the words a litany, an incantation. As if repetition could sand down her accent, could unmake her.

Jayshree shifted. 'You're heavy.'

Lena laughed but moved away.

Onshore, rain needled their cheeks. Jayshree kicked off her boots – army surplus, sturdy, bought for this – and waded into the shallows. 'There's a seal! It's making faces at me!'

Lena hunched under her hood. 'It so did not.' Her phone screen glowed uselessly. 'It's getting dark. We need to get going.'

Look at me, Jayshree wanted to say. Look at me the way you did at fourteen, when you held me, traced the henna on my palms and called it a map.

Another seal surfaced, whiskers twitching. Jayshree grinned. Lena fastened her coat.

The hostel room smelled of bleach and damp. Two bunk beds, red blankets thin as old scars. Their first reunion since the diaspora scattered them – Jayshree to London, Lena to California. They'd traded letters like hostages: Uni is fine. The cold takes getting used to. I miss mangosteens. Never the real words. I miss you.

Now, Lena unzipped her suitcase. A sari spilled out, the gold embroidery catching the dim bulb. 'For my cousin's wedding,' she said. 'Next month.'

Jayshree touched the fabric. 'You'll be beautiful.'

Their fingers brushed.

Return

The tide pulls Jayshree toward the rocks. She could let it. Instead, she swims back. On the beach, her phone buzzes – a message from Lena, sent hours ago:

Remember the seals? I saw them too.

A pause. Then: *I'm in London next month. Wear the blue sari. The one from home.*

Jayshree presses the phone to her chest. The sea exhales behind her.

She stares at the screen. Then, slowly, she begins to smile.

In the distance, a seal lifts its head from the water, as if remembering her too.

The Grammar of Wanting

There are things she wants to say, but the words curl up inside her like leaves in a fist.

She opens her mouth – once, twice – but nothing emerges. A syllable lingers on her tongue, then dissolves like sugar in coffee. She shakes her head. Not right. Not yet.

At work, she drafts scripts for herself: polite inquiries, rehearsed responses, the dry exchange of bureaucratic pleasantries. There, language is a transaction – predictable, practiced. But here, in this café thick with the scent of roasted beans and the murmur of strangers, words feel wild and untamed. If she speaks now, what will she unleash?

What if I never see them again?

What if I do, and the moment has passed?

The clink of a spoon against porcelain. The slow drip of the espresso machine. She watches as they stir their coffee, the liquid swirling like liquid amber. They pluck a strawberry from the plate, bite into it whole – juice catching the light, a bead of it trembling at the corner of their mouth – then chase it with a scoop of cream. The boldness of it makes her stomach flutter. I would never, she thinks. I'd slice it neatly, dab my lips after each bite. But then she notices the napkin folded on their knee. Ah. Prepared, but unafraid.

Their boots gleam under the café lights, polished leather holding the warmth of late-afternoon sun. Crisp chinos, a white shirt with sleeves rolled to the elbows – deliberate, but effortless. An unopened book lies beside them, spine uncracked; their phone, facedown, as if the world can wait. Outside, a bicycle bell chimes, and the wind carries in the scent of rain-soaked pavement.

She exhales. Just go over. Say hello.

But then – what? Ask to join them? There are empty tables everywhere, their surfaces wiped clean, waiting. The pretence would be flimsy.

Someone walks past her, glancing briefly, then away. Not rude. Not curious. Just enough to remind her: she is visible. She adjusts the strap of her bag, shifts her posture – small, automatic gestures of self-correction. She remembers – years ago, leaning too close to someone at a party. A hand on her wrist. A shared laugh. The silence that followed when someone else noticed. She had blushed then, deeply, instinctively, and never quite forgiven herself for it. She's better now, she thinks. But still, her body holds the memory of hiding.

They lift another strawberry, split it cleanly with the edge of their spoon. The sound is quiet but precise – a tiny snick of metal parting flesh. She watches as they swirl the half in cream, the white clinging to the red in slow, luxurious curls. Her breath catches. That's exactly what I would do.

A pause. The espresso machine hisses. The café's playlist shifts to something low and wordless, a saxophone tracing the edges of a melody.

As if hearing her thoughts, they turn – and smile.

Les Brookes

Three Chameleons and a Parrot

The bar at the Chameleon Club was besieged, one-thirty being the last chance to grab a drink and secure a pickup before closing time. Mark, in a soaked shirt with rolled sleeves, grinned wryly at Benjy, his fellow barman, as they took orders from the pack of noisy punters. This was the peak; the drift to the exit would soon begin, first by hopeful pairs, then by sad loners.

After work Mark often went to Benjy's for the night, though sometimes, after tipping him off and leaving him to lock up, he left with someone else. Benjy, easy-going, unassuming, never objected. He seemed happy to accept that they were no more than casual bedmates, though he sometimes dropped a hint that Mark might consider moving in. Mark was fond of Benjy; they were fond of each other. Mark looked to Benjy for support and words of wisdom. He needed a guide; someone to keep him in check.

Mark had another friend who came to the club every night. Jared was more than a regular; he was an addict. He sat in a corner all night with a single gin and tonic. He and Mark had met while working in a kitchen. Mark regarded Jared as a protégé, rather as Benjy regarded Mark, and was always advising him on who to approach and how to handle it. Jared was shy and diffident. He often left the club alone or with someone as desperate as himself, causing Mark to imagine yet another disastrous hook-up.

Tonight, just before the club closed, Mark drifted around collecting empty glasses and as ever dropped on a seat beside Jared. 'So what's doing?'

Jared smiled wryly. 'Not much ... as you can see.'

'What have I told you?' Mark said. 'Raise your sights. Choose someone you fancy and get in early. Don't wait till there's nothing left but scrag end.'

Jared looked stung. 'I don't,' he mumbled. 'Well ... not always.' He showed Mark a snap of himself with his arm around a weedy guy in thick glasses.

Mark frowned. 'Who's this?'

'That's Chris. He's nice. I met him here last week and we've been seeing each other. There could be some future in it. He's a free-lance programmer.'

'A first-rate geek, you mean. D'you go for *him*?'

'Sort of.'

'Sort of!' Mark snorted.

Jared shrugged and put the snap away. They fell silent.

'Now him,' Mark resumed, nodding at a young man in a plain black T-shirt leaning against a wall with a glass in hand. 'How d'you rate *him*?'

Jared took in the lean face and flop of blond hair, and nodded approval.

'Well, go over and speak.'

'Ah, no. I'm not in *his* league, am I? He'd brush me off.'

'Listen, mate, stop selling yourself short. It's a matter of taste. How d'you know he's not assessing his chance of getting off with *you*?'

Jared tittered and Mark walked off with a broad wink. But when he glanced back, he saw Jared trailing alone towards the exit.

'My place?' said Benjy as they locked up.

Mark smiled and nodded.

Benjy lived in a top-floor flat on Gloucester Road, a newish place, bright and spacious, with a balcony and a scatter of potted plants. Mark knew it well; it was his second home. On arrival, he and Benjy flopped on the sofa, their eyes drooping. Then they drifted into the bedroom, crawled under the duvet, and fell instantly asleep. All this was routine; talk and sex were for later.

Mark woke at ten-thirty to an empty bed. The bedroom door was open and faint strains of music came from the living room along with the aroma of coffee. He lay back and gazed at the ceiling. It was good to stop over at Benjy's, but did he want to move in? He liked having his own space, the freedom to come and go as he pleased, somewhere to bring guys back to. He was fond of Benjy, but moving in would inevitably cramp his style. On the other hand, it might be good to share with someone on a more permanent basis; this footloose life he was leading was shifting, meagre, a bit sad ...

He rose, pulled on his briefs, and drifted into the next room. Benjy, chomping into toast at the breakfast bar, turned with a smile. Mark kissed his crumb-coated lips and sat opposite. He poured a mug of black coffee and they gazed at each other.

'Phew, heavy night or what? We should give up this bar work. Try something cushier – like lion taming.'

Benjy chuckled. 'Ah, give over. You love it really. Flashing your big smile at all those lovely people.'

Mark bared his row of dazzlers. 'Flaunt whatever you have, I say.'

'So how's the shy Jared?'

'Same as ever. Still the wallflower.'

'You pep talk him every night.'

'To no avail. He showed me a snap of some guy he's seeing. A weedy little bloke with owlish eyes. God, what a waste! He underrates himself.'

'He certainly does. He's not unattractive. Quite cute, in fact. I often stop to chat to him myself.'

'Oh really?' Mark studied Benjy's face, his toast poised halfway to his lips.

'Yeah, I like him. He's simpatico. And you should stay out, Mark. He doesn't need a matchmaker. He's quite capable of making his own decisions.'

They lapsed into silence. Mark, faintly ruffled, got up and made more coffee. Then he turned and embraced Benjy from behind. This was the customary signal that they should go back to bed. Benjy glanced up at him with a smile.

Jared was absent from the club for several days. This was rare. Was he ill? Mark thought about phoning him, but recalled Benjy's disapproval of his tendency to meddle in Jared's life. Then Jared reappeared and Mark took a few minutes off to sit with him.

'Hey, where've you been? We've missed you.'

'Oh, you know.' Jared batted the question away. 'Just a bit down.'

'A bit down?'

'It's over, Mark. This thing with Chris. It'll never work. He's obsessed with chess. He challenges me every time we meet and I don't even *like* chess.'

'So nothing in common?'

'Nope. He watches fantasy films and reads sci-fi.'

'That's hardly a crime.'

'It's hardly an asset.'

They grinned.

'Hey, what did I say? Plenty of fish in the sea. So look around, raise your sights, and get in soon. Anyone you fancy?'

Jared blushed slightly. 'Well, yes, as a matter of fact.'

'Oh,' smiled Mark. 'So am I permitted to know?'

Jared hesitated. 'Actually, it's him,' he said, nodding at the bar with a bashful shrug. 'Your colleague.'

Mark looked thunderstruck. 'You mean ... Benjy?'

'Well, don't look so surprised, Mark. You told me to raise my sights.'

'Yes, but ...'

'Is he so far out of my range? I don't think so. We've spoken a bit and I've seen the way he looks at me. I reckon I'm in with a chance.'

Mark sat in silent wonder for some moments, his glazed eyes turned inward. Why was he so shaken by Jared's admission? He had no claim on Benjy. They were occasional bedmates, that was all. Didn't he often spend the night with someone else, and didn't he presume, without inquiry, that Benjy did too? All the same, it was clear to him that his feelings were aroused, that he *was* disturbed. His head buzzed with self-accusation. This was his own doing. Why had he called Chris a geek and encouraged Jared to aspire to someone better? What a meddlesome fool he was! How careless and inconsiderate! And how blind to his own affections!

'Well, you may be right,' he said, leaping up in agitation. 'Anyway, back to work. Catch you later.'

There was no time to confront his confusion for the next hour; the clamour was ceaseless. He looked around at closing time, but Jared had gone. He and Benjy washed up in silence, then turned to each other.

'My place?'

'Eh ... not tonight,' said Mark, feeling a need to ponder the situation alone. 'Morning visit from the landlord,' he quickly invented.

'Move in and we could *share* the landlord.'

'Well, well ... *there's* an offer.'

They grinned and ambled to the door.

'So Jared has reappeared,' said Benjy as they locked up. 'I spoke to him. He's broken with that guy.'

'I know,' said Mark, quelling another tremor of unease.

That night, back in his own bed, he slept fitfully, his mind fighting his tiredness. He was fond of Benjy and Benjy was fond of him, but had he failed to see *how* fond? Had he failed to look within, undervalued the person most dear to him? How would he feel if he were to lose Benjy, an outcome that was beginning to look like a possibility? Benjy was attracted to Jared, that much was clear, and the attraction was mutual. What if Jared made a try for Benjy, captured him and moved in? The thought made him twist in agitation. Not only did he bitterly regret now having encouraged Jared, he was starting to regret that he'd ever known him!

He woke very late the next morning and ate his usual breakfast of grapefruit and cereal. It was a fine day and, after a visit to the supermarket, he took a stroll in the park, glad of a chance to clear his cluttered head. He found an empty bench and sat in sunlight pondering his blunders and blindness, so entirely self-absorbed that he failed to notice the approach of someone who sat down beside him. He turned with a gasp of surprise.
'Benjy.'
'Don't be alarmed, I'm not stalking you.'
'Ah, what a shame.'
They chuckled.
'Am I intruding? You look sunk in thought.'
'I am.' Mark paused and scratched his nose. 'Benjy, I'm really glad to see you because ... well ... the truth is, I need to talk to you.'
'No call for an announcement.'
'Don't joke, Benjy, please. This is important.'
'Oh, sorry.'
'Look, the fact is, you're right. You've been right all along. I should stay out of Jared's life. I slammed his boyfriend and encouraged him to go better. And now ...'
'And now?'
Mark hesitated, unsure how to say what he'd never attempted. He was slow to reveal his heart, useless at sentiment ...
'Benjy,' he fished up at last, 'you remember you once asked me to move in?'
'Of course.' Benjy cocked an eyebrow. 'And actually, more than once.'
'Yes, well,' Mark swallowed hard, 'why haven't you asked recently?'

'I dropped a hint only last night, but you didn't take me up. You never take me up. I assume you have your reasons, though you never state them. For some time now I've supposed you were attached to Jared. I mean, you're always talking to him.'

Mark stared. 'Jared?' he gasped, frantically scratching the back of his neck. 'Jared?' He plucked at his ear. 'Oh no, you've completely misunderstood. I've never had *that* kind of interest in Jared.' He buried his face in his hands, then reappeared. 'Actually, I thought ... since *you're* always talking to him ...'

Benjy's eyes widened and he sat back in disbelief.

'If *I* had that kind of interest in Jared,' he said, 'why would I keep dropping hints to you?'

They gazed at each other, broke into splutters, and when the spluttering died, sat staring ahead like a couple of mystics having a vision.

'Funny old life,' quipped Mark.

'It *is*,' grinned Benjy.

They recovered over coffee and croissants at the park pavilion, where Mark talked too much, gushing with confession and spraying flakes of pastry.

'I've been a bloody fool, Benjy. Short-sighted, false to myself, and a bad friend to you and Jared.'

Benjy fixed him with a roguish grin. 'Oh well, don't beat yourself up, but now that we've established your idiocy, is it time to roll ourselves into some kind of statement?'

The following Sunday afternoon a taxi drew up outside Benjy's flat. The cabby unloaded the boot and received a generous tip. Mark stood on the step amid the clutter – holdall, suitcase, guitar, caged parrot, box of books – and rang the top bell.

'Hi,' came a gurgle through the intercom.

'Benjy, it's me. Can you lend a hand?'

'Of course.'

Mark waited, and shortly the door was flung wide.

'Welcome, flatmate!' Then, with wrinkled brow, 'Oh God, I hope that's all.'

'Just the essentials.'

They celebrated that night with a meal at Angelo's, the Italian place up the road. They went for lasagna, finished with sorbetto, and shared a bottle of Chianti.

'Salute.'

They raised their glasses.

'To Jared,' Mark proposed. 'The catalyst.'

'The what?'

'Oh, never mind.'

'Have you spoken to him since the break up?'

'Yes, I urged him to try again. To look at Chris with new eyes. I said there are worse addictions than chess.'

'Excellent. I approve.'

They skipped coffee, paid up, and sauntered woozily back to the flat, their thoughts turning to their new situation.

'Mark,' said Benjy. 'No offence, but the parrot. Is it always that noisy, and how do you avoid getting your heels pecked?'

John Grendel

The Boy Who Could Not See Himself

Once upon a time there was a messenger boy, the son of the farmer at a farmhouse near a river, near a hill, near a castle, the castle that ruled the shire. The boy had two brothers and four sisters. He worked as a messenger for the Lord. His name was Holkan. Everyone in the shire was impressed by his agility. Many an evening he could be seen galloping over the roads, through the fields on his dark horse, delivering everyone's messages, as well as instructions from the Lord.

Holkan's tragedy had started shortly after he could speak. When his oldest sister pointed a mirror towards him, Holkan only saw the room, with a vague blotch where his face should have been.

'You're mocking me,' his sister said, 'I can see you in the mirror.'

Yet whatever Holkan tried, he could not see himself. He looked into any mirror he encountered, he had leant forward over a pond, he had looked deeply into the eyes of his youngest brother, he had tried a piece of glass, a gem, the table silver, yet never did he catch a glimpse of himself.

His parents had sent for the doctor, then asked the witch in the forest, to no avail. At their wit's end, they paid an artist to sketch Holkan's face, but Holkan only saw an unintelligible jumble of lines. His father would not give up. He hired a wandering poet to describe Holkan's likeness, yet the words sounded like music to Holkan without anything that made him see himself. Pressing Holkan's face in a plaster mould had the same effect. Holkan only saw a crescendo of surfaces, but nothing that he could make sense of.

Eventually his parents gave up. Holkan became known as the boy who could not see himself. He got used to his brothers and sisters making fun of him. While they played games, Holkan was sweeping the floor, doing the dishes, feeding the cow, the pigs and the chicken, tending to the land, and preparing meals. His mother did nothing else but cry, his father nothing else but work. His father, convinced that Holkan needed a good fright to regain the sight of himself, subjected him to jokes such as pulling Holkan's chair away when he was about to sit down, or putting a rat down his collar.

When Holkan had been seventeen for a month and a day, he sped through a dense forest, past the borders of the shire, to deliver a message to another Lord in another castle. At midday he descended from his horse and sat down to eat on a fallen tree trunk.

Suddenly the leaves rustled. An old lady stepped out from under the trees.

'Who are you?' Holkan asked.

'Never mind. I know who you are, Holkan,' the lady said. 'I have known you since you were a baby.'

'Then you must know about my reflection,' said Holkan.

'I do,' said the lady. 'Do you want it back?'

'Yes,' said Holkan, 'I want it back, if I've ever had it.'

'If you'd like to regain it, you've got to fulfil three assignments for me.'

'Here,' she said, as she held up a golden ring with a white emerald. 'After you've delivered your message, ride to the blue pond in the forest between the shires, and throw this ring into the water. Linger a while, until you find something that I need, bring it back to me and I'll give you the three assignments.'

'The pond where they say the elves live?'

'Yes, that's the pond.'

Holkan got on his horse. After delivering his message in the other shire, he rode deep inside the forest. The path became narrower and narrower, until he had to duck to evade the branches.

When he reached the pond, he got off his horse and threw the ring in the water.

He stood there looking at the ensuing ripples for several minutes. He was about to go back when suddenly the water began twisting and turning. A greenish mass rose up amidst jets of water.

When the fountains had subsided, Holkan looked into the eyes of a fierce dragon, carrying the ring on his nose. Holkan moved backwards. The big green eyes of the dragon stared at him.

'Who is it that dares to call me?' the dragon asked in a deep voice.

'An old lady from the forest who sometimes sells us herbs,' said Holkan.

'Jalinda,' boomed the dragon. 'Why did she ask you to wake me?'

Holkan explained that he could not see himself.

'You wouldn't believe me, but some people are glad they can't see themselves.' The dragon smiled and lowered its head. 'Look into my eyes.'

Holkan did, but he only saw a blotch in the reflection where his face should have been.

The dragon raised its head and coughed formally, smoke coming out of his nostrils. He began to declaim: 'For now we grasp life only vaguely and in riddles. Now we see through a glass, darkly; through a mirror, obscurely. But then we shall be face to face with existence. Now we know only in part, but then shall we know even as also we are known by the universe.' The dragon coughed again and a whiff of smoke blew in Holkan's face. 'Crystal clear,' the dragon concluded. 'So it is written.'

Holkan wondered what it was all about, but he had learned not to start philosophising with clients, let alone with a dragon. He waved away the smoke. 'Jalinda told me I'd find something here that she needed.'

The dragon swam closer and pushed his nose forward. Holkan took the ring and put it on a rope around his neck.

'Wait a minute,' said the dragon, flames sputtering. 'There's one more thing.' His head disappeared under water.

When he resurfaced his jaws held what looked like a painting, covered in seaweed. He swam towards Holkan and put it face-down on the bank.

'This is for Jalinda,' the dragon said. 'It needs to be properly cleaned. You must not remove the weeds, you hear me, under no circumstances.'

The dragon went under, leaving the forest eerily quiet.

Holkan took the plate, packed it on his horse, and galloped back along the track.

Just as he reached the edge of the forest he was stopped by three horsemen, swords drawn.

The biggest one slowly glanced at Holkan and then over to the board covered in seaweeds. 'Well, well, what do we have here?' he asked.

'I don't know,' said Holkan.

'I don't believe you,' the headman said. 'Looks like a painting. Show it to us.'

Holkan descended from his horse and handed over the weed-covered board.

The headman held it up. 'Clearly the frame of a painting,' he said, as his two fellowmen came closer and looked over his shoulder expectantly. He wiped away the weeds. 'It's a mirror,' he said. Suddenly his face became deep red and then purple, his eyes started bulging out, staring into infinity. The same happened to his henchmen.

Then they fell forward. The mirror landed face-down on the grass before them. The men remained motionless.

Holkan picked up the mirror. He suppressed the urge to look into it. He put the weeds back in place with the mirror facing away. Then he tied it to his horse, face inwards.

When Holkan was back at Jalinda's the old witch shook her head. 'They should've known better. They'll have become headless horsemen by now.' She smiled wryly. 'You're not the only one who can't see himself anymore.' She looked pensively at the sky. Then she pulled herself together. 'Well, let's get down to business,' she said, taking the mirror and the ring from Holkan. 'You really do want to be able to see yourself, don't you?'

'Yes, I do,' said Holkan.

'There's a chance that you may not like what you see,' said Jalinda. 'There's risk involved, and perhaps some danger as well.'

'I don't know why, but I still want it, with all of my heart,' Holkan said.

'That's the right answer,' said Jalinda. She turned the golden ring around. 'Now you're ready for the three assignments. The first is to take this mirror and climb the highest tower of the Lord's castle. Tomorrow at dawn, when the first rays of the sun touch the tower, you need to break it. Whatever or whomever else you may meet on that tower, you must shatter it, come hell or water high.'

Holkan rode back to the castle, the mirror wrapped in a blanket. That night he slept in the castle's servants' quarter. Well before dawn he went up the steps of the tower, hundreds and hundreds of them, the twilight growing as he proceeded, the mirror under his arm.

As he was standing at the top in the half-light, a large black crow landed on a battlement. His piercing eyes looked at Holkan. 'What do you have there?' it asked.

'A mirror,' said Holkan.

'Can you show it me?'

Holkan hesitated.

'Come on, show it to me,' the crow said.

'Sorry, but I can't,' said Holkan. 'If you look into it you might die.'

'Well,' said the crow, 'why don't you simply look into it yourself? I'm sure it won't kill you.'

Yet whatever the crow tried, Holkan kept the mirror in wraps.

When, finally, the first sunray shone between the battlements, Holkan tore off the blanket, held the mirror facing the sun and then let it loose for it to fall onto the stones of the tower floor on which he was standing.

As he did so, the crow whooshed in front of the mirror. For a split second it looked into it. Then the mirror shattered into pieces.

Suddenly a magnificent white swan was flying above it, seeing itself reflected a thousand and one times in the broken fragments.

'I'm a swan! I'm a swan!' cried the swan formerly known as a crow.

Holkan collected the broken pieces in the blanket, said goodbye to the swan and walked down the steps, greeting the first guard patrol on his way out.

He mounted his horse and sped back towards Jalinda. After a few minutes he noticed a shade of whiteness on his right. He looked sideways and saw the magnificent swan flapping its wings.

Back in the woods Jalinda made tea for Holkan and served fodder to the swan. Then she put a cord with her ring on it over Holkan's head and hid it under his shirt. 'Your second assignment is to go the valley between the two hill ridges in the north. You'll find a river, and near the river a village, and on the edge of the village, just before the forest begins, you'll see an old tavern. At midnight tonight it'll be packed. One person will come to you and ask what it is you are wearing around your neck. You must show the ring and ensure they look into the emerald.'

Holkan went on his way, the swan flying by his side. At midnight he stood in front of the tavern. Through the window shutters warm light and the punters' murmurings were coming at him. A painted groundhog and the letters 'Forest's End' swayed back and forth in the wind.

Holkan walked in. Village people were chatting, standing around, drinking, playing cards, throwing dice, listening to a fortune teller. Holkan waded through the crowd and ordered a beer.

Holkan chatted with a farmer, who, after a couple of minutes, strangely seemed to repeat himself. When Holkan talked to the next few locals, the same happened. He asked them about it, but before they could answer a young lady walked towards the bar and stopped in front of him. She was well-dressed and looked glamorous.

The lady introduced herself, mentioned Holkan seemed new, exchanged a few pleasantries and then asked what it was he carried on his chest.

'You want me to get it off my chest?' asked Holkan. Excitedly Holkan took the necklace out from under his shirt. The emerald radiated a quiet light.

The lady looked closely, then shuddered and drew back. She started to cough. Smoke came from her mouth and nostrils, out of her ears and from under the hem of her dress. Her whole body became covered in a cloud.

Conversations stopped.

Holkan waved away the whiff. As it receded, a woman of at least ninety years old with piercing black eyes and a broom looked angrily at Holkan.

'Stop that light,' she said.

But Holkan kept holding the ring in front of her.

Her skin started to scorch. Pushing people aside she darted out of the tavern, releasing an awful cry.

The door slammed shut behind her.

Then everyone cheered.

'Thank you,' said the oldest man, tall, with a grey beard and bald head. 'The moment you walked in we knew that you could set us free.'

The old man explained all the village's inhabitants had been entranced in the tavern, for seventeen years, every night playing their roles as punters. When a visitor walked in, they became encapsulated in the spell. Nobody knew who had cast the spell or how to break it. But now they had seen her and they were free.

Holkan started on his way back to Jalinda, accompanied by the white swan and now also the old man, who had insisted on joining them.

When she heard what had happened, Jalinda smiled. 'It's been a long-running problem. That was Trajkalla, the wicked witch of the spaces below. Something told me that only you could smoke her out – it'll be a long time before she resurfaces.'

Jalinda revealed the third and final assignment. Holkan was to travel to the outermost shire of shires and visit the castle there. 'Among all the people in the castle there's one young man,' Jalinda said, 'who, when you look him in the eyes for seventeen seconds, will make you see your own face in his pupils. Your assignment is to find him.'

And so it was that Holkan went, accompanied by the swan and the old man. They travelled for seven days and seven nights. They almost got lost, but for the swan who kept them on their path.

When they reached the castle, the guards refused entry.

Holkan started pleading, at which the guards drew their swords and apprehended all three of them.

The old man showed one of the guards his ring and said: 'Please let us through.'

The guards froze, looked at the ring and then to the man. One asked him: 'Where did you steal that ring?'

'It is mine.'

The guards summoned the commander who upon seeing the old man startled as if bitten by a snake. 'Your Majesty, is it you?' he asked.

The old man was the king of the castle. He disappeared seventeen years ago, captured by the spell of the Forest End's Inn.

'Your baby son has come of age. He's on the throne now,' the commander said. 'But he's still mourning. He lives his life entirely alone. He's slowly dying of grief, not knowing what happened to you.'

They were brought to the prince. The old man – King Narcissus turned out to be his name – hugged his son for a long time. He told him about the quest they were on to find the eyes of one particular young man.

Upon hearing Holkan's story, the crown prince insisted on joining him to visit every last fellow in the castle. Man after man found Holkan staring in their eyes for seventeen seconds, but not once did Holkan see himself.

When they reached the very last prospect, the crown prince and the swan watched expectantly. Yet again, nothing happened.

Sadly they walked over to the King, who ordered the guards to search the whole castle from top to cellar and check every nook and cranny for an unseen young man – to no avail.

Suddenly the swan shot up. It started flying clumsily through the main hall. It seemed to have gone berserk. Holkan ran after it, and soon the crown prince was helping him trying to catch it.

They closed in from two sides, ready to jump at the swan, but it shot away. Holkan fell and the prince tried to catch him. In each other's arms they fell on the floor. They had to laugh. The prince's smile caught Holkan's attention. Holkan looked into his eyes and was mesmerised.

After what seemed an eternity, but were a mere seventeen seconds, he saw a blotched figure forming on the lenses of the prince's pupils, which slowly morphed into the face of a young man he had never seen before but who somehow felt very, very familiar. Finally, he had come home.

Beauty is in the eye of the beholder, they say. Holkan was enchanted by the view. He and the prince stared into each other eyes a little more, discovering a new world.

Soon after, they became engaged and then they married. Jalinda and the swan were their witnesses. Holkan's parents, brothers and sisters were also present, wearing their Sunday bests, trying to find ways to put down Holkan's newfound happiness while not endangering their shares in his newfound wealth and royal life. Holkan took them into his heart, realising this was the only way they knew to express their love for him.

Holkan and the prince became the happiest couple in all of the shires. Holkan could see himself now in a mirror, brightly, in the water, sharply, in the reflection of an emerald ring, radiantly, in the prince's eyes, lovingly. He was now the boy, the young man, the man who could see himself – although now he knew the view, he didn't need to look anymore. For the first time in his life he realised how beautiful, how perfectly imperfect he was the way he was, and it felt great.

Holkan and the prince became King and King Consort and lived happily ever after. They raised seven sons and daughters, all of whom they employed as messengers. They became grandfathers and then great-grandfathers.

One day, when their days as young men were a faint memory, they rode together to the old forest in Holkan's birth shire, and into the old forest to the pond in which the elves lived and a dragon slept, and in front of the pond they dismounted.

Following the King's ancient family ritual, holding each other's hand, they bent over the water and looked at each other's reflection, and then they bent over a little more, and then still just a tiny bit more to get a better view, until they darted forward together, met their reflections, and were swallowed by the water – never to be seen again.

Allison Fradkin
Soar Spot

You know something?
I got sand.
That's why I came to the beach.
I heard they were running low. Heh.
Speaking of hearing things,
I wish I had some tunes.
That tribute to transformation, 'I Am Changing,'
would really hit the spot right now.
Well, not the *sore* spot.

But I don't mind listening to the sound of my own voice.
I never really noticed it before, but it's ... present.
Pleasant. Much more mellifluous
than something off of your Greatest Hits album,
which includes such scintillating singles as
'Diss You Much,'
'Proud Marry in Haste, Repent at Leisure,'
and the pièce de *no* résistance,
'You Can't Stop the Beatdown.'

Except I can. I did.
I stopped the beatdown.
You knew my motto:
Batterer up, three strikes *I'm* out.
You'll never have the pleasure of seeing me cry anymore.
Or the pain of seeing me smile.
In fact, you won't see me any kind of way, ever again.

See, you thought our song went:
I'm tellin' you from the start
I can't be torn apart from my guy.
But see, that is unapologetically uninspiring.

So on my album, the song goes:
I'm tellin' you from the start
I can't be torn apart by my guy.

I know the first time leaving is the hardest –
first is the worst and all that –
but once you go black-and-blue,
you – *I* – never go back.
So you might think that this is one of those
'If at first you don't succeed,
try, try again' initiatives,
that they call it escapism because
it's nothing but a fantasy.
But I know something you don't:
I can take the *y* off 'emergency'
and put an *e* there instead,
and then I've earned
a resurgence of emergence.

Words to live by.
Which is why I'm going to beat the odds
my first time out.
Well, maybe not *beat* 'em,
but *overcome* just sounds so
underwhelming.
I got guts for days.
Weeks, months, and beyond.

I can't take all the credit for my courage though.
Got to give gratitude to Sofia
– from *The Color Purple*,
not *The Golden Girls*.
Her song 'Hell No,'
about refusing
to be cruising
for a bruising,

is what got me to make tracks in the first place.
A person hears something often enough,
she starts to believe it.
She starts to repeat it. Out loud.
I'd croon, you'd cringe – and criticize:
I know why the caged bird sings.
She's a Maya Ange-loser.
Come on now, don't pout.
You know I'm only teasing,
and still I get a rise out of you.

And what did I ever get out of you?
Nothing but another bouquet of your
sorry-not-sorry-ass flowers,
the kind perfect for playing
that time-honored game of
He Shoves Me, He Shoves Me Not.
That's right – I'm playing games *without* you,
and guess what?
I can identify 'em.
None of that baseless accusation B.S.
What games was I ever playing with you, huh?
Trouble?
Aggravation?
Pac-Man?

Well, since you neglected to specify,
I picked my own game to play:
Pack-Your-Bags-and-Leave-That-Man,
where every woman's a winner.
Now that's something to sing about:
He's got no power
No power no more
Over me.
Formerly sung by The Exciters,
presently sung by The Exiters.

When did I get to be so
infuriatingly inspirational?

Must be when I realized that
I am the wind beneath my
uncaged wings, that
underneath the coat of war paint
I applied to the bruises
was a brave face
just waiting to be put on.

Someday, even when those bruises
are gone but not forgotten,
they'll still be souvenirs of survival,
and they'll still be a sore spot.

But now that I'm no longer under
your skin, your thumb, or your spell,
I can spell that word a little differently:
s-o-a-r.

Hell yes.

Challah If You Queer Me

When you're a teenager – or, more maturely, a young adult – you are completely at the Mertzy of the meshugenahs that are your mishpocheh. Yeah, I know – I've got some 'splainin' to do. On the sunny side, I've got minimal complainin' to do. At least in regards to my coming out, which happened the gay – uh, day – of the first night of my sixteenth Hanukkah.

So, picture a nostalgic nuclear family, not unlike the kind you'd find on a black-and-white boob tube. 'Which episode should we enjoy this evening?' Dad queries, perusing a pile of VHS tapes. "Job Switching"? "Lucy Does a TV Commercial"? "Lucy and Ethel Buy the Same Dress"?'

'How about "Gaycation from Marriage"?' I suggest, my stomach twisting like a shofar.

Mom schmears cream cheese on a Tam Tam, as if daring me to make like a matzo and crack. 'Is that the one,' she asks, noshing on the hexagon, 'where the gals are quarrelling with the guys and Lucy asks Ethel if she wishes there were something else to marry besides men and Ethel answers 'F yes!' or something a little more fifties-friendly?'

'No, that's the one where Lucy and Ethel take a hiatus from their husbands and move in with each other,' Dad mansplains in his customary chivalrous manner. 'Then one night, they get all gussied up and pay a visit to their spouses, and Lucy says she hopes Ricky and Fred have as gay an evening as she and Ethel are planning on having and then ... Wait.' As Dad's synopsis stops, his eyes grow wider than yarmulkes.

The size of Mom's eyes matches macaroons – suspiciously smaller.

There's an explosion of silence, unheard of in a Jewish household.

Suddenly, I feel like the filling in a blueberry blintz: ready to come out at the slightest provocation.

'Mom, Dad,' I address my absurdly attentive audience, 'I have some seriously super news to share: I'm gay.'

Now I hope and wait – and worry that I've just committed a Sapph-faux pas.

How will my family react to my declaration of lesbi-independence?

Will they regard me like schmutz on a schmatte?

Kiss my keppie like everything's kosher?

Or offer some verkakte-mamie advice like: 'Don't be daffy, Allie, at least date a non-goy boy before you make it official'?

While Mom and Dad – or, more formally, Judy and Steve – turn their wheels like Tevye's milk cart, I start schvitzing like an ice cold bottle of Dr Brown's cream soda. Maybe they'll do a bottle dance in honour of the unexpected uncapping of my secret?

And then … Judy winks at Steve, and it becomes queer – uh, clear – that the abba who knows best has been looking to the ima who knows better for approval.

I should've known Mom knows.

In our house, we don't practice Judaism.

We practice Judyism.

'Better late than straight,' the aforementioned mensch guffaws.

'Take me to the WC – the water closet being the only acceptable kind – and call me relieved!' Dad cavorts, his dance a maniacal mishmash of the Horah and the Hokey Pokey.

'Now we don't have to fret about you knocking boots and getting knocked up,' Mom marvels, twirling with equivalent merriment.

'And I don't have to compete with another fellow for your attention,' Dad discovers. 'I have the privilege of being the only man in my little girl's life.'

I must be hearing things – which is good, I guess, since I'm hard-of-hearing – but my parents don't really think that my similarities to Sappho are boffo, do they? I mean, it's not like I anticipated yelling, but I definitely did not foresee this degree of glee and kvelling.

'The point is, Allie,' Judy says, and I brace myself, because the woman makes more points than a Star of David, 'we have bupkis to worry about.'

Dad's face contorts as if he's just imbibed his first spoonful of Vitameatavegamin. 'Nothing at all?' he kvetches.

'Don't worry – we'll think of something,' Mom pledges, and Dad perks up pronto.

But then, much to my chagrin – though thank heaven for hearing impairment – they begin to sing a vibrant, validating, verbose version of the *I Love Lucy* theme song. 'I love lezzie and she loves me / Queer as happy as two can be / And chaim is heaven, you see / 'Cause I love lezzie / Yes, I love lezzie / And lezzie loves me!'

'Oh, honey,' Mom coos, until something shoos the smile off her face. 'Stand up straight, my little mezuzah,' she demands. 'The one and only thing we expect to be straight about you is your posture.' I sigh but comply, her cue to reply with a harrumph of triumph. 'Oh, honey, you're home.'

As my parents embrace me, squashing me like the childhood of a girl at her Bat Mitzvah, I realize that the bloom isn't off all the heteros. In fact, just because one's family is nuclear, doesn't mean they'll *go* nuclear at the news that there's a lavender menace in their midst.

'You know,' Dad muses, 'we should have our own family-friendly TV show: *The Lucy-Lezzie Comedy Hour*.'

'I can see the episodes now!' Mom enthuses. ' "Wonder of Wonder, Queer-acle of Queer-acles," "Lucy and Ethel Put the Lez in Klezmer," and the Hanukkah special to end all Hanukkah specials ... "The Labia Menorah"!'

And with that, I am out.

Hongwei Bao
Long-Term Relationship

'What are the secrets to a long-term relationship?'

The speaker is in his late fifties, dressed in a grey suit with a dark blue tie, looking mature but still handsome. He picks up a perfect-bound paperback from the neatly stacked pile in front of him. On the cover, two big, red hearts sit next to each other with a significant overlap. Below the hearts are some big words printed in a flashy golden colour: *Long-Term Relationship for Couples*. The name David Gregory underneath. 'There are four Cs', David Gregory opens the book and reads out from the content page: 'Communication, connection, commitment ...'

I yawn. I look around. The room is full, which is surprising given it's a sunny Saturday afternoon, I seem to be the only one who's not paying attention. Everyone else has their ears erect like small antennas trying to catch every piece of information transmitted through the air current. The woman sitting next to me is oversized and occupies a portion of my leg room. She's even jotting down notes in her yellow Moleskine notebook. I take out the mobile phone from the pocket of my jeans. I swipe open an app, and then quickly turn off the volume. Within a few seconds, David Gregory's voice floats in the air, like the quiet humming of the traffic outside. I'm chatting with a middle-aged guy named John on Grindr. His profile is next to mine on the app.

'Hey, what's up?'
'Chilling. And you?'
'Bored to death.'
'Fancy meeting up? I'm in the Vic.'

The Vic is only a few doors away from the bookshop. A spontaneous afternoon date at a pub sounds like a much more appealing idea than sitting through a tedious talk.

Slowly, I pick up my Adidas body bag from the floor, lean aside to the woman, and gesture to the aisle. I squeeze out an apologetic smile as she reluctantly puts down her notebook and moves her body aside. I mumble a quiet 'sorry' as my legs brush hers. I manage to put on a straight face while I walk towards the door. I can feel the burning stare from the audience and from David Gregory behind my back. Who cares? Write a better book!

All the trouble is worthwhile. Looking slightly older than his picture and profile age, John is reasonably attractive. He says he's from London, and it's his first time in town. He takes an interest in my life as I tell him that I recently broke up with my ex because Joe didn't want a long-term relationship – 'What's a relationship if two people aren't committed to each other?' I asked rhetorically as he was packing his bag. 'People change, situations change, and relationships change – this is a fact. Why can't you just accept it?' With these words, he had left the flat.

John is a sympathetic listener. He nods frequently, his grey eyes filled with warm empathy. I'm slightly surprised by my own candidness in front of a stranger I only met half an hour ago, but having such an attentive listener gives me unprecedented courage and confidence. To be honest, I hadn't got a proper chance to process the trauma of a break-up until this moment. The confession feels cathartic. I desperately need it.

Before it's my turn to ask about his life, John takes a quick glance at his watch. 'I've got to go,' he says. 'Perhaps we could meet up later this evening for some fun, at your place?'

We exchange our phone numbers. In front of the bookshop, David Gregory is pacing back and forth in slight agitation. He stares at me when he sees John and me waving goodbye. John walks up to David Gregory, gives him a big hug: 'Darling, how did the talk go?'

Blind Date

'I've got to go,' I take a glance at my watch: 'It's getting late.'

'Oh, it's just a quarter past ten,' Paul says. 'Do you have to get up early tomorrow morning?'

'No, I work from home,' I reply. 'I'm a games developer. I create video games.'

'Fascinating,' he raises his eyebrows. 'You don't look that nerdy.'

I smile in embarrassment, trying to figure out whether this is meant as a compliment. I decide it is.

'So I imagine your place must be full of interesting stuff.' He waves his arms in the air to indicate an exaggerated size.

'Some, not much,' I chuckle, 'and certainly not that big. You were describing an antique computer from decades ago. Today's computers tend to look pretty slim.'

'Tell me,' he pushes his beer glass aside. 'What interesting stuff have you got at home?'

'I've got a high-powered computer,' I answer, unsure what he was alluding to.

'Not that kind of thing,' he says with a flourish, 'the gay stuff.'

'I don't do drugs,' I shrug my shoulders. 'I've got some poppers in the fridge.'

'Interesting,' he raises his eyebrows again. 'Do you use them often?'

'Sometimes, not very often.' I answer quickly, deliberately lowering my voice, conscious that I'm in a pub, surrounded by strangers.

'What are you into?' he looks at me, seemingly oblivious of the crowd.

'Ahhh,' I blush, feeling the conversation is heading towards an unknown territory. Earlier we had a chat on Recon and decided to meet up here. 'I'm into both vanilla and kinky. Some BDSM stuff, you know.'

'I'm intrigued,' a twinkle in his eyes. 'What toys do you play with?'

'Some handcuffs and ankle cuffs, made of leather.'

'Ummm. Nice. I can feel them,' he lifts his wrists and shakes them in the air, as if he could feel the weight. 'I can't escape. What shall I do now?'

'You can do nothing,' I follow his tone and get into the scene. The background noise seems distant and unreal. 'You'll follow my instructions, whatever I ask you to do.'

I can visualise him stripped naked, face down and blindfolded, helplessly hogtied on the bed.

'I'll flog your bottom with a cane, slowly and steadily, then work things up.'

'Ouch.' His body twitches a bit, a thin layer of sweat glistens on his face. 'Does it hurt?'

'A bit,' I say. 'Not too much. You'll love it.'

'Ummm ...'

I think of something: 'What's your threshold?'

'I'd say ... medium.' A slight hesitation. 'I've only done this a couple times before.'

'How did you like it?'

'I liked it. Great fun,' he said. 'It was ... exciting, very liberating too.' He quickly adds: 'I'm trying things at the moment, still need to figure out my sexuality.'

'That's OK.' I pause for a few seconds. He's my type and seems adventurous enough. I decide to take my chance.

'Would you like to have some fun tonight, at my place?' I ask.

Paul seems slightly taken aback by my words. His facial expressions freeze. A few seconds of silence feels like hours. Then he relaxes his lips. A grin appears on his face. He looks me in the eye and nods: 'Why not?'

I wrap my arms around his shoulders and give him a firm hug. I can feel his warm breath and thumping heart. 'Trust me. You'll be fine. We'll have a great time.'

Blue

That afternoon I browse Grindr out of boredom, I'm drawn to your profile. You are not particularly good-looking but there's something about you that catches my eye. You remind me of someone, perhaps a friend. I send you a message: 'Nice shirt!' I should have said: 'I love your blue eyes.'

We meet at Paddington Station on a Sunday afternoon. It's an autumn day. The sky is grey, and the trees are all yellow and brown. The station is full of people. A young couple is taking pictures in front of the bronze statue of a bear. Perhaps they are also new to this country. As an international student studying art at a London university, I've just embarked on the difficult journey of living in a foreign country. Everything feels new. The English weather is predictably wet and cold. People are constantly busy and impatient. I can't even understand my professor's accent completely. I hadn't expected living abroad to be such a lonely experience.

It hasn't taken you long to find me in front of a newsagent. I'm carrying a rainbow-coloured bag. I bought it from one of the shops in Soho, a sex shop perhaps, with lots of eye-opening toys on display. Soho is next to Chinatown, a place that feels both familiar and strange to me. It looks Chinese enough but is not the China I'm familiar with – its language, its food.

We sit down in a café, next to a window. My rainbow bag attracts a few random looks from passers-by. It's my first time to carry the bag around in public. I feel exposed. You are talkative. I'm fascinated by your profession as a film-maker. How do you make films? What kind of films do you make? You say you are doing it freelance and are constantly looking for new projects. How can anyone make a living like that? I wonder but am too polite to ask.

You are curious about my life as a gay man from China. I tell you about the booming gay scene in Chinese cities: the bars, the clubs, the parties, the underground queer film festival, and the unsuccessful pride event where the organisers got into trouble with the police. You laugh. I notice you have a nice smile. That makes me feel more relaxed. We discover a shared interest in films: Fassbinder, Warhol, Almodóvar. ... Despite linguistic and cultural differences, there's still a shared vocabulary – call it a queer cultural heritage if you like – between the two of us.

You want to show me your DVD collection, so we take a bus to your flat, a small bedsit located in South London. You put Derek Jarman's *Blue* in the DVD player. The shimmering blue light immediately fills up the room. It's a strange film; not much is going on: the screen is deep blue; a baritone voice talks hypnotically in the background. But that does not matter. Bathed in blue, we kiss and then lie in our naked existence. The heat of our bodies warms up the cold air in the room.

We kiss each other goodbye later that evening. I rush to the tube station to catch the train back to my dorm. In front of the ticket barrier, I search all my pockets for the blue Oyster card. A faint light flashes on my phone. It was lovely to meet you, you message. 'Shall we meet again?

Suddenly, London doesn't feel alien anymore.

Elizabeth (Beth) Lister
My Life on Shifting Sands

I was born in 1934, Elizabeth Janet, to be known as Beth, at Troutbeck Bridge in the Westmorland that is no more.

Until I was six we lived near Sandside, on the River Kent Estuary, and the sands were dangerous: the wave of the tidal bore carves deep channels.

Toujours cette anxiété, cette sensibilité.

1941 – Wellbeing

My mother was back from six weeks in hospital with a new baby sister. We had moved and were living in the railway-station house at Arkholme, on the Carnforth-Leeds line, no electricity or hot water. How little I understood of my mother's hard life.

There was sunshine. A farmer's wife liked me to visit her and she gave us 'beestings' milk from the cows for rich milk-puddings. We gathered mushrooms in the early mornings. Dad grew leeks. There were cowslips and primroses, and a brook in a meadow.

The woman teacher liked my seven-year-old self. We sang, *Golden slumbers kiss your eyes,* I knit a doll for my baby sister, I learnt copperplate writing with pen-and-ink, and how to do sums in pounds shillings and pence.

1942 – The Hurt

My dad got a better job, two stations, and rented a house in the village of Glazebury on the edge of The Moss, flat fields, and visible red-brick cotton-spinning factories in the distant town of Leigh, Lancashire.

Wartime. Two uncertificated women teachers, and a male headmaster. Back to using pencil, doing sums in Hundreds, Tens and Units and printing.

I wasn't liked. I spoke RSP (Received Standard Pronunciation) and not with a Lancashire accent.

In Junior Two, fun with peeping at privates ended when a note was found by the cleaners; 'Meet me on the rec for a fuck, Beth,' and I hadn't written it.

The headmaster divided his class between the two condemnatory women teachers, took me into his empty classroom, would not believe my pleading that I hadn't written the note and said, 'Now show me what you showed the boys.'

I have read that the sexual-predator recognises the vulnerability of his victims and this was so with my Junior School Headmaster. He isolated me, shamed me and I experienced 'being sent to Coventry' – accused, shamed, defeated by malevolence, and having to keep a secret from my parents who would have chastised me.

1947 – The Hurt Continues
Children went for holidays to their relations and had to behave and be helpful; so it was at holiday time in Windermere, where I stayed with my aunts, where my grandfather was confined to an attic bed with his painful rheumatism ... like a spider waiting for his young prey as she went upstairs to bed.

I ran up and down the stairs for my aunts, with his meals and medicines.

My bed was in a room on the same floor. At bedtime he got out of bed and asked for a cuddle. He wrapped his arms round me ... I tried to sneak up to bed on other nights, but he always heard me, and the cuddling went on.

Would my aunts have believed me?

1955 – A Religious Shift
Alsager Teacher-training College, Cheshire.

Four of us stayed to talk after most students had gone to their rooms. Bill said, 'You have to ask Jesus into your heart.' Dorothy and Hilary were nodding in agreement. Bedtime.

It didn't occur to me to doubt what Bill had said. What was there to lose when one felt a failure, had backed out of the English Honours' Course at Leeds University, after passing the first-year exams, and continued to hide behind a wall of seeming confidence and capability? I knelt by my bed and closed my eyes. I never knelt to pray by my bed!

'Jesus, will you come and live in my heart?'

A glorious shining light filled my being. and all felt well.

'You never asked me about that night,' I said to Bill.

'I didn't need to,' he said. 'I saw.'

In 1958 I met Thomas Anthony Lister, Tony, when I joined the staff of a new school in Oldham. *Fool, absolute ignorant young fool that I was.* He had a failed marriage of short duration and was waiting for a divorce. My parents were horrified and sad.

Lovers, in 1959, I agreed to share his flat. I agreed to everything that he decided ... which began an absolute agony of guilt and an effort to keep the secret from the school authorities and my friends on the staff. It was beyond my strength; I needed the doctor and tranquillisers.

We married.

Tony was appointed to an English Lecturer job at Alsager College, and where there were attractive women on the teaching staff. *If one was to examine pain I wonder, where on the scale of 1-10 would the agony of unfaithfulness be placed?*

1961

I taught English, Art and Drama at Brierley Street Girls' Secondary School in Crewe.

1967, age 33

I learnt to drive!
Freedom!

1971

Two children, one diabetic sheepdog, resident mother-in-law and my husband's two known love-affairs later ... I said to Tony, *'Please leave me'*, and began life as a single-mother with my six-year-old and two-and-a-half-year-old daughters. I re-trained to teach Primary School children. *Will anyone wonder what happened to the resident mother-in-law? In 1971 (I think) she jumped from the upstairs window to kill herself and died in hospital the very next day!*

1972. Divorce, age 38

The girls and I lived positive, happy years, and loved our holidays in our caravan next to Granny and Grandad's van, at Towyn Abergele, and our Youth Hostelling. Ventures ... me never without the Librium capsules.

1984, age 50

A room, with dark-brown lino on the floor, the Counsellor at MIND in Stoke-on-Trent was helping me.

I lay on my back on the floor, washed up, hopeless, with my head on a cushion. Counsellor John sat without speaking, with his hand resting on my stomach chakra.

'Nobody loves me,' I said, and the tears ran down the side of my face and wet the cushion.

It was quiet in the room and I thought, *'That's not true. My family and my friends love me.'* It's me that doesn't love me!

My body appeared to be covered with a net of shimmering gold.

1985

That was the new beginning, and the me that was learning to be me realised that I am bi-sexual.

I took myself to a gay club in Hanley, Stoke-on-Trent, the 141 Club, met some friends and danced with Shirley who was a nurse.

I moved in with Shirley, into her very old, rented cottage and sold my house. We adjusted.

1987

I had a breakdown and was retired.

Shirley retired from nursing.

We were in touch with our children. Shirley had two sons. Our children worked at different jobs and eventually found partners.

I joined a women's writers' group where we laughed a lot. I wrote and acted my play *IMAGO* at gay clubs, the Pankhurst Centre, and a Green Room theatre in Manchester.

I painted pictures in acrylic and exhibited them.

By 1996 I needed too much time to follow my creative pursuits to be a loving partner and left Shirley to live on my own. We stayed best friends and learnt to play folk-music together – me the piano-accordion and Shirley the drum. We played for the Stoke-on-Trent Molly Dancers.

In 2000 I disturbed the peace by having a love affair with a man, and decided to get away from Stoke to where my younger daughter had moved: Berwick upon Tweed.

My grandson was born, and I could be of help in his early days.

I played my accordion in the Northumbrian Folk Competitions, learnt to play the concertina, and wrote a winning song!

2002

I moved back to live in Stoke on Trent.

2004, age 70

'Did you know you are a writer?' Lilian Mohin, founder of Onlywomen Press, asked. She had phoned to say she wouldn't accept the first manuscript I'd attempted.

No, I didn't, but the age of seventy was a good time to start.

'Did you know about GAW?' a gay friend asked.

No, I didn't, but there were good friends to be met there and I'm still a member. I enjoy travelling to London to GAW meetings and reading at special events.

I wrote poems and articles and five lesbian novels (published by Paradise Press).

2018, age 84

I move to live in a downstairs flat in Chirnside in the Scottish Borders, near my younger daughter: she works with teenagers with special needs. My grown-up grandson lives and works nearby. My elder daughter moved to the area. She is a nurse.

I'm still a member of GAW but now that I live in Scotland and am old ... I can't get to the meetings I so enjoyed.

2025, age 90

No more driving ... a smart blue electric-scooter to get up the hill that is Chirnside.

I knit, garden and write ... morning emails and weekly letters to Shirley who had a stroke and is in a nursing home, daily emails to GAW member Kathryn. I keep in touch with friends and am a member of the local Church of Scotland. I enjoy learning ... the Spanish language, Anglo-Saxon language and life, about the world from travel and history documentaries, Wikipedia and books: for relaxation, I enjoy watching a good film and nice little murder series where each death is solved in an hour's episode.

I haven't too many years left to live and am making the best of them.

I have enjoyed living in different houses, a bungalow, and flats. I am now in a flat but am not promising to stay here.

My life equals the effect of shifting sands.

The next move will shift me out of this life!

The Authors

Author Biographies

TALIM ARAB is the author of *Sexual Mathematics*. Born in London and raised in Australia, he is a Fellow of the Royal Society of Arts and a passionate lover of pianos, ballet, opera, and fine coffee.

HONGWEI BAO is a queer Chinese writer, translator and academic based in Nottingham. He is the author of *Queering the Asian Diaspora* (nonfiction), *The Passion of the Rabbit God* (poetry), *Dream of the Orchid Pavillion* (poetry) and *Self-Portrait as a Banana* (poetry). His flash fiction 'A Postcard from Berlin' was a runner-up for the Plaza Prizes 2023.

CRAIG BINCH is a 45-year-old nurse by profession. He joined GAW's flash fiction writing workshops in 2024 and enjoyed the experience. He says, 'Exploring Flash gave me the opportunity to flex my creative writing skills and challenge myself in different ways. It has been a springboard, and I won't stop.'

CJ BOWMAN is an Irish writer who lives and works in London. He holds a Masters-of-Arts in Creative Writing. His short story 'Thump Thump' was shortlisted for the Bridport Prize 2024.
    Find him on instagram @conor.bowman

LES BROOKES lives in Cambridge UK. He writes poetry and fiction, and his work has appeared on webzines and in anthologies published by Cambridge Writers and Paradise Press. He is the author of *Gay Male Fiction Since Stonewall* (Routledge) and blogs at www.lesbrookes.com.

JENNY BULL works as a gardener and their writing practice explores being a parent, LGBTQIA themes, and reflections from the garden. They studied Fashion Design at Manchester Metropolitan University, cycled to India from the UK and survived growing up during the Section 28 era. These poems surfaced during a pivotal personal moment in mid-life and are their first poetry submissions.

ROSS BURGESS lives in Scotland with his husband, Peter. Burman. An item in their 20s, they never quite lost touch, and came together again in their 70s. They now share an elegant Edinburgh flat, a 17th-century house in Fife, and an enthusiasm for churches and ancient buildings. Ross, retired from IT, concentrates on writing, editing for the Falkland Society, and designing/typesetting GAW publications.
Website: www.peterandross.uk

C. J. CASS-HORNE, based in London, has written a poetry collection *Dandelion Tea* and an acclaimed short story anthology *Tulip Tears and Other Short Stories*. With years of writing experience under his belt, he is now preparing a memoir that promises to share an engaging narrative about his family.

KEVIN CROWE has had fiction, non-fiction, book reviews and poetry published in many outlets and is the author of the short story collection *No Home in This World* (Fly-on-the-wall press) and former editor of the Highlands LGBT+ magazine *UnDividingLines*. He has regularly read his work in public and has worked with musicians and visual artists.

STEPHANIE DICKINSON trained as a primary school teacher in her thirties, which took all her time and energy! Retirement brought the opportunity to develop a range of diverse interests, focused on writing: poems, short stories, also co-editing two anthologies: *We Want to Tell you How...*, poetry and prose celebrating women's loves, lives and landmarks, and *Flash Dances*, flash fiction.

JOHN DIXON has published two volumes of short stories *The Carrier Bag* and *Whispering Campaigns*, and two poetry collections – *Seeking, Finding, Losing* and *Fancy That*. In preparation he has a novel, *Push Harder, Mummy, I Want to Come Out*, and a selection of diary entries.

JEFFREY DOORN, born New Jersey, now lives in South London with his civil partner. Work published in *Gawp* and *Gaze, Queer Haunts, People Your Mother Warned You About, The Best of Gazebo* and local publications. Edited *Lost Places*. Co-edited *A Boxful of Ideas, Slivers of Silver, Oysters and Pearls* and *Coming Clean*.

ELEANOR (NOR) DOW is a doctor living in Glasgow. They write songs, poems and short stories, but rarely release them to the wild. They found out about the Gay Authors Workshop through GLADD, the UK association of LGBTQ+ doctors and dentists, and hope to contribute more pieces in the future.

IAN EVERTON was a pioneer. He came out at school aged 14. In 1971 he founded Sheffield Campaign for Homosexual Equality. Gay Men's Press published his novel, *Alienation* in 1982. In 2022 he married Syd, his partner of 50 years. Ian died in 2024, having fought failing health and social workers with equal ferocity. He is greatly missed.

JOHN FAIRLAMB Harare-born and a devoted Christian, John found his faith challenged when he realized he was gay. Resolving this internal conflict, he now lives contentedly with his partner in Walthamstow, where he enjoys his profession as a gardener.

DAVID FLYBURY: born Suffolk 1963, moved London 1984, 1997 met hubby, married 2021; now occupied by the normalities of domestic tranquillity, plus internet. Novels, *Six Miles to Whatawhata, The Dalliance,* and short-stories, *Fragmentarium,* deal with growing up, coming-out, relationships, death, travel, Art, mainly ... oh, and sex.

ALLISON FRADKIN has a gay old time creating poetry, prose, and plays that (sur)pass the Bechdel Test. She has contributed to *The MockingOwl Roost, Eggplant Emoji, The Queer Gaze, Vita & the Woolf, Snowflake Magazine,* and *Gnashing Teeth;* collections *Frozen Women/Flowing Thoughts* and *Sapphic Eclectic.*

JOHN GRENDEL writes short stories and other short fiction with a magical realist touch. *The Boy Who Could Not See Himself* is his first foray into fairy tales.

EMILY HAY is a lifetime south-east Londoner, a queer parent, insider-outsider and urban romantic. Her poetry and prose has been published by *Lancaster Litfest*; *Coffee House* poetry magazine; *Riggwelter Press*; *Aôthen Magazine*; the *Lavender Review*; *Paragraph Planet*; City Lit *Between the Lines*; and as winner of *Greenwich River of Words*.

ZEKRIA IBRAHIMI writes: I am an elderly pensioner preferring amateurishness and chaos. I am the grey, ugly opposite of all 'love' is said to be. In literature, as in life, I deserve the rotting coffin and mouldy earth that will inevitably confine me. The grim epitaph on my cracked tombstone? FAILURE WAS ALWAYS MY AIM.

BODICEA ICENI, the cycling poet, born and raised in London. As an emerging writer, her journey commenced in 2023 at a women's writing circle. A practitioner of vipassana meditation, she employs eastern philosophies to inform her world view and writing. She currently writes poetry, short stories and plays. Co-editor of *Gold*, a commemorative poetry anthology to be published by Paradise Press.

RAINER KING is a queer writer of colour with a passion for creativity and storytelling. When they aren't exploring nature, reading or expressing themselves through writing and painting, they can be found relaxing with their beloved cat, Bailey.

ROBERTO LISSA lives in London. His first novel won a special mention in *Spread the Word*'s Life Writing Prize 2021 and was long-listed for the Grindstone Literary Award 2022. He is currently working on his second novel.

ELIZABETH (BETH) LISTER, Beth, born 1934. Bright, sensitive, obedient, abused. Successful book-learning hid her non-value of self. Marriage and two daughters, divorce at 38. Help from MIND at 50 and realised she's bisexual, a painter, a writer, a knitter, a gardener. Lives in Scotland near her daughters. She has published five books with Paradise Press – including *Prisoner 537*.

IRENE LOTTA, an older queer soul, lives in the Scottish Highlands. Her memoir, *My Plastic Jesus Umbrella*, reflects her ambivalent but irrevocable ties with a God she has wrestled with for over sixty years. The memoir will be available in early 2027 but her poetry and short stories over many years embody struggle, survival, and moments of glory and joy.

CATHERINE MEADS writes: I am a Professor of Health at Anglia Ruskin University, and a long-term LGBTQ+ activist and researcher with around 30 academic LGBTQ+ publications. This is my first foray into poetry.

SUSAN MILLER is a long-standing GAW member who lives with her wife and little black cat in Brixton, London. She really enjoyed her chance to try her hand at poetry. She's addicted to cosy crimes, and is keen to try writing one. A sub-editor of news, sports and business stories who loves the fun of creative writing.

GILLIAN JANE MORRIS is a retired GP and hospital doctor who specialised mainly in Paediatrics and Psychiatry. Her professional interests now are holistic medicine and hypnotherapy. Her hobbies include reading, writing, art, music and theatre. She lives in Edinburgh where she went to school and University.

PATRICK C. NOTCHTREE is an author of prize winning gay based novels as well as some non-fiction on diverse subjects. He lives in North-East England with his wife of 55 years and has his son's family nearby and a daughter in the USA with her family.
    Website: www.notchtree.com

ADRIAN RISDON's heyday was in the 1970s, when he directed Antony Gormley in verse-drama, drank with Peter Ackroyd and commenced his role of amanuensis to the blind poet John Heath-Stubbs. From 1980 onward, however, Adrian's luck changed. He now lives in an Almshouse of Noble Poverty in Winchester, and writes.

HASTIE SALIH is a GP and member of Jericho Writers, the Royal Society of Literature, Exiled Ink and GLADD. She has published short stories, poems and two novels – *Dahlia and Carys* (2023), *The Cradle and the Cage* (2025). Hastie

has lived in Wales, Germany, Belgium, and now Essex with her family and adopted cat.
Website: www.hastie-salih.com

PETER SCOTT-PRESLAND: writer, director/performer, activist. Worked for Capital Gay, and other LGBT+ publications; founded *Homo Promos Theatre Company* and has written many award-winning plays. Books: *Amiable Warriors* – the early history of CHE; *A Gay Century*, two volumes of unreliable vignettes of 20th Century gay life. Co-edited the flash fiction anthology *Flash Dances*.

LEIGH V TWERSKY lives in London, where he was born. His poems and short stories have appeared in *Chroma* magazine, *A Coup of Owls* and other Paradise Press anthologies. His debut novel, *Olympia Heights*, is a gay-themed dystopia set in a future Britain.

ELSA WALLACE (1939-2018) lived in Africa until she was thirty, moving to East London in 1969. In 1978 Elsa co-founded Gay Authors Workshop (with her partner Kathryn Bell, Michael Harth, and others) to support LGBT+ writers. Her publications include a novel *Merle,* a novella *A Short History of Lord Hyaena*, and short story collections *The Monkey Mirror, Ghosts and Gargoyles, Kissyface.*

Kathryn, by whose permission Elsa's work is here printed, continued as GAW secretary, sole-editing the GAW newsletter, contributing there and to GAW anthologies. In 2024 she received the ILGCN award for her work. Kathryn died in August 2025, aged 91.